THE NIGHTMARE CHRONICLES:

THE AGE OF DARKNESS

The Nightmare Chronicles:

The Age of Darkness

L. M. Mendolia

authorHOUSE®

AuthorHouse™
1663 Liberty Drive
Bloomington, IN 47403
www.authorhouse.com
Phone: 1-800-839-8640

Published by AuthorHouse   04/15/2013

ISBN: 978-1-4817-3348-9 (sc)
ISBN: 978-1-4817-3343-4 (hc)
ISBN: 978-1-4817-3347-2 (e)

Library of Congress Control Number: 2013905380

FOR MY FATHER

This is not a story. Well, for you it may be, because who knows how many years have passed since these events have taken place, if they have taken place at all. It all depends on whether my talents have deceived me, I suppose. At this very moment for me, however, it is not a story. It is more of a prediction, a testament of the things that will come to pass, as I have seen them. I am telling you now, because there must be some documentation of the future as I see it, and there is no guarantee that I can recall all the facts as fresh in my mind as they are now. I cannot say that these proceedings will occur exactly as I have seen them, but I will say this: it is very seldom that I am wrong.

I studied much by way of chemicals and potions as a young man. My father was an adventurer and alchemy enthusiast, and at a young age I began to I follow eagerly in his footsteps. However, my life has lead me down a much different, though no less dangerous path than his. While his love for the chemical arts led him to an early grave, mine lead me to so much more.

I am an alchemist, an apothecary, a medicine man of sorts. A wizard, a sorcerer, as some may say. In years past, many people have come to see me for anecdotes and medicines. For healing, for murder, who knows . . . I never ask questions of them and they never ask questions of me. Those who come to see me are not the moral sort. In my youth I was well liked enough, but as time went on people have grown to fear me. "Wizard," they whisper under their breath fearfully, as they scuttle away and lock their doors and windows.

Over time my practices have earned me great respect and, even worse, great power. There comes a time when someone who gains too much knowledge and power must make a decision. *They can use their supremacy for one of two things: good or evil. As for me, well, that is not for me to say. No man would ever admit that what he has done is evil. The only thing I will say is that over the years I have developed many gifts and talents in the midst of my studies and practices, and have put them to great use in my behalf. Gifts that, when combined with rage, regret, and vengeance, can be deadly. Gifts that no one man should ever have such control over. One of which is this wretched 'sight'.*

'Sight,' as I call it, though ironically enough, it appears out of the darkness. It begins with a deep sleep. A sleep laden with sorrow, fear, fatigue, and anger. It is an unimaginable silence, a lifeless stillness, an irrevocable emptiness, as if dead. Then, the cloudiness, the spinning, the warped perceptions, and out of the chaos swirling immensely through my restless mind: an image, images of past, of present, of haunting details. Images that are so real, I'm there. I see, I hear, I feel; I perceive the unperceivable, then, the anxiety, the agitation, the stress, and, ultimately, the insufferable pain, pain that itches underneath my skin as if trying to claw its way out through my pores. My breathing stops. I awake with a start, in a cold, noxious sweat, my head spinning, and I am left alone, in the dark, with my nightmares.

I scribble them down in a state of frenzied detail and drink to wash the haunting images from my psyche, but they never leave. And worse, sometimes, they repeat themselves, a haunting, nagging reminder of the licentious existence in which I have submersed myself.

My sight is not a gift, as some may say. It is a curse, a curse which I have grown very accustomed to. I have no control over what I see or don't see. It is not a ritual practice where I light candles and close my eyes and whisper incantations under my breath. These visions occur at any time, day or night. They show me memories of the past, things happening at the present, and what may or may not be in the future. They not only depict events concerning me, but they show me others, scenes involving those I know, and often the exploits of strangers whom I'm destined to meet. They are sporadic and random, haunting. They leave me to sort out what is real and what is an invention of my own mind.

These are not dreams or fantasies; they are nightmares. In the world that I live in now, there is no room for dreams and fantasies, because nightmares are all that ever play out. The only thing that is worse than having a nightmare is actually living it. And so I write these nightmares down in my record: a chronicle of things to come and things that have been. A chronicle of the dark and gruesome world that I have created.

There was once a time when this world was a happy place. When the sun actually rose at dawn, and when it set, everyone slept and had sweet dreams. The sun never shines here now, and I can't blame it. Why should the sun waste its time on such a corrupt and destructive place? There are no flowers in bloom. Instead, bare branches and stems are coated with a bitter frost. There is always a harsh chill in the air. There is no such thing as spring and summer, and never a happy holiday. It doesn't even snow, because even snow can be beautiful. The only snow that exists, curiously enough, drapes itself across the side of one particular mountain, to serve as an obstacle for trespassers . . . but we will get to that later.

For many years, the people have lived in shadow, and most people live in fear. There is little color in the world, and little light. Color, if any, is pallid and dim. It seems that only things touched by magic or sin give off radiant hues. It has been dubbed 'The Age of Darkness,' and I, myself, may be the one to blame for it.

The entire world is haunted by wickedness and sin. Creatures of the night always stalk the land and feed off chaos and turmoil. Nature and the environment have conformed to the immorality and sin of the society in which we now live. There is no happiness and hope; there is no bravery or expectation. At least there hasn't been for many years . . . until now.

It doesn't seem that the world will continue on the way it has for the years past; things are going to change. The birth of the twins has upset this chaos: out of wickedness, the birth of heroism and valor. Nearly thirty years ago the birth of the twins signified the fulfilling of a prophecy: the twins would arise and end the reign of terror in this world and enter it into an age of peace. Years ago I vowed to break it, vowed to weaken the group that meant to keep the brothers safe, and since then I have endured many successes.

But this team of heroes has grown stronger, and the two brothers have grown into men. They have made it their mission to seek me out and destroy me, in order to instill peace and happiness in the world once more, to end the darkness. They will come for me and I will flee; there will be a battle and there will be a victor. I know this because I have seen it.

This nightmare is different. It predicts the future. It has come to me in a series of installments over the past few weeks. After each episode, I have meticulously copied every exact detail, with more care and exertion than I ever have before. I have added thoughts, insight, and back-story in order to make it all clear and discernible.

I have written this manuscript as a testament of things to come and things that have been. This is a record of my ultimate vision, the finality of such which is justified through the relevance and significance of the events to come. Included are sections from my diary, accounts of my past life, which I have filed meticulously among the existing pages of my manuscript. I have also complied, at the conclusion of the manuscript, some of my previously documented nightmares, which are recognizable by the manic scrawl of one awakened in panic. They have been advantageously footnoted at relevant points. All of these documents, I hope, may serve to better understand my story.

This manuscript serves one purpose and one purpose only: to help the one for whom it is intended to better understand and, ultimately, to forgive.

It is still yet uncertain whether or not my vision will play out as I have seen it.

But this is what I have seen.

J. J. V

I

THE ESCAPE

It will all begin with a knock at my door. I am sitting at my great oak desk, writing feverishly as the minutes slip away. I should be preparing for my departure, but no, I must finish, it is of utmost importance to me.

I stop and strain my mind to try and remember every last detail, and everything is pivotal; he must be able to understand someday.

The clock is ticking slowly, slower than normal it seems, as my heart fills with anticipation. I hasten to write as much as my memory will recall. My mind is intense and my heart beats faster. My head aches and my hand is tired and sore, but I cannot falter now. I have to get it all down. The face of the clock stares back at me as the silent ticking clicks in my brain. The candle by which I write is fading with the fervent movements of my pen.

I glance at the dusty old grandfather clock in the corner and the minute hand creeks forward another interval. It is almost midnight, the bewitching hour, that lowly hour when everything foul comes out into the night.

There is a fire blazing in the hearth, and Vesta, my cat, is lying in front of it toying with a spider as it tries to escape her fateful grasp. She is a beautiful creature, though older than I can recall at the moment; a rare Archangel Blue, a breed yet to be discovered in fact, with a shiny, silvery, bluish-black coat and bright, shimmering pink eyes. She is long and lean, playful, yet sly, and every bit a predator, evidence of which is shown as she bats and swats at the frantic spider.

All is quiet; the only sounds are the rain coming down in soft droplets on the windows and the crackling of the burning fire, combined with the light scribbling of my quill pen and the faint, nervous beats of my pulsing heart.

My home is fairly modest, though perfectly comfortable. It consists of only the mere necessities of a lone man. It is an intimate setting, made up of one great room and a smaller loft above. In one corner rests a small bed layered with clumsily knit quilts that are moth eaten and frayed from Vesta's endless scratching. There is a great wooden library full of books: many old dusty volumes, the spines of which have seen the same fate as my bed quilts, books that have been read and reread over the many years. I am extremely well-versed in literature, as well as philosophy, theology and science, which is symbolic of many long, lonely nights.

The dusty shelves also include various handwritten journals and notes from my work. Many of these journals consist of my diary entries and nightmares. They are a record of all the experiences I have lived through and the horrors I have seen in my sleep; a compilation of the scariest yet most intimate details of my past and the future. I call them 'The Nightmare Chronicles' for that is what my life has been: no less than an intense, insufferable nightmare.

Luckily, I have been able to locate and compile a few of the most important documents to include in this manuscript. These include carefully selected pieces from my personal diary, pieces which will add detail and shed light on my past. Also, I have created an appendix of excerpts from my nightmare chronicles. I have grown accustomed to waking up in the middle of the night, in a fit of panic, and recording the details from my nightmares, which, as it turns out, reveal more of the truth. The rest of my writings, unfortunately, will be lost.

All of the papers belonging to my manuscript are piled neatly before me upon my great oak desk which is set against the wall adjacent to the library, and it is at this desk that I sit now. My desk is littered with additional stacks of papers and quills, as well as inks that have spilled along the surface and floor. A series of candles line the topmost edge of the desk, each with cold hardened wax cascading down the stem. My personal seal lay nearby: a silver coin with a large 'V' inside one star; the nautical star, a symbol of my younger days, which I've no time to discuss now.

There is also a vial of glittering black dust. I stare at it for several seconds, thinking heavily and debating whether it should be put to use.

A minute iron cauldron, no bigger than an ink jar and caked with gray ash and bits of charcoal, smokes slightly in front of me. An equally small glass jar sits next to it, the contents of which are a vibrant orange powder. I carefully scoop a teaspoon of the powder and sprinkle it into the smoking cauldron atop the smoldering charcoal that lies within. After a brief moment, the cauldron emits a pleasant perfume into the air. As it does, more thoughts become clearer and my memories begin to flow once more. I rotate my neck and rub it slightly, then continue to write.

I scribble something, cross it out, rewrite it, then crumple the paper and toss it exasperatedly into the waste basket next to my desk. This basket, made of old wicker, is a ghastly sight if any. The bottom of it is stained black from ink, and it is filled with various materials, mostly crumpled up pieces of paper with half-written "visions" on them. A radiant silver dust sparkles from within the heap; burned matchsticks, ashes, and some twine also find shelter amid the paper. Two empty corked bottles top the pile, one broken in three pieces and the other containing a green residue dried to the sides. These residues, among other things, were created by my own hand.

There is a work table up against the far wall, which is filled with similar bottles containing liquids and powders of different colors and viscosities, as well as various utensils and equipment. Many sinister things have been created here, many perverse ideas brought to life. It is hard to look at this table, for it is a reminder of the life I have created for myself. How many lives have been hurt or lost due to the makings from my very hands?

Too many.

A warm fire is in the hearth next to me, though dwindling in the late hour. There are pots for cooking stacked up next to the hearth as well as my black cauldron, a few worn cloaks hanging from the wall beside it. A great woven rug in lay the center of the floor, and in front of the fire sits a beautifully carved oak chair with intricate designs etched into it. Forgive me for divulging such details about matters—which are, seemingly—as insignificant as the attributes of my home, but this is the last time my eyes will look upon them.

I look up from my writing a moment and stare anxiously out the window. How much longer? What if they get here first? Impossible, in these woods. I hope . . . .

My small, desolate cabin is set in the middle of the forest where the trees grow so dense that one cannot even attempt to enter it nor would have ever wanted to. Only the bravest, or else the most foolish, have ever attempts it. (There is such a fine line between the two.) The forest is sort of like my own labyrinth, an endless maze of trees and vines, making it difficult to find your way in, and once you are in, finding it impossible to get out. My house, like the Minotaur, is lurking somewhere in the midst. It is even possible at times that my cabin may not be in the same place one day as it was the day before. This forest is full of magical trickery and illusion. The wood has claimed many lives of travelers and hunters who have gotten lost in its depths. Only I and a few allies know the way.

Until now, no one else even knew my home existed in the refuge of all these tall trees. It has been a safe haven for some time now, but it is no longer. My whereabouts have been discovered, and as I sit here trying desperately to finish this manuscript, I am eagerly awaiting what is to come.

I sit quietly, thinking, nervously waiting to find out whether all that I have seen is about to become a reality. My visions, or nightmares, which become more frequent with my older age, are rarely wrong, though I've found that small changes are possible when the outcome is already expected.

I look down at my sore hands: aged, worn, and corrupt from many years of affliction. I have not aged well. I appear older than most my age, the consequences of the life I have chosen to lead.

I take a few moments to reflect on the past, and to ponder, sadly, what is going to happen within the next few hours, days, and further on, if that time is destined to come.

I look about the cabin remorsefully; soon all of this will be lost. My apprehension thickens when I am disrupted by that fateful, gentle rapping at the door. The time has come.

I put down my pen and move anxiously to the door. I put my left ear close as if to listen to the breathing of the presence on the other side.

"Who's this tapping at my door?" I say through the great wooden door. Tension builds in my chest as I await the answer.

"It's me, sir." The familiar voice comes from outside. I relax and breathe a sigh of relief. It is safe, at least for now.

I open the door to reveal a well-built young man who is dripping wet with rain and standing in front of me. Man, I say in respect for him, for he really is just a boy. Under his hood you can see the dark silhouette of his handsome face and pale blue eyes beneath a mess of soft brown hair.

"Locke, please come in," I say as I allow him to come inside and remove his drenched cloak. "What took you so long? It is such a relief that you made it here unharmed. What news do you have?"

Locke takes a minute to catch his breath, holding his wet cloak over his arm as soft droplets of water descend from the fabric and create a small pool at his feet.

Locke is quite lean yet solid, not an inch over six feet tall. His arms are toned with muscle; he has broad shoulders and a proud, toned chest. His build is that of a young man who has worked hard all his life. Locke is the type of person who, should a stranger see him on the street, would immediately be misjudged, as most of the world, in its ignorance and arrogance, misjudges. Even those who know him as a casual acquaintance might develop an ill-opinion of his character. What many do not know is that despite his tough exterior, Locke has a gentle soul and a caring heart.

I cannot help but envy him.

Locke is just a few months past his twentieth birthday (or so I have estimated), yet he has the mind of a scholar from years of study and travel. He has spent many years under my tutelage, as well as—reluctantly as I was to condone—under the instruction of schoolmaster in the village. He is quite handsome, with striking features, welcoming eyes, and a charming smile that would make any young lady take notice.

I often wonder, sadly, what would have become of him if it were not for me.

I stare at him now as he stands in the doorway, tired and wet, and feel most extraordinarily thankful for him. He made his journey in haste no doubt, for the news he brings is unpleasant yet imperative.

"The league has figured you out," he replies.

"Someone supplied them with information?" I ask, already knowing the answer.

"Yes, sir, the old man Janus. He has opened the doorway, thought they'd spare him if he talked. Damn fool."

"And I suppose they disposed of him."

"Yes, sir, they beat him half to death and burned his house down. Then they hung him by the neck just after they questioned him. I saw him hanging in the town square just yesterday while I was passing through."

"A just punishment for a murderer . . . and a two-faced traitor."

The news is no surprise to me. It is just as I have seen[1]. Janus, beaten severely and confessing everything that he knew: what I had done, what my future plans were and, most importantly, where I was hiding. The fool. Within minutes of his confession he was strung up like a flag in the village square, a symbol of what happens when you oppose the league. Either he really was that dense or he preferred hanging over what I had planned for him. Though I'm not a mind reader, I would bet on the latter.

"Gruesome sight," Locke says, shifting uncomfortably. "His eyes were popping out of his head, and funny, in death, they seemed to turn sort of pink in color."

"Interesting . . . though deserved, no doubt."

"After all you've done for him. I can't believe that he would turn on us like this. That's so like him though, always working in two directions, trying to do what's best for him, that stupid son of a bitch."

"Watch your tongue," I say sternly. "Nothing displays unintelligence more than the profound use of curse words." As much as I adore Locke, he has the tendency to speak quite foully at times, a trait he no doubt picked up from his teenage cohorts and the slinky areas they frequent. He makes

---

[1]   Nightmare #846

an honest effort not to, but stress and anger often let the demons come out of him.

"You already knew he was dead," Locke continues, pushing aside my previous statement, "and that he confessed everything?"

"I've seen it."

"In a dream?"

"A nightmare."

Locke looks at me concernedly. "You've been having nightmares a lot lately. What other things have you seen?"

"It is not for me to say," I reply with a gentle sigh, "I do not wish to put any further stress upon you. If you knew the things I know, well, just be happy that you don't. But I do assure you, my dear boy, you have nothing to fear in all of this. That is all that I will say for now, please do not ask again."

One thing that I do appreciate about Locke is that he does not pry or demand information he feels worthy of knowing. He is trusting and loyal, and has full confidence in me.

He takes this as the end of the conversation and hangs his cloak up in front of the hearth to dry. "Do you think this has time to dry?" he asks. "Shall I add another log to the fire?"

"No need," I say as I rub my palms together. A gentle, tingling warmth emerges from my hands. I face the palms of my hands towards the dying embers in hearth and the flames reignite, a bright orange and yellow inferno intensifying in both heat and height.

"It should be dry in no time," I say smugly.

Satisfied, Locke wipes the remaining sweat and rainwater from his face. He sits down at my desk and I in my wooden chair by the fire.

I pick up my pipe, which, prior to this, rested patiently on the floor beneath my chair, along with a small vial of dense purple powder. I sprinkle a bit of the dust into the chamber and light it, inhaling the smooth, aromatic smoke in long, deep tokes. It tastes of blueberries and pomegranates. Delicious, yet incredibly light.

As I puff from the end of my pipe, a sparkling violet smoke rises up out of the smoldering ashes in the chamber. The smoke ascends, spiraling and swirling in all different directions, creating patterns in the air. It is quite hypnotic, and such a beautiful shade of purple, with various pleasant smells that seem to change with the desires of those of whom it wishes to appeal.

I close my eyes and allow the smoke to flood my brain and erase my thoughts. For a few relaxing moments, it produces a feeling of total comfort and innocence. A welcome contrast for a mind so clouded with angst and corruption.

At the sight of the sinuous rings floating in the air, Vesta's ears perk up and her attention is diverted from the spider. She watches carefully, faithfully, in a sort of trance. Her head and body stay still as her shimmering pink eyes follow the winding smoke. Within minutes, the entire cabin is filled with purple vapor, and tension ceases to exist.

Locke wipes more sweat off of his face with a handkerchief which is tucked up inside his sleeve. He brushes away his dangling brown locks to reveal a finely stress-lined forehead. He looks as anxious as I felt only moments ago.

I extend my arm to offer a puff off my pipe, but he refuses it.

"I don't need to smoke that shit," he says, pushing the pipe out of his face. He's right; I realize it may be good for one of us to have a clear mind, and he is clearly frustrated with my sudden aloofness at such a crucial time.

"Vincent, we must leave, immediately," he begins telling me. "They are coming; Janus told them the way through the woods. You delivered a nasty blow and the league has been severely maimed, but Roman is out for revenge and is even more fueled to bring you to your demise. They have been searching around for three days."

"My woodland friends have served me well," I reply. "They are as lost as can be."

"Not exactly." Locke's tone is growing more and more urgent. "Listen to me, Vincent. Janus gave them pretty specific instructions. They are nearing us, despite the distractions. As I was on my way, I noticed them not far from here. I slipped past them as no more than a hushed whisper, invisible to the ignorant eye. The rain is making it harder for them, but no doubt they are getting closer by the minute. We haven't much time, the quicker we move the better off we'll be."

His face looks tired and desperate. I know what great risk and effort it took for Locke to come, and all of his years of helping me have made it very dangerous for him. He is a good young man. Well, not necessarily a *good* man, when you're speaking of leading a life that is morally acceptable by society and God, but a good man in the sense that he offers immense loyalty and trustworthiness to those dearest to him. He has done so much for me and I owe my life to him.

Well, mine as well as others, perhaps.

"I believe everything in order for my departure," I say as I put the pipe inside my robe. Vesta, disappointed at the disappearance of the dancing smoke, returns to hunt for the spider which has conveniently scurried away.

"Good, sir," Locke replies, "but we have far to go and not much of a head start. So if you would please, sir, gather whatever it is you need and let's go."

"All I need is my manuscript," I say in seriousness, "a few essential materials,"—then, in a more delightful tone I announce—"and my cat!" I sit down again at my desk to finish the last few sentences of the final entry. In the meantime, Locke begins barring all of the windows and the door; he rips up sections of loose floorboard and nails them in crossing patterns across each possible entryway.

I glance through the pages one last time. As I write the last passage I cannot help but look up at Locke, who is working methodically, putting so much of his effort into saving me and risking his life. I suppress much emotion as I scribble the final lines.

Locke finishes and looks at me in earnest.

"I do wish I didn't have to rush the ending," I say, half to myself. "It is far too hard to recollect the proper facts and details if your mind is being distracted by haste."

"Or if your mind is clouded with smoke," Locke interjects dryly.

"However," I say, brushing his last comment aside, "it is imperative that I finish it now. I may not get another chance. I think I got it all right, just a few final notes . . ." I finish writing and then shuffle the loose, tattered pages together.

"Oh, and I almost forgot," I say, turning back towards my bookshelf. I rifle quickly through a tattered volume and rip a few random pages from it. These I carelessly append to the back of my pile of papers.

"I expect we will need these few extra pages," I say. I am speaking more to myself than Locke, who looks thoroughly confused.

I close up my manuscript and tie the crimson ribbon tightly around the leather binding with double knots, so that none of the pages may fall out. Then, after dripping some hot, black wax onto the cover, I press my seal into it creating my emblem.

I fill a cloth satchel with all of the necessary provisions for our journey. My manuscript is the last to be tucked away inside it. Locke secures the satchel about his him and then pulls on his wool cloak, which has dried completely.

For myself, I collect a series of potions and powders—including the vial of glittering black dust, not before fingering it gently and pondering the possibility of using it—all the essential accoutrements to facilitate my skills, and a small silver skeleton key from my bedside table. I secure them all inside the inner pockets of my cloak.

Locke proceeds to assist me as I pull on my heavy black cloak around my shoulders and I fasten the shining metallic emblem at the front, which is shaped like a star and embossed with a 'V.' I secure the hood over my head, covering my long, gray hair. In the night, the hood casts a dark shadow which hides my pale, aged face. All that is visible are my sparkling violet eyes.

"Vincent, you still haven't told me where we are going," Locke says, surely intending it as more a question than a statement.

My reply is blatant. "And now is not the time."

Everything seems to be in order until, suddenly, there are voices in the distance. They are rowdy, angry voices. They are loud, and worse, nearby; they seem to be getting closer by the second. The boarded-up windows make it impossible for us to get a glimpse of the intruders, but it is apparent that we haven't a moment to spare.

With a quick, frightened glance at me for approval, Locke begins pouring gasoline all over the walls and floor, soaking every inch of the wood.

My poor, humble home.

In just a few minutes' time there is a loud banging against the door. The wood splinters and bright light from flaming torches is visible through the cracks under the doorway. Locke looks at me in panic.

Another loud *SLAM!* and *CRACK!* More splintering wood and the door budges slightly.

"Quick, Vincent!" Locke yells as he pushes against the door with all of his might. His voice is desperate and petrified. "We must go now, before they break down the goddamned door!"

Locke runs to my desk and, with all his strength, pushes it across the room towards the door, papers streaming off of it and scattering themselves upon the floor. He wedges the desk up against the door, providing an additional barricade. It should buy us a bit more time, but not much. It is such an aged and rickety piece of furniture.

I rush to my bed and reach underneath one of my feather pillows, procuring a small, black velvet satchel with a radiant silver cord. I put the cord around my head and neck and tuck the bag into my cloak, so that it hangs securely from my neck, just at heart level.

The men outside continue to smash against the door with brute force. Locke is pushing with all his might, his back up against the desk, his muscles tensed and straining with every ounce of energy and strength.

I take one last look around my home and begin to roll up the carpet in the middle of the room revealing a small iron latch in the wooden floor. The latch is rusted, deprived of use over the past several years.

Just outside, the mob grows angrier and more violent, and the door is finally beginning to give in. The door, the desk, and Locke begin to slide slowly forward as the men push their way in. I can hear the cries of the men: they will show me no mercy. We have only a few seconds.

I open the trap with some difficulty, and then turn towards Locke and the heaving door. I raise my palms so that they are facing towards the chaos and take a few deep breaths.

"Locke!" I yell, my voice barely audible amid the commotion, "now!" An invisible force erupts from my palms and Locke moves away from the door, which now refuses to budge against the shoves from the opposite side.

Locke moves quickly, as I do not know how much longer I can hold them. The door will stand only another moment. Without breaking my contact and concentration, Locke assists me in stepping backwards, down inside the hollow ground. Only my hands remain above the floor.

The door is now being shredded by a sharp axe and we haven't another moment to lose. The commotion has become manic. Locke crawls down after me and readies himself to strike a match.

"On the count of three!" Locke shouts.

"Wait!" I say loudly, but Locke fails to hear me.

"One!" Locke yells, readying his matchstick and stone.

I push with all my might through my arms, but the strength on the other side of the door has become too great. The rising tension, coupled with my fear of losing Vesta, has weakened the force.

"Two," Locke says in succession.

"Wait! Vesta!" I shout again, looking about frantically.

"Three!"

Then, something magical happens. A sequence of events occurs in the blink of an eye: all in the same instant, Locke strikes and tosses the match onto the gasoline soaked floor; I collapse, releasing the invisible barrier; the barricaded door gives in to the pressure and shatters as it is broken in by the intruders; I then see the light hit the furious face of Roman and his hard, brown eyes, just as the entire house goes up in flames, and we shut ourselves down underneath the trap door which vanishes into thin air; all of which happens just after my dear cat leaps into my arms, the tormented spider dangling from her mouth.

October 28ᵗʰ, '54

I went to Janus, tonight, to offer fair warning, but it was in vain. I knew, as I have known all along, all these years, that he would one day betray me.

I held his neck tight in my grip and pressed his back against the ivy-covered brick wall. We were in the back alley of the town inn, a dark, secret place where I knew I'd find him, drunk no doubt, and alone. I grabbed him as he was stumbling home from the tavern, swift and shadowlike. He did not even know what happened until he was backed up against the wall, in the back alley, my hands clasped tightly around his treacherous throat.

Janus's feet dangled inches above the ground. He did not fight me, he just hung there, like a cat being held up by its scruff, staring idly back at me. I stared deeply into his pale, pink eyes, trying to read is thoughts. I looked at him in complete seriousness, and he looked at me in complete shock.

"I am warning you, Janus, I see all, and you are not fooling me. I know you look both ways."

"I am not going to say anything, I swear!"

I could feel the blood rushing to his head, and he struggled to breathe.

"If you think they are going to just let you off easily, with a quick confession, you are wrong. They are not as good and honest as you think."

"I promise you I am not going to say a word!" His voice was desperate, but I learned long ago not to trust him. He would say anything to anyone that would get him out of trouble. Yet this time he was more than simply 'in trouble.'

"Why do you not trust me? I have been a loyal friend of yours for years! I have helped you. We have helped each other!"

I let him go and he dropped, choking, to the floor. I watched him as he made a pitiful attempt to rise but could only pull himself upon his knees.

"You take me for some kind of fool!" I spat.

"I do not, I do not!" he replied desperately. "How could I, Vincent? I am your friend. I swear!"

"If you think for one moment your body will not be swinging by the noose the moment you open your mouth, then you are even more brainless than I imagined!"

"I will remain silent Vincent!"

"You helped me gather information against them. You led me to their hiding places. They will not be sympathetic towards you."

"I know it," he said, through pathetic sobs. "I am loyal only to you, Vincent. There must be someone else helping them!"

I considered the possibility of this for a moment. Someone else was helping them. But who? Haram? No. Certainly not Locke . . .

I knew it was Janus. My sight does not fail me.

I bent down to his level, grabbed the back of his head, and drew his face close to mine. I spoke slowly, deliberately, emphasizing each word.

"If you say a word, I will kill you. I will murder you with such ferocity that you will wish they had offered you an easy death." I let go of him and stood back up.

He was clearly horrified by my anger. Tears streamed down his cheeks and he wiped the long strands of copper hair from his face. I could smell his sweat, his panic.

Janus sat motionless, apparently tired from the struggle. His chest heaved and his baggy clothes hung loosely from his limp body. He seemed to take a moment to think and tried to assemble a clear and rational thought. I waited. After a few moments, he spoke.

"What do I have to gain from telling them where you are hiding? They will offer me no silver, no gold, no freedom, no mercy. I am at your mercy, Vincent. I am well aware that if my tongue slips, my life is at stake."

"Just remember who helped you collect the debts owed to you these last few years, who held men at your mercy while you collected what was rightfully yours and while you took your anger out on them for their delay, and who hid you after things went too far."

"I remember!" he cried urgently.

"Really? I'm not so sure, so I'd like to give you a small reminder."

"Please, Vincent, no!" But he was suddenly silenced. I grabbed him by the shoulder with my left hand and held my right hand to his forehead, pressing my palm gently between his eyes. My hand emitted a steady electric jolt.

16

Janus screamed in agony. I released him and he fell once more, his face hitting the ground. I kicked him as hard as I could. He lay motionless.

I bent down, grabbed Janus by the hair once more and pulled his face up to meet mine. He was barely able to open his eyes, but somehow managed to do so. This time, they were shimmering—no burning pink—as if on fire.

"Let that be your warning." I let go of his hair and his head dropped back down. I left him there, laying face down on the floor, unable to move. He would be paralyzed for several minutes, which gave me enough time to disappear without being noticed. Before he was able to lift his head again, I was gone.

As I made my way back through the winding forest, staggering with exhaustion, I pondered the effectiveness of my threat.

I don't know why I wasted my energy on him; I know what is going to happen. I have already seen the whole thing played out in my latest nightmare.

II

THE PROPHECY

Locke and I sit in silence as we listen to the commotion overhead. There are muffled yells as the men scramble about and then out into the woods again. There is no doubt that the house is completely engulfed in flames by now, and there may be a few casualties. Better for Locke and me, I suppose. They won't be able to find anything . . . anything that is of importance anyway. What's more, they won't be able to find their way out of the woods very easily either. This buys us more time. Some will not make it out at all, if they are separated. Poor souls, they sealed their own fate by daring to come into these woods, especially on a night such as this.

Locke and I are surrounded by darkness. Pitch black. This corridor was built years ago with the assumption that we may need an escape route someday. I was lucky enough to make the acquaintance of and employ a group of naive young sailors who were quite eager to earn a handsome compensation while at port for the winter months. It took them nearly the entire length of their leave to complete it. Unfortunately, once they finished and sailed out again, their ship was met by an unforeseen storm and capsized, killing every one of the young men for whom I owe a debt of gratitude.

One might also understand that news of my secret passageway would defy its purpose, so precautions had to be taken.

The corridor is at least six miles long; it runs deep beneath the forest and comes up and out into a small village just outside the forest. This village can be very dangerous. It is inhabited only by the darkest of beings. I say beings because 'people' cannot apply sufficiently to everyone.

Many of the good citizens from years ago have moved on, left their homes to ruin. Those who remain are those who have little trepidation, and little conscience.

I have been there many times on, shall we say, 'business.' I used to meet with colleagues in secrecy at the old inn and had to be very careful in doing so. I ceased entering the village several years ago, when the risk became too great. There are many who desire the great talents and powers such like I possess. Some of these colleagues can turn out to be conspirators as well. Janus was one of them, and look at what happened to him. I have since been sending Locke in my stead, though I know it has been difficult for him as well.

Locke looks extremely uncomfortable; he is claustrophobic. Though he never admits his fears, I know that when he was a small boy he got trapped inside a vault from which he was trying to steal some money. He was locked in that three-by-five foot vault for three days until I discovered him, nearly dead.

It wasn't the first or last time I needed to save his life.

"Breathe," I say, resting a hand on his shoulder. Locke takes several deep, soothing breaths.

"It is goddamn cold down here," Locke says, shivering in the darkness. He feels around along the wall for a few minutes and then produces a small torch. The matches are nowhere to be found.

"I can take care of this," I say as I reach into my pocket. I reveal a small dose of a luminous yellow powder. I sprinkle it onto the torch and then, with a slight snap of my fingers, spark a flame that ignites the torch. Locke takes the torch and holds it out ahead, illuminating the long passageway ahead of us.

The walls are lined with stone, covered in moss and dirt. At our feet, there are several collections of bones and skeletons of all the rats and various small creatures that had hoped to find food in the corridor and failed. Vesta delights in all of the spiders scattering around about our feet. I reach down and tickle the back of her ears and she purrs softly. She then traps a particularly large spider under her paw and lays down to chew on it.

Locke and I stare ahead, into the silent and desolate passage. I am extremely fatigued from the previous ordeal, but now is not the time to be weak.

"Well, come on then," I say reluctantly. "We've got a long trek ahead of us."

Locke lets out a heavy, exasperated sigh and takes the lead as we begin our journey into the darkness.

Fearing that she is being left behind, Vesta abandons her spider, leaving it dead on the ground. She runs far up ahead of us, her tail swishing back and forth in delight. She turns back to ensure that we are following her, her pink eyes aglow in the shadows.

After about two hours or so of walking I become very tired. I am old and weak, especially in this intense situation. Locke seems to have calmed down his claustrophobia quite a bit; he is no longer in such a rush and obviously tired as well.

"May we stop a moment and rest?" I ask. Locke comes to a stop and places the torch in a hook upon the wall.

"Are you feeling alright?" Locke asks as he takes my bag from me.

"I'm fine," I reply. "Just a bit tired. I should very much like to sit down for a few minutes and catch my breath." Locke sets down the satchel and, grabbing me by the arms, helps me to lower myself to sit down onto the floor. The floor is hard and wet and cold. Locke gathers a few scattered twigs and leaves and constructs a small fire in the center of the corridor, using the torch to light it. Vesta, delighted by the sight of the fire, immediately curls up into a little ball just beside it.

Locke heaves a great sigh. He slumps down to the ground and props himself up against the stone wall. He stares at the fire, transfixed, as the flames dance and writhe about.

"So what is your plan?" Locke asks at last. "I mean, now that the league has destroyed your home, where can we go? Are we just going to keep running?"

I search for the best reply, because I already know how this will end. "Locke, we have a few things we need to do. Then we will make our way out of the country. I have a few places for us to stay, and a few people we may confide in, but I will meet Roman and the league eventually. I have already seen it happen."

"But without both of the twins? Can the prophecy be fulfilled?"

"That is exactly what the prophecy has foretold."

"I'm sorry," Locke says quietly. "I guess I don't exactly understand what the prophecy has foretold, I have only picked up things from others' conversations. I have to admit, I am ignorant of what to expect."

I was afraid of this, and have avoided this moment for a long time, for Locke's sake. Up until now, he has been courteous in not asking too many questions and trusting me with this knowledge. Although, it was inevitable that Locke would have to learn the truth. Locke has spent many years doing things for me without too much inquiry. It was easy when he was very young, but the older and wiser he becomes, the harder it is for him to be content with his ignorance.

"I suppose it is time I told you, Locke, what exactly you have gotten yourself caught up in. I think it is only fair that you know the truth, and that I give you an opportunity to make a choice."

I take out my pipe and light it. I puff it gently and allow the scent of the spices inside it to soothe my aching bones and cloud my head.

The prophecy itself is quite clear in my own head. I have mulled it over so many times. Scrutinized and memorized each precise word, pondered the meaning of each exact detail.

Locke waits patiently, as if understanding the meditation needed before regaling him with the tale. I take a deep breath and then begin the recitation.

"The prophecy was foretold by an ancient oracle that lived in the old world. They say that she was the daughter of one of the muses. She was both very beautiful and extremely repulsive, though no one alive had ever laid eyes upon her. She had lived for two hundred years in a cave at the top of the highest mountain by the sea. The mountain was so tall that it extended into the heavens, and it had two distinct sides. One side of the mountain, facing the sea and the sun, was warm and inviting, yet it was smooth and sleek and impossible to climb. But the other side, the side in which she dwelled, faced away, towards the valley, and never saw the sunlight, so it was icy, and cold and dark. This side was full of sharp, pointy crags. One could only climb up this threatening side, and so, only the bravest of men dared to call upon her.

"One night in late autumn, an old man ventured out to see her. He had been drinking heavily for days, after having a terrible nightmare. He climbed and climbed up the jagged rocks of the mountain in the icy storm, and though death reached its gruesome hand out towards him several times, the man resisted the temptation to grab hold, and he made it to the top.

"He went to the witch and asked for her permission to enter the cave. She acquiesced, but told him he must first render himself sightless, for she never let anyone see her face.

"The man agreed and blindfolded himself with a piece of cloth that he ripped from his own garment. He entered her cave and could see nothing, yet he felt the warmth of her blazing fire. The inviting flames licked away the frost that covered his skin. Once he was comfortable, the witch offered him a seat and asked for what had he come. His response was this:

"'Great madam, a fortnight ago, I had the most terrible dream. I dreamt that, many years from now, a terrible evil will reign over the world. There will be darkness and shadow and the wicked will live in triumph and the good will live in fear. I dreamed that this evil will be of my own flesh and my own blood. Please, tell me, for the sake of my ancestors to come, will this terrible age come, and will it last forever?'

"The seer closed her eyes and hummed silently. She then opened her mouth to speak but no words came out. Suddenly, though the man didn't see it with his own eyes, a voice arose from the fire between them. The voice was soothing and beguiling, and the man listened intently, in a trance. His whole body became suddenly aware of the closeness of the woman, and the sensuality exuding from the oracle enveloped the old man's body.

"From the fire, a voice rang out, and the voice answered the man.

"'There is a she-wolf who has roamed the lands for hundreds of years. She only comes out when the moon is full. She herself will wrong a human man, a man of your flesh and your blood. This man will grow angry, and powerful, and wicked. Many years from now, the world will be in terrible ruin, and the great wizard will start it all. But amid this horror, the she wolf will, on the eve of the full moon, give birth to two cubs. These twins will grow fast and strong. They will hunt for the evil wizard.

One, the wizard will defeat with ease, while the stronger brother continues the hunt. The evil wizard and the stronger son will meet in battle, on the night when the moon is full, they alone will duel, and the better of the two will decide the fate of the world.'

"The man turned away from the oracle even more very distraught than he was before he had come. But before he could go, the seer made him promise he would not reveal what she had predicted. However, the temptation her voice created was too overwhelming and he turned slowly around and lifted the blindfold to catch a glimpse of the beautiful and hideous beast.

"What he saw is unknown. But he returned to his home, visibly sickened and agitated. He spoke to no one. Inside the comfort of his home, he wrote the prophecy down. The prophecy was recorded and passed down through generations of the old man's family. For many nights, he brooded over what he saw, and the temptation was too great to resist. He told a close friend one evening of the oracle, and the man immediately retreated to go catch a glimpse. The friend never returned.

"Less than a week later, while the old man lay sleeping, the oracle approached him in his bed. She gouged his eyes out with her bare hands, for she was angry that he had deceived her by lifting his blindfold to see her. She then left his eyes out as a sacrifice, and, in the night, the she-wolf came and gobbled up the old man's eyes. The scent of the man's flesh and blood was forever imprinted in the she-wolf's memory.

"Since the old man could no longer see, he was cursed with gruesome nightmares for the remainder of his life and he passed these nightmares down to all of his children. He never spoke of the oracle again, taking the memory of what he saw and the curse she had left upon him to his grave."

Locke sits, stunned. "How can you be sure this story is true? All this with Roman and Remy, it may just be a coincidence."

I laugh at his innocence. "Locke, I have heard it many times. It has been written, and do you not see it unfolding right before your very eyes?"

"So the birth of Remy and Roman," he asks, "the 'cubs,' they grow strong and come for you, and one you will defeat with ease?" He sits, amazed. It has already been done.

"Exactly."

"And the full moon, it is approaching." Locke states.

"Yes. 'On the night of the full moon, the two will meet in battle.'"

"But Vincent, your fate is not sealed by this prophecy; she said, 'the stronger of the two will decide the fate of the world.' That could very well be you! You have powers Roman could only dream of!"

"This is true, Locke; it does not necessarily mean that I am doomed. However, Roman is much stronger than Remy was. He will not be killed as easily."

"I don't understand the whole 'wolf' part," Locke says, perplexed.

"You will." I state matter-of-factly. Locke looks at me uncomfortably, as if he does not wish to ever find out what it means.

"How can you be sure the prophecy will come true?" he says.

"I know," I reply, "because I have heard the prophecy myself long ago, but also, because I have seen it. Did you not realize, the end of the story, the man is cursed with nightmares that are inherited by all of his descendents?"

"You don't mean . . ." Locke begins, stunned.

"That is exactly what I mean. He was *my* ancestor."

I allow Locke time to process all that he has learned. He looks tired and deep in thought, as if he is working it all out in his brain.

"But," Locke says, "it also said that the she-wolf would wrong the man, turning him evil. What does that mean?" I do not reply to this and Locke realizes that I do not wish for conversation to continue. This is a silent agreement that exists between us. When I choose not answer, he accepts it.

"The nightmares," Locke says, choosing a different topic of discussion in order to relieve the tension. "you have had them all of your life?"

"Not as a boy, no," I reply sadly, thinking back to the time. "They were my father's burden then. He used to have the most horrific nightmares. In his sleep, he would scream and claw at the air and wake up in a cold sweat."

I wince as I think back to those gruesome nights: the writhing, the screaming, the blood as he clawed at his skin—leaving such thick scars—as if he were trying to rip the vision out of him. I shake my head, relinquishing the painful memory.

"The same is true for you, is it not?" Locke says.

"You've seen?" I ask, somewhat embarrassed, yet also feeling, for the first time in a long time, slightly vulnerable.

"Several times," Locke shyly admits. He too seems embarrassed, as if he has intruded on some intimate affair. "Did it scare you, as a boy?"

"Well, yes," I confess. "They frightened me; overwhelmed me. I longed to know what my father dreamed of, but he never spoke a word of it to anyone. He never wrote it down either, as I have done."

"When did they start for you?"

"When my father died. That very night, in fact. I remember it vividly[2]. I had the most horrific vision of his death, as though I were him, living it as it happened. I was actually there to witness his death, and it was gruesome indeed, but as awful as that was, it was nothing compared to living it through a nightmare. Do not ask me to describe it. It is, to this

---

[2]   Nightmare #I

26

day, the only one I have failed to write down. All I can say is . . . it was so very real. I felt his pain. The nightmares, they continue to be that way."

"And you've had them ever since?"

"For the most part. They stopped for a short while, when I was about your age. But their absence, unfortunately, did not last long."

"Well, luckily you don't have a child to pass them on too," he says innocently.

"Yes, luckily." I voice constricts as I say this and I choke lightly on the words.

"Do things in your nightmares always happen as you see them?" Locke asks.

A knot in my stomach tightens.

"I do not wish to answer any more of these questions," I say.

Locke looks away, slightly hurt. Perhaps he felt some sense of trust in my honesty, which is a very rare occurrence. I keep so much else from him.

"This is a really big deal." Locke says dejectedly, still staring in the opposite direction. "I know not everything is my business, but how could you not tell me this? When are you going to trust me? I am not Janus I think I have proven myself to you on countless occasions." I can tell it is taking great courage for him to say this, as he fears my reaction.

"It is as you said," I say to him. "Not everything is your business. I tell you what you need to know at the proper moment. And nothing more." He does not respond to this, and I know that I have truly hurt him. What he doesn't know, is how sorry I am for doing so. "And as for your 'proving' yourself to me, that remains to be seen, Locke." This statement is completely untrue, but Locke's whole existence is based on proving his worth to me, and I say this only as a tactic to motivate him. Complacency on his part is dangerous for me. It is a dirty trick, I know, but a necessary one.

"Why don't you close your eyes for a moment and try to catch some sleep, sir," Locke says finally. "I'll keep watch. We only have a few miles left to go."

"Thank you very much, Locke," I reply. "However, it may be better the other way around. We should be alright for a few hours time. Your strength will be much more beneficial than mine, as the very little I do have left is dwindling by the hour. Besides, it has been weeks since I've had any sort of sleep at all that has not been disturbed by visions, so I shouldn't expect to catch any now. I shall wake you if it is necessary."

Locke rests his head back against the damp wall. In a second or so, the pale blue of his eyes fades away as his eyelids close and he drifts into sleep. *Poor, poor boy.* I sit beside the fire and warm my hands over it. The hours slip past us, as Locke sleeps soundly next to me, and I sit, hypnotized by the dancing flames in front of me, in a state of semi-unconsciousness.

My head swirls and fills with meditative cloudiness. It floods with a memory so real, that for a brief moment I feel as though I am there . . . .

We are sitting by the candlelight of my cabin. I am slumped forward in a chair, clearly weak, and Locke pours me more tea. My hands shake as I attempt to lift the cup. Locke helps me by lifting the cup to my lips, and I sip the warm liquid.

"It is done then?" he asks.

"Yes," I whisper.

"You should have let me come with you."

"It was not your task. You have helped me enough."

"What now?"

I look up at Locke wearily.

"I must prepare for retaliation," I say. "I am sure they will come for me eventually. I do not wholly trust Janus; I am sure he will tell."

"Have you seen it?"

"Not yet, but I am sure it is coming."

Locke looks worried.

"I will have to leave you," I say.

These words seem to trouble him immensely.

"I'm coming with you," he says without hesitation.

"No." I shake my head but refuse to look him in the eye.

Locke is clearly insulted by this rejection. He slams his fists on the table so ferociously that I wince slightly, but I say nothing. He sits back without another word and turns to stare off out of the window, deep in thought. My trust means everything to him.

I sip my tea quietly, not daring to look at him.

"Vincent," he says at last, leaning forward again. He places a hand on top of mine. My hand gives a slight lurch at his touch, but I do not move it. I stare down at my tea cup. "Look at me, Vincent."

I look up at the boy across from me; my sparkling violet eyes meet his pale blue ones. His face displays courage and, at the same time, fear.

"What else do I have?" he asks, his voice breaking. "You are the only person I trust, the only person I care for. I do not care if it kills me. I am coming with you. I will do whatever it takes, you just tell me when."

The memory, and the emotion evoked by it, overwhelms me. I cannot control myself, and suddenly my head nods forward and my eyes begin to dim.

Not now, Vincent, not now. I attempt to perk myself up. I can retain my consciousness for only a few minutes before my mind begins to wander away again and my eyelids start to sag. *NO! NO! NO!* Too late. My eyelids close and my eyes roll into the back of my head and then it comes. I open my eyes to glimpse the ominous presence ahead.

A figure in the darkness approaches: a bright white form of mist in the distance. Those eyes, those brilliant blue eyes, they come closer and closer. As if in a trance, I rise steadily to my feet; no, I am *pulled* steadily to my feet, like a marionette, with no control of my own. My chest tightens and my heart begins to race faster and faster; it's beating, banging violently against my ribs. I can't breathe; everything around me begins spinning and spiraling. The figure comes closer and closer and my drooping head is raised and the two brilliant blue orbs penetrate my own tired eyes and the light engulfs me and then . . .

And then . . .

Darkness.

September 22ⁿᵈ, '54

It was pitch black. Not a sound could be heard as I crept up the winding staircase to the topmost tower. The cobwebs created a soft barrier for me to pass through. My eyes, sparkling in the darkness, lit a violet path in front of me. I knew he was here. I had seen it.[3]

As I ascended the steps, I stepped carefully over the corpses of those few who dared to stand between me and my prey.

My heart pounded lightly in my hollow chest. I saw the faint glow from the fire coming from the room at the top of the stairs. I reached into my cloak and dusted my violently aged hands with a light, radiant, silvery powder. They immediately began to tingle and burn. First a white hot, then an ice cold. It was working.

I reached the top of the steps and skulked surreptitiously into the circular room. The room was empty. I admired the tall stone walls and steeped ceiling. There was one lone window slightly ajar at the peek of the round room. The fire crackled and I considered my own reflection that lingered amid its flames. A brisk wind snuck in through the open window.

Then, suddenly, I felt a sharp blow to my back. I stumbled forward a few steps but remained standing. I turned slowly around and faced Remy. The young, handsome figure stood tall over me, sweat dripping from his chest and face. His soft brown eyes were filled with both determination and fear. I knew he was behind the door, I saw it before I entered the room, but sometimes I like to toy with them. He didn't say anything . . . he just stared at me.

Remy and I stood face to face. I could read him like a book. He wanted to kill me. He wanted to take thirty-two years of misery out on my bones. He breathed heavily and his muscular chest expanded with confidence and retracted in fear. He eyed me up, like a lion sizing up a weak antelope right before the pounce. I just stood . . . . I could feel the blood from my wound trickle down my back. We stood facing each other in silence for a long time. Remy made the first move.

---

[3]   Nightmare #844

He lunged at me and tackled my weak frame to the floor. I took one swift blow to the face and spit a tooth onto the floor beside my head. Remy stood over me and held his sword to my throat. His face was overcome with fear and angst. I looked back at him and sneered as I noticed, in my peripheral vision, the clouds disperse outside. At that moment Remy froze, his face swathed in the bright gleam of moonlight that streaked abruptly through the open window. His eyes turned a deep black and began to slowly dilate, absorbing the whole whites of his eyes. I felt his skin turn hot and all the hairs on his body stand up. He had a look of ultimate terror on his sullen face and his breathing stopped as his mouth hung open rigidly. He stood paralyzed, and his sword dropped to the floor; his eyes were pitch black and empty as he stared right through me. I had a brief moment to make my move. My hands burned with impatience.

With a flash of violent white light, Remy flew into air, smashed into the ceiling and fell to the floor. In one quick angelic movement, I slipped from the floor and hovered over Remy, who laid on his back, bleeding from his brow, his black eyes glaring up at me. He lifted his great arm and I raised a hand, the force from which withheld another blow from the weakening hero.

With much energy, Remy's paw-like hand was forced to the floor. I then closed my icy hot hands around his throat without actually touching his skin. My palms grew white hot, and a radiant silver mist erupted from my palms, spinning in ringlets around his neck. Remy's whole body tensed and his neck burned from my fiery grasp. He writhed and twitched on the floor beneath me, choking on air, but my grip was tight and unforgiving. His body released pools of sweat and his flesh continued to burn. Remy began to scream and cry and howl in agony, and I stayed still, my gaze transfixed on his eyes, which faded from black to wholly white. I leaned forward and whispered gentle words to him: "You are no hero; this world will never see peace. I know what you are and I have won. I know your weakness. Your brother will come and he will join you in hell."

Remy's eyes glossed over and his body relaxed; his eyes rolled back in his head and his breathing ceased. I let go of his neck and in an instant, as if being pulled by some great force, I flew backwards out through the open window into the darkness.

III

THE SCHOOLMASTER

"Vincent . . . Vincent," I hear a voice say. I cannot see. Everything is a foggy blur. I am lying on what feels like a blanket, though it is undoubtedly on the floor. I can hear whispers beside me, and the pungent smell of some soft, aromatic herb fills the room. "Vincent, can you hear me?"

It is Locke. My muscles relax, comforted by the sound of his voice. He is with me. He is always with me.

"I can hear you," I say softly. "But I cannot see you." My mouth is dry and my voice is cracked. My head aches and a pulsing pain shoots up and down the back of my skull.

"He has been blinded," a second voice says. "I believe it is only temporary." This second voice is unfamiliar. The voice is somewhat cold, as if a soft breeze emerges, floating about with the spoken words. I try to open my eyes and bright sharp light pierces through my irises and into my brain. I groan in pain.

"Keep your eyes closed, Vincent!" Locke says, covering them with his hands.

"I thought you said this has happened before," the cold voice utters.

"It has," replies Locke. "Just a few times before, but never this bad. I was asleep myself when I was roused by his movements. He got up and stood, staring blankly ahead for a few moments and then he just dropped to the floor. He started in a fit of wicked convulsions. He was mumbling uncontrollably, something incoherent to my ears. He was speaking in a strange language. I think it was Hebrew or Latin or something like that. Though I couldn't make out what he was saying, it was apparent that he was repeating the same phrase over and over. And when his eyes opened, they were blood red. Then he went still and cold. He usually just passes out. I picked him up and carried him the rest of the way here. I didn't know where else to go."

"It was wise of you to bring him here," the unfamiliar voice says.

"Vincent doesn't trust many people, but I knew you would help us."

"You said there was a light?" the cold voice asks.

"Not one that I can see," replies Locke. "But he sees it, he mumbles about the 'white light.' Then he starts speaking those same foreign words."

"This is very peculiar," says the cold voice. "In all my years of teaching and study, I have never seen such a thing as this. However, I have heard of similar things before. Demonic possessions have been occurring for centuries. That light may have been a Gidim."

"Gidim?"

"The ancient Sumerians believed that diseases or bodily sicknesses were caused by sickness demons, or Gidims. Christian cultures believed in similar possessions, only the demon was the devil."

"It doesn't seem to make sense," Locke says. "If the light was the devil, or one of these Gidims, why would it be white? Isn't the devil associated with black or red?"

"I don't really think the devil has a color preference," the schoolmaster jokes. "Besides, it may have been an illusion. It is popular belief that one sees a white light before death to symbolize the entranceway into heaven.

The white light in this case may have been a disguise to lure Vincent in towards death, and then it began the possession."

"I really don't think Vincent would fall for that shit," Locke says blatantly. "I'm sure he doesn't truly believe he is destined to go to heaven, if there is such a place. God has never done anything for him. If Vincent was ever faced with an angel, he'd probably spit right in its face."

The ache in my brain lessens and the soreness of my eyes begins to soften. I crack my eyelids a little, and a little more, and eventually I am able to open them. My blurred vision allows me to make out two faces standing over me. One of which contains the soft, pale blue eyes belonging to Locke, and the other is one I am oddly, eerily familiar with, but I cannot place it with a name.

The schoolmaster has an inimitable look about him. His eyes are of the most glowing, pure green. I've seen them before[4].

The schoolmaster's hair is a mixture of ebony black peppered with streaks of radiant silver. His face is chillingly pallid, complimenting the ashy white pallor of his neck and arms and, presumably, the rest of his body. His eyebrows dance atop his brow, one curving up sinisterly while the other sinks low over his eyelid. His mouth is perfectly shaped into a thin, sneering grin. He is tall and lean, and remarkably well-groomed. He is wearing black trousers with black and white striped suspenders over a deep velvety purple shirt; his sleeves are rolled neatly up to his elbows. A black bowtie is secured in a perfect knot at his neck. According to Locke, he had always been an eccentric dresser, something that became more and more outlandish the more educated and cultured he became. I notice his matching purple top hat and tailed waistcoat hanging on the back of the door.

---

[4]   Nightmare #712

I stare at him deeply as my eyes focus. Again, I sense some recognition in his face, in those striking features. The thought weighs briefly on my mind, for I cannot place it, and I forcefully dismiss it.

But, I cannot help but think: *Those eyes.* I shiver. *Where had I seen them before?*

"Vincent," says the schoolmaster, "I do not believe we have ever had the pleasure of meeting." He extends a bony hand toward me. "Bienvenue. Welcome. I am Professor Ollam Fuil. I am the schoolmaster in town, and served as such for Locke when he was a boy."

I reach up to grasp his hand, but withdraw in shock. His fingertips are icy cold, and I shiver once more. Sensing my discomfort, Ollam retracts his own hand with deliberate slowness, as if insulted by my squeamishness, and places it behind his back. He stands rigidly, erect.

"It is regrettable that Locke has recently abated coming to study with me," Ollam says. "He is very intelligent, and a fine young man. Although," he relaxes now, "I see he got his looks from his mother!" Ollam laughs haughtily, satisfied with his joke. Locke gives a weak smile, and I cringe.

"That may be true," I reply irritably, "as Locke never knew his parents. Therefore, I guess we will never be sure, will we?" Ollam stops suddenly and swallows, had his face the ability to exude color, it would be flushed with embarrassment.

It was true; I had, a few years ago, forbid Locke from continuing his lessons with Ollam. I had always had a sort of contempt for the man, though I had never met him in person. I rued some of his teachings and the ideas he was putting into Locke's head. Yes, I wanted Locke to be well-educated, and I hadn't the time to instruct him myself, but his mind was mine for molding, and Ollam threatened that. Locke was very taken with him, and would often come to visit me with stories of the things the brilliant Professor Fuil had taught him. It left a bitter taste in my mouth. There was a short period of time, in Locke's early adolescent years, when he began to rebel against me. Locke insisted that Ollam had his best interests at heart, but I could not allow him to corrupt Locke any longer. I had the sinking feeling he was working to turn Locke against me, though his motive for that escaped me. As soon as I felt that Locke had acquired sufficient knowledge, I prohibited his attendance at school, under the guide that I needed more help from him, help which Locke was all too eager to provide. Ollam was not pleased.

Suffice it to say, he was ever keen on meeting. And now that I am finally in the schoolmaster's presence, the look of him and his snide remarks corroborate my previous judgments. The fact that he is insulting me in presence only adds fuel to the fire. And I do not play well with fire.

"Je suis désolé," Ollam says. "My sincere apologies. I have known Locke a long time, but he has never spoken to me about the death of his parents. One of the greatest lessens in education: no matter how much you think you know, there is always more to learn."

"You can discontinue the French," I say, "as I am now well aware that you speak it, and there is no need to show off." Rather than being offended, Ollam appears fairly pleased with himself, and he curves his thin lips into a complacent smirk.

I sit up, thoroughly annoyed, more so at Locke for bringing me here than with this foolish man. My head continues to ache, though dully.

I look around me and instantly recognize my surroundings: a large stone schoolhouse with high arches that resembled the gothic architecture of the late 12th century. I had been here once before, to collect Locke after his lessons, though, at the time, Ollam failed to make an appearance.

It is one great room with several small archways leading to separate quarters. There are great wooden double doors leading to the front of the hall. Rather than the traditional desks, there are long wooden tables and chairs in rows. Along the stone walls are shelves of books and various pieces of equipment.

The walls of the hall extend high to the ceiling and are covered in a thick grey dust. The ceiling ascends and comes together into two large points on opposite sides of the hall. There are many large, intricately designed stain-glass windows. Peculiarly enough, the windows, which were designed to allow floods of golden rays to pour in, are instead dark and shaded, letting little light into the massive hall. It is murky and cold. The school looks more like a great gothic cathedral than a schoolhouse.

It was designed by Ollam himself to resemble the structures from his previous country. He had come here succeeding the previous schoolmaster, the one I knew as a young man, and had the old schoolhouse demolished. He had this grand structure erected in its stead. I assumed at the time, and still do, that Ollam wanted to make his presence known. He certainly knew how to make a grand entrance.

Though his ancestors hail from Ireland, Ollam once lived in France, many years ago, which explains his fluency in the language. According to Locke, Ollam lived there throughout his child and young adulthood. However, some sort of unknown dangerous situation forced him out of the country, and after several years of traveling the continent, he ended up here. That was near about forty years ago. How old is he exactly? I can't really determine it, but he has aged gracefully, or barely at all, with the exception of those strikingly silver streaks through his hair.

"I apologize for the lack of a proper resting place," Ollam says. "I rarely get any sleep myself and do not feel that you would find my personal sleeping quarters any more comfortable."

Locke helps me up off of the floor and walks me over to one of the tables. Vesta, who was hiding in a corner of the room, darts under the table and begins rubbing her back affectionately back and forth across my leg. I reach down and pet her soft gray fur, and she purrs delicately.

Ollam leaves briefly and comes back with a glass of water for Locke and two glasses of wine, one for himself and one for me. Mine is a white, translucent and yellowish in hue, his, a red, thick in viscosity and deep crimson in color. I take a long sip from the wine and my headache begins to subside. It is sweet, with a hint of peach and mango flavors. Ollam drinks nearly the whole glass in one long gulp. A trickle drips down the side of his chin. I watch as he delicately wipes it away and licks the remnants off of his finger.

Locke passes on the water. He is staring off at the wall. His hands are shaky and he bounces his heel lightly at the floor. After a few minutes, he gets up suddenly and heads towards the door.

"Where are you going?" I ask nervously.

Locke turns around, his eyes looking weary and anxious. "I need some air," he replies and goes out of the room.

I turn to Ollam, who is eyeing me suspiciously. "He looks terribly troubled," I say, less angry now that my concern for Locke has overridden my dislike for Ollam.

"You gave him quite a fright," Ollam replies. "He just needs a little air, a chance to catch his breath. He will be all right. He was up with you all night. Didn't sleep a wink."

Ollam looks at me and me at him. I study him: his prominent features, his suspicious grin, and his glaring eyes. It all leaves me with a bit of uneasiness in the pit of my stomach.

"How long was I out?" I ask finally, breaking the silence.

"Quite a few hours," Ollam says. "I believe its mid-afternoon, though I have not looked outside. Not that it matters, as I sometimes forget. I must say, Vincent, I am quite pleased myself with the lack of daylight around this part of the country."

"Day is as good as night around here."

"Precisely, and we have you to thank for that, don't we?"

"It would be awfully presumptuous of me," I say sharply, "to assume that I alone have had any effect on the environment."

"Suit yourself," he says smugly. I glare at him once more, his expression still carrying a sarcastic smile. "I enjoy it either way; I was merely thrying to give credit to where I assumed it was due."

I roll my eyes. Usually I reveled in the fact that I did in fact cause such a powerful phenomenon, but the fact that Ollam was commending me for it lessened the glory of it, and I denied any involvement out of spite.

"He carried you a long way, you know," Ollam says accusingly.

"I'm well aware of that," I snap back, resuming my previous aggravation.

The tension from my bad mood causes another awkward silence, though Ollam seems unmoved. We continue to stare at one another, squaring off in a silent battle, each of us plotting our next move. Ollam remains silent for a few moments longer, as if he is pondering his next words carefully.

"You depend quite a lot on that boy . . . don't you, Vincent?" he says to me at last. I try to look undisturbed by this sudden accusation.

"The older I get, the more valuable a companion he proves to be, yes."

"He's been with you a long time though, eh?" The tone in which he delivers this question has changed to genuine curiosity. It is apparent that Ollam is attempting to ease the tension with casual conversation, and for a few moments, out of sheer fatigue, I decide to let my grievances rest.

"I have known Locke since he was a young boy," I say. A scrawny, misfit of a boy; about seven or eight or so, I'd say. He was ever so devious and cunning, yet very smart and resourceful; no family, no one to care for him. He lived on the streets and ran around with a pack of misfits like himself, although they, unlike him, had a warm meal and a place to sleep at night.

"The first day I met him I caught him trying to pick silver from my pockets in the village. When I'd noticed him for the first time, he got away from me quick enough, but I chased him down three alleyways. He was a quick little imp. Unfortunately for Locke, however, I had a few, shall we say, 'tricks' up my sleeve. With a few flicks of my fingers, the boy was rendered immobile and the coins were back in my pocket easily enough."

I smile at the memory, though it is somewhat fabricated. It was not my pocket he was trying to steal from, but that of another unsuspecting villager. And it was certainly not the first time I met Locke. By this time, I had already known him for a few years, and he was not trying to pick my pocket, but that of another man in the street. At the time I found Locke to be most irksome, but I now look back on it with fondness. I wonder if Ollam can sense my deceit.

"He followed me home that evening," I continue, "and wanted to know more about my gifts. I struck an accord with him: if he ran a few small errands for me, I would tell him more about my trade." I use the word "errands" lightly, as well as "trade". Ollam knows very little about the true meaning behind these words. Or so I think.

"And he has come to your door every day since I presume," laughs Ollam, recalling the story as Locke had once told it to him.

"Yes, something of that sort. I took to giving him a hot meal and place to sleep every so often. Though I wouldn't say I'd actually taken a liking to him. I'd be lying if I said I'd always enjoyed his company."

"Yes, yes, Locke can be quite a handful," Ollam advises, "especially given his choice of extracurricular activities." With this he laughs aloud and reaches for a silver case from his breast pocket. He pulls a cigarette from the shiny case and does not yet light it, but instead twirls it between his long, slender fingers. "He was especially troublesome once he hit his teen years. Do you remember when he got into that fight at the pub? What was he . . . thirteen? Fourteen? Locke certainly was not an intimidating young lad, but he gave that brute a licking for sure." Ollam laughs proudly at the thought of a young Locke thrashing a man nearly twice his age.

"Yes, yes, of course I remember. He came stumbling back to my cabin with scrapes and cuts all of his face and hands. It looked as if he had been in a fight with a hyena."

"Handy work on your part though, eh Vincent?" Ollam acknowledges my efforts at healing the boy's wounds with a smile. "He came to school the next day looking good as new."

"Yes, well, I have a way with my hands," I state with confidence. "Locke has grown into quite a powerful young man. And he has certainly matured much over the past few years."

"It's a shame you stopped allowing him to come see me," Ollam says. "He has always been one of my favorites." It's true, that after a time I ceased allowing Locke to go into the village to attend school. It may be vanity on my part, but I felt I had much more to offer him by way of an education. I have also, in the past few years, become more and more paranoid and distrusting. I do not believe many people know of Locke's association with me, but after the recent nightmares of this particular journey began, I have felt more compelled than ever to keep our acquaintance a secret and also to keep him well protected.

"No doubt you feel quite helpless without him?" Ollam says. With this, the conversation takes a sudden turn and the previous tension resurfaces. I take a moment to ponder the meaning of the question. Ollam, though a great mentor and teacher for Locke, is definitely not someone I am willing to trust. I wonder how much he really knows.

"The boy has done much for me over the years," I say carefully. "Though I cannot say I feel at all 'helpless', as you put it, Ollam. You would do well to know that I am quite able to fend for myself." Despite the forwardness of this comment, I wonder if Ollam can sense my anxiety has arisen with Locke's departure from the room.

"Everyone has times of weakness, Vincent. And weaknesses are what make people destructible. Remy has realized that the hard way, no doubt."

Ollam leans back curtly in his chair and finally lights his cigarette. He draws a long pull from it and allows the cloudy smoke to escape delicately from his lips. A sneer creeps across his face, and I cannot help but suddenly feel uncomfortable.

I stare at him for a moment. How does he know about Remy? What exactly is he getting at?

"Oh, I meant no harm in the question, Vincent," he suddenly remarks, sensing my obvious unease. "I was just making an observation. Please, do not feel offended. I am certainly not trying to meddle in your personal matters. It's just that, well, to be quite frank, everyone in the village knows about your current, shall we say, 'state of affairs'. And I was merely satisfying my curiosity."

At the conclusion of this remark Locke re-enters the room and shakes the rain off of his cloak. I cannot help but feel a little more at ease upon his return. I try not to let Ollam notice.

"It looks like the rain is finally starting to let up," Locke says. "It's about time. It rained all night."

"Oh good," Ollam says, feigning concern. "That should make your travels much easier.

Locke sits down and his stomach gives a loud rumble. "Sorry," Locke says, clasping his hand to his stomach. "I haven't had anything to eat in hours."

"How rude of me!" Ollam exclaims. "You *must* be hungry, after such a *long*"—he emphasizes the word long, and looks directly at me as he says it—"journey this evening. And in the rain! Allow me make you something to eat." Ollam quickly puts out his cigarette and goes out of the room, disappearing into one of the side corridors. Locke stares at me intently, concernedly, and I wonder what he is thinking.

"Why did you bring me here?" I snap at him. "You were foolish to get this Ollam involved. I suppose he knows we have fled the league."

"I thought we could trust him," Locke says earnestly.

"I'm starting to think you lack proper understanding of the word," I say. "We have many enemies, Locke. You cannot trust anyone but me. You would do well to remember that." Locke looks dejected, clearly remorseful for having upset me.

"I'm sorry, Vincent." Locke looks up apologetically at me. "I really didn't know what else to do. You still haven't told me where we are going. I didn't have any other options. I just did what I thought was right." We sit in silence for several long minutes. I am angered by his stupidity, and Locke looks ashamed.

"I was worried about you," he finally admits. "This was different from last time. I wasn't sure you were going to wake up." I feel a slight tinge of remorse for the boy. Despite his rough exterior he really does have a gentle heart, and where that came from I've no idea. He certainly did not learn it from me.

"There is only so much I can do on my own and . . ." Locke looks down at his feet. "And . . . I . . . I was afraid I might lose you this time. I trust Professor Fuil; he's taught me everything I know."

"Bah." I am disgusted. I taught him everything he *really* needs to know, though I've kept many dark secrets over the years.

Ollam returns with three plates of steak and potatoes, another goblet of wine for me and one for himself, as well as a mug of ale for Locke. He also sets down three sets of silverware. The steaks are done extremely rare, almost completely raw.

I wait until Locke and Ollam are deep in conversation before I, disgusted by the blood seeping out of the bottom of my meat, place my hand over the top of the steak, and within a few seconds a faint heat radiates from my palms. The meat slowly turns from bright red to a light pink, and I am able to eat. I take a few measly bites and give the rest to

Locke, who has already devoured his steak and is eyeing Ollam's untouched potatoes.

"I never was a fan of starches," Ollam adds as he scrapes the spuds onto Locke's plate. Locke gives him a grateful look and continues to eat ravenously. "I do love a nice rare steak though. I'm ever so grateful that I could share it with the two of you. It has been so long since I've seen you Locke, not since you've left school, I think." Ollam stops and watches Locke carefully. Locke seems to be having trouble cutting through his steak. With a quick slip of the knife, he makes an incision in his forefinger. A small trickle of blood seeps from the cut. Ollam winces, and sits up a bit straighter.

"Locke," Ollam says. "Vincent has just been regaling me with the story of the first time he met you." Locke looks down at his food, slightly embarrassed; it is apparent that he is unaware of the story to which Ollam is referring. Ollam continues, "I remember the first time I met Locke as well, the very first time he came into my school, as if it were only yesterday." Ollam shoots a sideways glance at Locke. "It was nearly one o'clock in the morning and I was on my way home from visiting some colleagues of mine. It is a routine of ours, actually, to get together for a few drinks one night a month and discuss academics. Anyway, I was on my way home, and as I approached the steps of the schoolhouse I noticed him, a boy of nearly eleven; he was trying to wrench open one of the lower windows next to the schoolhouse door. I snuck stealthily up behind him and grabbed his hand and whipped him around. You should have seen the look on the young lad's face!"

Locke laughs. "You scared the shit out of me for sure, Professor! Although I'm sure I could have gotten away; you had four or five glasses of wine in you at least. I was watching you at the pub, drinking away. So I decided to check your place out. I don't know how you saw me, it was so dark out! There is no way you could have been able to see straight."

Ollam is silent for several seconds; he seems as if he is in a sort of trance as he stares, his eyes transfixed on Locke's bloodied hand, which moves animatedly as he speaks.

"Ollam, are you alright?" Locke asks, confused.

Ollam snaps suddenly out of it. "Uh . . . yes . . . quite right," he says. "I may have been somewhat incapacitated, but my sense of smell is always quite alert. I could sense you were there."

"You could smell me?" Locke is amazed.

"Oh, of course," Ollam replies. "And so," he is speaking to me again, "I walked with him for a bit, and lectured him the whole way about criminals and the importance of education and how the mind is the most important tool to being successful in life. And don't you know Locke showed up for school every day since! I even had to send him home several times on the weekends!" Ollam laughs heartily and takes a sip of his wine.

"So Vincent," Ollam says to me, trying to change the subject while staring again at the wound on Locke's finger, which has yet to stop bleeding. "Tell me, what brings you out of your wooded abyss? You seem unable to get very far these days without getting into a bit of trouble. I didn't expect you to be wondering about, given the state of things."

"If you must know," I reply, "I was chased out."

"By whom? If you don't mind me asking."

"The league is always after me, Ollam. I believe, according to your previous statement about my 'state of affairs', that you already know that."

"Of course, of course. Well if it's all out in the open then, enough dancing around the subject. I am only too eager to help you, Vincent. I taught Remy and Roman as well, you know, when they were young. Bastardly annoying little children, you know? Always displaying chivalry and good will and all that, and never showing up for astronomy, as if they were too good for it. Pah!" He is still looking at Locke's finger, which Locke has now been attempting to bandage with a napkin. Small

46

beads of sweat have begun to form around Ollam's forehead, and he tugs uncomfortably at his collar. Nevertheless, he continues his speech.

"And to be honest," he says, "As I have already said, I quite like the world the way it is now, never any sunlight, much more cool and comfortable don't you think?" He again notices Locke struggling to clot the blood from his cut.

"Can I help you with that Locke?" he spits out, unnaturally, his voice cracking a little. Locke looks up at him, confused by his sudden urgency and momentary loss of composure.

"No, I'm alright," Locke insists. "It's just a little blood."

"Your blood is quite potent," Ollam replies, swallowing. "I mean, it is potent in color. It's very red. You must be very healthy." Ollam is still staring at the finger. The sight of the blood seems to bother him or fascinate him, I can't decide which, but as the minutes go by, Ollam's face grows slightly paler—if that is even possible—and more eager. In contrast to his whitening skin, I notice, peculiarly, that his eyes have become darker and his pupils have somewhat dilated. I wonder if he may become sick. I also begin to wonder if perhaps there is more to Professor Ollam Fuil than he has been willing to admit. If my intuition serves me correctly . . .

After a few minutes of silence, he looks at me again.

"I want to help you in any way possible," he says. "I am quite fond of Locke, having taught him all those years, and, whether you realize it or not, you have done me a favor or two in your time, Vincent. My schoolhouse is always a safe haven for you."

"I appreciate your hospitality," I say. "Nevertheless, I do not wish to burden you any longer. Besides, it is not wise to stay in one place for too long."

"What is our plan, Vincent?" Locke asks. "We cannot stay much longer, the league is sure to find us soon. I certainly do not want to put Professor Fuil in danger." Locke has a nervous look about him. I notice

Ollam staring at Locke intently, his eyes never leaving the young man's face.

"We must leave at once," I reply. "Roman is coming for me, and he must not find us. It has been hours since we escaped, and Roman at least, I'm sure, has made it out of the forest. I can only assume he will expect us to come to the village. We must be off." Turning to Ollam I say, "Ollam, I am eternally grateful for your help. Come, Locke, we must be going."

As we get up, Ollam stands abruptly.

"You cannot leave, Locke." His eyes are cold and threatening, his dark, widening pupils still transfixed on Locke. The sarcastic grin he donned all morning has vanished and has been replaced by a grave expression. "You must stay; you are not safe with him."

"What are you talking about, Professor?" Locke questions confusedly. "*He* is not safe without me." Locke is obviously unsettled by Ollam's ominous countenance. He takes a few steps back towards the door as Ollam slinks forward and turns to towards me. "C'mon, Vincent."

"I said," Ollam repeats, very slowly and deliberately, "that . . . you . . . can . . . not . . . leave!" Ollam is facing Locke, his fists clenched, and his eyes have an urgent, hungry look in them. Locke begins to back toward the door. Before he can take another step, Ollam grabs Locke's arms and forces him back against the door. His face is stern and his eyes are now completely black, the whiteness around them bloodshot. Locke tenses with the pain of his grip.

"You are not leaving," Ollam repeats; his voice is rash and sinister, almost robotic in tone, as if it is no longer Ollam speaking but someone else through his body. I rise to my feet, and Ollam turns his head around towards me, maintaining his grip on Locke.

"You cannot win, Vincent," Ollam says. "You will not win. You have no one on your side. Roman will find you and Roman will kill you. Shape shifters are everywhere; no one is as they seem to be. I warn you now: *you will be betrayed.* Janus was only the first. You have been betrayed once, and you will be again. This is certain." He gives a sideways glance at Locke.

"It is best you go on alone," Ollam continues. "I will not allow Locke to go down with you. Besides," he looks to Locke and his lips curl into a grim sneer, "I am still quite hungry and would like Locke to stay for a second helping."

Ollam's eyes are eager and saliva seeps heavily from the corners of his pale lips. What happens next is quick and intense. I raise my hands towards Ollam, but he releases Locke in time and turns towards me. He swipes his hand through the air and the surprising force from his hand knocks me off of my feet and up against a wall. My frail body slides helplessly to the floor. Ollam lunges suddenly at Locke, slamming him up against the wall and leans in towards him, his mouth open, bearing razor sharp teeth. Vesta hisses viscously, all of her hair standing up.

At the same moment, I press my palms together and then turn them outwardly at Ollam. Locke ducks down as white blasts of light shoot through the air from my direction and tear into Ollam's side. The deep gash in his waist spills black blood intensely and Ollam looks up at me with a sneer.

The wound then, amazingly, begins to heal itself. The blood ceases to flow and rapid scabbing occurs. New skin regenerates as tiny threads of white flesh stitch themselves back together over the spot where the old flesh had been torn away. Within seconds the whitish skin is whole and smooth, with not even a scar to show where a deep gash had existed only moments ago. Ollam looks up, unscathed, and sniffs at the air.

Then, without hesitation, Locke grabs a poker from the fire place and swings it at Ollam's head. Ollam turns around quickly and reaches up to grab the poker, stopping it dead mid swing. Locke struggles for a moment, but his great muscles cannot compete with the miraculous strength of the thin schoolmaster. At once he lifts the poker and Locke into the air and hurls them both across the room. Locke crashes into a table, splitting the wood into pieces and spilling its contents all over the floor.

Ollam slowly turns to me, blood dripping from the corners of his black eyes. "I could take care of you now," he says, "and save Roman the trouble."

I raise my hand, though weakly, and another stream of white light erupts from my hand. Ollam leaps backward through the air, feet over head, and lands on all fours on the far wall. He hangs on like spider, his limbs bent at awkward angles. He looks down at me and again, smiles.

In one last desperate attempt, I release another jet of white light, but Ollam leaps away to the adjacent wall. The light shatters the wall where Ollam clung moments ago, and pieces of debris clatter to the floor.

Ollam waits for further assault, but I'm exhausted. He then begins a deliberately slow descent down the side of the wall the floor. He stands upright and looks over at Locke, who is struggling to raise himself to his feet.

Sure that Locke is no longer a threat, he walks over to where I lay, weakened on the floor. He does not see Locke reach out and wrap his bloodied hand around a splintered piece of wood.

As Ollam approaches me, I raise a quivering hand. He chuckles lightly and leans in closely.

"Your silly magic tricks are no good here, Vincent," he whispers. "You have no power over me, give up and go, or I will have to kill you first. You know you are failing; you weaken with every passing day, with every emission of your power." He creeps closer and closer. "You may fool others, but you do not fool me." He is upon me now, and he kneels down to meet my face. "You really are not as scary as everyone thinks." He tilts my head to the side to expose my neck. He opens his mouth bares a row of long, razor sharp teeth. "I can't imagine that this . . . ."

Those are the last words he speaks, for a large wooden stake erupts from the front of his chest and black liquid spurts out of the wound. He looks down at his chest, and clutches the protruding stake. He looks up at me, with fear in his eyes. His whole body begins to tremble, and, piece by piece, as if crumbing like a marble statue, his skin begins to fall away, revealing rotted, steely muscle and bone.

And then, quite suddenly, a loud *Crack!*

And he disintegrates into a pile of dust.

Behind him, Locke stands, his chest heaving, as he tries to catch his breath.

I couldn't help it really. The anger engulfed me. Another failure.

Locke just stood there, knowing he had let me down yet again, and stared at the floor while I thrashed about.

I whipped my right hand to the side and a chair flew across the room and shattered against the wall. I whipped by left hand in the opposite direction and a glass vial followed the chair; glass shards flew in every direction.

I clasped my palms together—they were glowing and white hot—and threw flashes of light, blowing a hole in the wall right next to Locke's head. He flinched, but did not move away. He did not scream. He just stood there and took his punishment.

I stopped my tirade and stared at him. He stared defiantly back at me.

I whipped my hand again in a slashing motion and, though I was at least ten feet away from him, a gash appeared across Locke's face.

This was too much for him to bear.

Locke dropped to the floor and covered his bleeding cheek. It was then that I broke.

I walked over and knelt down next to him. I lifted his chin to my face and saw not only the blood dripping from the wound that I inflicted, but the watery tears threatening to descend from his pale blue eyes. Locke held it in; he tried to stay strong.

But he broke.

"I'm sorry," he said, shaking.

I put my palm against his cheek and felt the warmth surge through my arm, out of my palm, and onto his flesh. Within seconds, the gash had vanished.

"I need that jewel, Locke," I said to him, in a calm, yet assertive tone.

"I know," he said. "I did not mean to fail you."

"It is I who have failed you, Locke. You are not quite yet a man, yet I send you to do a man's work. Perhaps you are not ready."

"No!" Locke said. "I am ready. I will find it for you. I will not let you down."

"Close your eyes and relax," I said and he obeyed. I put my hand on his forehead and his head fell back as he slipped into a deep sleep.

I reached into my pocket and took out a vial containing a glittering black dust. I tilted Locke's head back and opened his eyelids. I sprinkled the dust into his eyes and placed my palm on his forehead once more.

"I'm sorry," I whispered as I released him.

"Sorry about what?" Locke asked as he opened his eyes.

IV

THE TAVERN

Locke sits staring at the black ooze and dust that cover his hands, a look of disbelief on his face. He then slowly helps me to my feet.

"Are you alright?" he asks me.

"Fine, my boy, thank you. For a moment there, I thought he had me. Though, I don't think my blood would have satisfied him."

"Lucky he threw me into that table," Locke said. "Or I wouldn't have had such a nice piece of wood to impale him with."

I give Locke a few moments to collect his breath and then we decide to have a look around the schoolhouse. As I do, I cannot help but become suddenly overwhelmed with a sense of dejection.

I have only ever been in here once, long ago, and my stay was brief. I was a young man, and I came here to seek instruction from the current schoolmaster at the time. He turned me away, because I had no family and no money and would not fit in with his current pupils. He did, however, allow me to take several volumes to study on my own. I had to teach myself all that I know, and thank him for giving me the opportunity to do so.

At the same time, I swallow a sense of loathing for the man. How different things might have been.

Locke heads for the kitchen and I make my way through one of the passageways to, what appears to be, Ollam's small laboratory.

It is a small room, dimly lit, with bottles and dead animals everywhere. On the dissection table lay a line of corpses, the remains of small animals sliced open, exposing their innards, and neatly pinned to the table. Each of which has been drained of all of its blood.

Along the table are an array of flasks and bottles, each filled with an unmistakable crimson liquid.

Suddenly my attention is turned to Vesta, who is pawing at wooden trunk in the corner and mewing pugnaciously. She then takes a few steps backward and hisses at the trunk. Her claws bared, she leans back and her hairs stick up as her tiny fangs glisten.

"What is it, my sweet?" I walk over to the chest and open its lid. In an instant, the most horrific stench erupts from the trunk, and I double back in a fit of hacking and coughing. Vesta is maniacal in her fear and anger, though she dares not take a step closer. I have never seen her act this way before. I cover my mouth with the sleeve of my cloak and inch apprehensively towards the open chest. The sight made me vomit instantly.

Curled up at the bottom of the huge chest lay a wolf, slain, and cut open down its front. Though the rotting flesh remains, it has been completely drained of its blood. The wolf's eyes are white, and its body rigid and ice cold, though the most peculiar thing of all is what I see about its neck. I lift a tuft of fur and notice a thin ring around the neck. This is not just a ring, but a wound, that seems to have been burned into the skin. Suddenly, the thought strikes me as I whisper the word, "Remy . . ."

"Vincent!" Locke calls from the other room. He comes rushing in, so out of breath he can barely get the words out. "Torch lights! In the distance! We have to get out of here!" I close the lid to the trunk and make my way from the room.

We move as quickly as we can, slinking quietly out the back doorway. Luckily, the procession of torches passes the schoolhouse by and continues on down the road.

Locke and I creep out into the eerie night. We move as shadows: silent, dark, and looming. The silence in the air is frightening. The harbor is visible in the distance, and I notice a large ship is docked. There is some bustling and shouting about it, but other than that the night air is still.

As we walk, I ponder the disturbing facts behind what I just saw. How is it possible that Ollam had retrieved the body? And did Roman know? Surely it was done out of spite. Disputes between Ollam's and Remy and Roman's kind have been written for centuries.

"Vincent, where are we going to go now?" Locke asks.

"If I am not mistaken, an unfamiliar ship is currently tied up in the harbor?"

"Actually, yes. I noticed it yesterday."

"We will need to stop there first to retrieve something."

"And then?"

"Then, we shall go and visit an old friend," I say. I use the term 'friend' very loosely, though Locke needn't know this yet.

"Perhaps we should lay low for another hour or two," Locke cautions me. "They must be getting tired. It's been nearly sixteen hours since they burned your cabin down. They should be going off to rest soon, I'm sure. You know, to come up with another plan for locating us and such."

"We cannot be too sure Locke. And I'm hesitant to stay in one place for too long. As you have already have noticed, we seem to have few we can depend on. No, Locke, I think we must continue on."

"Come on," Locke insists. "It'll only be for a few minutes. I think we could both do with a stiff drink after that ordeal."

As much as I detest the idea, I cannot pretend that the thought of a relaxing, sedative drink is beguiling.

"Fine," I say.

"I know just the place," he remarks. He starts off down the road and I follow. "The League would not be caught dead there. Or else, they might find themselves as such."

We walk down the main road, past the rows of houses; I cannot help but recall the way that this town has deteriorated over the past few years. It is a street that was once populated by bustling shops, cafes, and cheerful townsfolk; it is now quite run-down and dilapidated. Most of the "good" people have moved on and left this a desolate place. Many of the houses are now either boarded up or else terribly vandalized by young men, most of whom Locke has been guilty of fraternizing with.

We approach a tavern at the corner of the street. It is a tall, stone building. The windows are all broken and the sign above the entranceway hangs by one chain—the other having been broken—so that it dangles helplessly, threatening to fall at any moment. A cacophony of sounds erupts from behind the great wooden door: raucous laughter, clinking glasses, shouts, and stools scraping across the floor.

"Have you ever been here before?" Locke asks me.

"No," I lie. I had been to this particular pub just once before, looking for Locke, in fact.

"One of my favorite spots," Locke says enthusiastically. "You're in for a treat; I think the men in here are just our type."

"I don't consider a bunch if rowdy mongrels 'my type,'" I reply nastily.

"I only meant that they won't give us a hard time. They're no friends of the league, that's all."

Locke pushes the door open, revealing a scene of ragged and drunk men engaged in rowdy activities, and within seconds of us entering the bar, the place falls silent. In all directions the men stop and turn to stare at us. We make our way through the crowd and approach the bar. Locke, obviously feeling uncomfortable, turns around and faces the crowd. Many sets of suspicious eyes scrutinized the pair of us, most of them were unthreatening and dull, but a select few of them, I noticed, were bright and glowed, though not nearly as vibrantly as my own.

"Does someone in this room have a complaint?" Locke demands of everyone in the room. His eyes narrow and his jaw clenches in a way that I have never seen before. Locke's confidence and courage exude in this type of environment, which is somewhat of a refreshing contrast to the demeanor he has in my presence. After his assertion of dominance, the men turn around and return to their laughter and enjoyment.

The tavern-keeper, behind the bar, is no longer the same man from a few years ago. This man is middle-aged, tall, and has a full head of burnt red hair. He has small, dim eyes with no traces of color in them. He dons an open-collared shirt with the sleeves rolled up just above his elbows, revealing sculpted muscles on his chest and arms.

He stands proudly in front of rows of wooded planks, which play host to an array of glass bottles, all different shapes and sizes, and containing liquids of various colors and viscosities. There are two great big kegs of beer turned on their sides, foamy ale dripping from the taps. Above the tavern-keeper's head dangle hundreds of glasses.

"Locke!" The tavern-keeper shouts jovially, reaching for the boy's hand. His accent is of a thick, Gaelic sort. He reaches over the bar and grasps Locke's hand tightly, giving it a hearty shake. "Good to see yeh, laddie! It 'as been quite a few weeks since I've seen yer face 'round here."

"I've been taking care of a few things, Olchobhar," Locke says with a laugh. "You know, the league has been out in full force lately. Vincent and I are on our way out of here."

The man's smile immediately diminishes as he looks from Locke to me. His neck muscles tense; he swallows hard.

"Vincent," he says, almost in a whisper. It is as if he is looking at a ghost as he surveys my aged face. A week ago, I would have enjoyed causing this man to feel so uncomfortable by my presence, but, as precious seconds tick away, I am instead becoming increasingly annoyed with his hesitation.

Locke senses the discomfort and tries to break the silence.

"Look," he says. "We just need a little something for the road. We don't plan to stay."

The tavern-keeper, Olchabar, breaks his gaze at me and looks back to Locke.

"Right then, well, I think I 'ave just the thing." He reaches under the counter and retrieves two small glasses and places them on the bar. He then disappears into the back for a few minutes and emerges with a small crystal bottle in his hand.

Olchabar uncorks the bottle and pours a light, indigo liquid into our glasses. I watch him suspiciously, and I see that he notices my scrutinizing glare. As if he has read my mind, he reaches under the bar and pours himself a glass as well. He then lifts the drink in the air, clinks glasses with Locke, and takes a sip. Locke drinks his down in one gulp and coughs violently for few seconds.

"Carefull now." Ochabhar laughs as he pats Locke on the back. "Not so tough now, are yeh? Think you can drink with the big boys. Think again!"

"What the hell was that?" Locke asks, through smaller coughs.

"Old family secret." Olchabar begins to refill Locke's glass, despite his previous reaction. "You know," Olchabhar says as he puts the stopper back on the crystal bottle, "that Brogan 'as been in several times over the past few nights."

"Brogan?" Locke says inquisitively.

"Aye, laddie, the big burley one. A right brute if yeh ask me. Thinks 'e's something of a threat around here. Comes in ordering people about like anyone in this part 'o town really gives a shite about who 'e is or what 'e wants." With this he casts a sideways glance at me, as if looking for some sort of praise or approval.

"Why would this Brogan show up here?" Locke asks. He lifts his drink and sips more carefully this time. "I thought the league wasn't welcome in this part of town."

"Aye, well, you know they just tromp around wherever they's feel the need to," Olchabhar says. "I wouldn't be surprised if 'e came in tonight. 'E's been meeting up regularly with a woman from just outside of town. Gets a room upstairs for a few hours, but never stays the night. She's a real tramp, piece 'a work if I've ever seen one." Olchabar laughs deeply.

Vesta, who has perched upon the bar, hisses loudly at him, her hair standing on end.

"Oh, ah, sorry, Vincent," he says nervously. "But the cat's goin' to have stay outside. Bar policy an' all."

Vesta looks at me, innocently, her head cocked to one side, pink eyes shimmering. I nod at her, and she, understanding the orders, leaps delicately to the floor and slinks slowly outside, pausing momentarily at the door to look back at me with an expression of disapproval.

"Anyways," Olchabar continues. "I suppose Brogan's just getting his kicks at a place that he feels won't degrade his character in front of the league."

Locke chuckles at this bit of perverse information.

"An' besides," Olchabhar adds, "Brogan's a right-bit closer to our type o' crowd anyway. I hear the only reason 'e's workin' for the league in the first place is out of sheer anger. Jus' wants free range to harm an' bully anyone 'e wants with the league's protection. He really don' give a damn about Roman 'er any of 'em."

"Really?" Locke asks.

"Aye 'tis true," adds a man sitting at the end of the bar. He has been silent and inconspicuous until now, but this conversation seems to have aroused his interest. He is old and scrawny, hunched over his own glass. His white hair hangs straggly in front of his face. His eyes are vibrant orange. "I hear he is out for blood. After the death of his father, Evander, he wants nothing but to take his anger out on anyone and everyone."

Evander. A name I haven't heard in a long time. It makes me cringe. Evander was the one who started the league. It was he who first heard of the prophecy and located the twins. It was he, with all his bravery and valor, who decided he would raise the boys and teach them to fight so that they could fulfill the prophecy. It was he who started the league to protect them.

He spent years evading me, moving the boys around from place to place, adding more and more 'warriors' to his secret circle. Many of them have fallen victim to me and, after a time, fewer and fewer men were feeling brave enough to join and fight for the common good.

Evander was convinced he'd hid the boys' secret from me and that at the proper moment he would release their relentless fury upon me, unsuspecting.

He was a fool. And fools are easily disposed of.

His son, Brogan, is another name I know well. He never cared much to support his father's cause; he felt no need to interfere, that is, until things became personal. He's a sworn member of the league, not for good or justice, but for vengeance[5]. How alike we are, he and I.

"What happened to Evander?" Locke asks Olchabhar.

"*Murdered*," the old man says in a sinister whisper, elongating the pronunciation for dramatic effect. "No one knows by whom or for what reason, but the truth is his father was murdered in cold blood and Brogan

---

[5]   Nightmare #556

has been bloodthirsty ever since. He beats and tortures, but no one ever defies him. He has no allegiance to the league; he simply uses them as protection while he wreaks his vengeance and seeks out his father's killer."

"And yet the league chooses to employ this type of barbarian?" Locke asks, disgusted. He has just drained his second glass and Olchabar reaches for the bottle mechanically, refilling Locke's empty glass. "What a bunch of hypocrites. I thought they were all about bringing light and peace to the world."

"Yeh don' understand," Ochabhar puts in, "Evander is the one who started the league in the first place! Swore to protect the twins 'til they was old enough an' train 'em up."

"And so Brogan feels," the old man continues, "that the league has no choice but to allow him to remain in their company."

"That's a bunch of bullshit if you ask me," Locke states matter-of-factly. It is clear that the spirits are now starting to affect him. "He's looking to do Vincent and me in and hurt other people just because somebody knocked off his dad? My dad's dead too and you don't see me running around slitting people's throats. Though, I wouldn't mind a chance at his."

Locke cracks his knuckles defiantly and the two men laugh.

"Oh you'll have your chance I'm sure," the old man says.

I listen carefully to the conversation without comment but choose to focus my gaze not on the tavern-keeper and Locke, but rather on the drink in front of me, which I have yet to taste. Instead, I swirl the contents of the glass and admire the whirls of color.

I sniff the alluring liquid which occupies my glass; it has soothing aromas which I have never sensed before yet they are sweet and inviting. I take a small sip and instantly feel a burning in my throat as the liquid slides delicately down my esophagus. It is sour, sweet, and bitter all at the same time. I feel a sudden warming in my bones and my muscles relax. I let my eyes close and allow my mind to wander into a deep trance. My head clears of all thought and distress, but swells with a series of vague, cloudy images.

I see Locke's pale blue eyes staring back at me from across the table. The eyes remain still, but the form around them changes.

They morph into a young woman, a pretty young face with light, golden locks. The face was smiling, but then the image morphs again around the pale blue eyes.

This was the same young woman but a look of sheer terror upon her face. Then, she morphed again around the constant stare of the eyes, and her face goes cold and still.

The image changes one final time. The blue eyes continued to remain unchanged, but the face that materializes this time is that of another young woman, comparably beautiful and innocent, with long, light brown hair and soft, pink lips. The eyes, which have since remained unchanged, become a more brilliant blue and, now, they sparkle.

Then both the face and the eyes begin to die away.

The memory fades into nothingness and I slowly open my eyes, but all that is visible to me is a blinding white light. It fills the room. It comes nearer and nearer and a burning sensation fills my body. My eyes stare, transfixed, ahead at the luminosity just feet from my face. I try to speak, but I am frozen. I cannot move. I cannot think. I feel weak; my heart is pounding outside of my chest. I feel the glass slip from my hand and clatter to the floor. I hear a faint murmur of voices beside me. They grow louder, and louder, and louder, and then . . . .

I fall.

The rain fell heavily last night, and given that Locke had not been home at all since last evening, I was beginning to worry. This was the first time, in many years, that this opportunity presented itself, so I did hesitate in sending Locke out for me. I knew he had had some trouble, though I was not yet sure how severe.

Although the morning hours were approaching, they brought no light. The nights have been getting longer and longer, and the days darker and darker. It is bitter cold, and the fallen rain quickly turned to ice as it hit the frozen earth. I gazed out my window, looking at the thick of forest ahead. The trees look dead, frozen in time as the world grows ever more sinister.

"I suppose I should go find him," I said, half to myself, half to Vesta, who sat at my feet. I quickly grabbed my old woolen cloak and headed out the door.

I walked for miles, pondering what could have happened to the young lad who has always been so faithful and so exceptionally useful to me. I saw in my vision only so little. I knew Locke had made it to the tavern unharmed, and I knew he had met the right men. But I also knew he was nervous, he would not be able to get what I had asked for, and that he, perhaps, had been seriously harmed in the whole ordeal.

As I approached the town I sensed a stiffness in the air. Several people in the street stopped and stared. A young mother, at first glimpse of me, rushed her child along into the nearest establishment. As I passed on down the frozen dirt road, passersby stepped back out of my way, as if the mere closeness of me might do them harm. Shutters closed, and doors were locked; the town seemed to shut up all on its own.

And I smiled, reveling in the triumph of their fear.

I walked up to the tavern at the corner, a large, stone building with gray shutters and a large oak door. The wood of the door was old and withered. A bleak sign hung above the entranceway, though the words were faded and no longer readable. I surveyed the surrounding area carefully and then approached. I raised a cautious hand and pounded heavily on the door. A frightened voice came from the inside:

"Who's there?" someone called from behind the large barred door.

"You know who it is," was my reply. "And you know that if I need to break this door down myself, there shall be hell to pay." At these words the door slowly creaked open to reveal a short, nervous looking man. He was extremely pale faced, with snow-white hair around the sides of his head, the top nearly bald. He had faint hazel eyes, and a thick, bristly mustache. His hands were trembling as his short stubby fingers fiddled nervously with a bar rag.

"You've seen a young boy around here last night," I said. It was not a question, for I had already seen that Locke was here[6].

"I'm s-sorry?" he stuttered.

"A boy, barman. Are you deaf? A fifteen year old boy. Thin, pale blue eyes, quite handsome. You have seen him." Again, my tone was assertive rather than questioning. I looked at him hard. I saw, in his faint hazel eyes, which were spread wide with angst and terror, the glow of my own sparkling violet ones reflecting back at me.

"Y-yes," he replied. "He w-was here, he sat at the bar for an hour or two, and I served him s-several pints. Then a group of sailors came in about m-midnight, and he left with them." He looked extremely frightened, and he should have been.

"You usually serve alcohol to fifteen year-old boys?" I said in disgust.

"I-I . . . ."

"Never mind, barman," I spat. "You said something about sailors?"

"Yes, s-sir. A group of them, about f-four or five, I'd say."

"You're sure? What did they look like?"

"They were all quite tall, with tanned skin and black hair and beards. They were all d-dressed in ragged clothing. The leader, he was the fiercest looking of the lot. He had, I think, a scar over his left eye, and in it was a shiny glass sphere. His right eye was a gruesome yellow color.

"And then?"

---

[6] Nightmare #823

The barman took a deep breath. Then he said, "And then I heard them say their s-ship was leaving tomorrow for the islands off the main land, that they wanted the boy to come with them. There was some k-kind of discussion between the men and the boy, that which I could not hear. Then they grabbed him up and took him outside." This was new information to me, for my vision had stopped before the "sailors" had entered the tavern. "N-naturally I was quite conc-cerned for the boy's safety, so I followed them out."

"Naturally," I said, knowing that it was far from concern, but instead mere curiosity that provoked this man.

"They took him down that way," he said while pointing in a direction around the corner of the building, "and then they were gone."

I stared at him suspiciously for several seconds after that. And he stood facing me, sweating, anticipating my next move.

"Very well," I said, and I turned away from him. As I walked in the direction to which he pointed I heard the door quickly shut and bolt back up behind me. Again, the sense of his fear intrigued me.

And so, I thought to myself. Locke met them, as I had seen in my nightmare. They must have the jewel, and know he is looking for it. I wonder if the rest was true as well. If it was . . . .

I turned down the way and noticed, far off towards the bay, that there were no ships in the harbor. The men Locke met up with last night were clearly gone. I walked on a little further in that direction until I noticed a huddled mass on the ground. Damn . . . it was true.

I approached and saw little movement from body that lay on the icy earth.

I pulled the woolen cloak from the ground to reveal Locke's motionless body. I touched his skin, which was hard, and cold. He was not dead, but only barely alive. He had cuts all over his face and a fresh bruise around his right eye. A stream of dried blood flowed from his mouth. A chunk of hair was missing from his scalp. I stared, pitifully, down at the boy at my feet, and I shook my head. I shouldn't have waited so long.

I searched his pockets; they were empty, as I had feared.

I knelt down beside him and removed his shirt, revealing long, think scars across his chest. How much more will this poor boy go through on my behalf? I wondered. I pulled a vial of glowing green liquid out of my cloak, uncorked it, and took a small sip. I then laid my hands on his chest and closed my eyes. Within a few minutes, his chest began to rise and fall heavily, yet slowly. His skin warmed beneath my touch. His eyes fluttered open, and the pale blue irises stared blankly up at me.

At that I searched through my cloak and retrieved a small bottle containing a black powder. I removed the cap and, pulling back Locke's eyelids, sprinkled a tiny amount of the substance into his eyes. I placed my left hand onto his swollen forehead. Within a few seconds his eyes closed again. I got up, walked away from him, and started the long journey home. After a few yards' distance, I turned to look back where Locke's body lay and saw Vesta sitting beside him.

While back at home in the comfort of my cabin, I pondered how to rectify the situation. I sent Locke on this quest; I knew that I was putting him in danger. And what's more, he was not successful. No matter, he would not remember.

I lit a pipe and let the soft ringlets of smoke float about and danced about in the air. I sat, thinking, both angry with Locke and yet, somehow, concerned for the boy. Within a few minutes, there was a knock at the door. Locke emerged out of the darkness, looking tired, and weak.

"What has happened to you?" I asked him angrily.

Locke lifted his hand to his forward and pushed the brown locks back off of his face.

"I have no idea," he replied.

V
THE THIEVES

A splash of cold water rushes upon my face and my senses return instantly. I shake my head and see both Locke and Olchabhar bending over me. Locke has a water jug in his hand.

"Vincent," Locke says; his concerned countenance becomes clearer as my eyes refocus.

"I am dreadfully sorry," I say, rubbing my temples. "That is quite a strong concoction. I seem to have lost myself for a moment." The tavern-keeper picks up the empty glass, which remarkably, has remained intact, and mops up the spilled liquid with a dirty cloth.

Locke helps me to my feet and dusts a few remaining droplets off of my cloak.

I look around and notice that the entire room is staring at us. The old man at the end of the bar turns away, swallows the last of the contents of his glass, and gets up from the bar. He nods to Locke, but stares daggers at me as he passes by.

"Can I offer yeh a room for the night?" Olchabhar asks, though reluctantly.

"We really must be going," Locke tells him, shifting uncomfortably from the stares of the onlookers. "What do I owe you?"

"On me tonight, Locke," Olchabhar replies.

"Thanks, Olchabhar," Locke says, reaching out to shake the tavern-keeper's hand. Olchabar grasps Locke's hand and pulls him close. He says, barely audibly, as if hoping I wouldn't hear, "I can keep you safe, yeh know."

"I appreciate that," Locke whispers politely back, but with assertion that he has no intention of taking up the offer.

Olchabhar pulls back, looking let down.

"Safe travels for yeh then," he says in his normal volume, which suggests his relief that the offer to house us for the night was declined. "Hope to see yeh again soon . . ." The tavern-keeper pauses for a moment before adding, ". . . alive." He shakes Locke's hand with both of his, pats him roughly on the back, and then glances once more upon me, his face displaying suspicion and concern. Then he turns to Locke and says, "Why don't the two-a-yeh slip out the back way there, lad." He gestures towards the doorway behind the bar.

"Thank you," Locke says sincerely.

"An' Locke," Olchabhar adds, "be careful, eh. There 'ave been some strange men comin' in an' out the past few nights."

Locke nods in gratitude and, with my arm hoisted over his shoulder, begins to walk me out. Stares follow us as we slip behind the bar and disappear through a dim hallway. We leave out the back entranceway and stumble into a dark alley. Vesta rejoins us, rubbing her back against my leg.

"Locke," I breathe tiredly, "I need just a moment." Locke lets go of my arm and I slump down to the ground. I pull a vial from my pocket containing an emerald green liquid. I take a sip and put the vial back into my cloak. I drop my head so that it sits upon my knees, and Locke crouches down beside me, resting his weary hand on my shoulder.

"You alright then, Vincent?" he asks, concerned. "You saw the light again, didn't you? That's twice in twenty-four hours. It seems to be getting stronger."

"My dear Locke," I sigh. Everything else is getting stronger around me while my aging body grows weaker and weaker still. "I am beginning to think this is a winless battle we have decided to fight."

At these words Locke sits down next to me and stares up into the black night sky. He takes a few deep breaths and looks over at me.

"We can't give up now, Vincent," he says. "You know that you are powerful enough to stop them. We just need the proper help. You said we need to retrieve something from the ship in the harbor. Just tell me what it is. I will find it."

Locke's words are reassuring. He is right. He is sticking to the plan.

"I cannot reveal it to you now," I say. "But it is of utmost importance. What I am looking for lies within the hull of that ship."

"But, how can you be sure?" Locke asks.

"I saw it.[7]"

"Recently?"

"No, many years ago, actually. However, it would have been foolish of me to attempt to retrieve it myself."

"You should have asked me," Locke says. "I would have tried to help you."

I remain silent.

"I believe it is somewhere on the ship," I repeat. "We must go there now and find it."

"Well," Locke says, rising to his feet, "what are we waiting for?

---

[7]   Nightmare #828

"I suppose," I say, "that we are waiting for an old man to catch his breath."

Locke laughs and grabs my hands, and pulls me up.

"C'mon," he says. "We're not going to get anywhere just sitting around here."

Just then, a chilling voice comes out of the darkness.

"You're not going anywhere."

Standing just ahead of us are four men. They are tall, with dark hair and tanned skin. One of the men has a long, braided mustache, and several gold chains reveal themselves behind an unbuttoned shirt. The other two look almost exactly the same; they are both short, and have long beards and rags tied about their heads. They each have a gold band through the right nostril. All of the men appear dirty and are wearing ragged, loose clothing.

"I believe I've met you before there, eh Locke?" The man in the front of the pack smirks. He moves into the moonlight, revealing his features more clearly to me. His lips form a sinister smile, revealing several crooked and cracked teeth, one of which is made of gold. He wears a patch over his left eye and a thick scar extends down over it from forehead to cheek, leaving the impression that this is the reason the eye is missing. His skin is darker than the rest, suggesting many long hours in the hot sun.

"Haram," I say to myself in a whisper.

I feel Locke slowly push me behind the stack of wooden crates next to the tavern. I slump down to avoid being seen.

"Who are you?" Locke says fiercely, standing alone now, facing the group of men.

"Oy, you hear that mates?" the leader, Haram, calls to the men in behind him. "This lad doesn't recognize us." The other men roar with laughter. It is apparent, by their wavering stances, that all four of them are drunk. The leader turns back to face Locke.

"Well, allow me to refresh your memory, boy," he says.

The three men walk out from behind and form a circle around Locke. Haram pulls a long sword from his holster and holds it up to Locke's throat.

"You surely remember this, don't you boy?" he says. "Where's your old man Vincent? I thought for sure he'd be comin' for us after last time, seein' how we've found what he tried so hard to get and," indicating Locke, "which this son of a bitch tried to steal from us." He presses the blade of the sword deeper into Locke's throat so that a trickle of blood seeps out. "But we roughed him up pretty good, didn't we boys?"

His cronies begin to laugh.

"But he didn't do anything about it, did he?" Haram says to Locke. "Maybe he really doesn't give a shit about you. Or perhaps he isn't so eager to make trouble, since he knows what power I have in my possession."

I shake my head in amusement. He may possess what I desire, but he has no idea how to use it, or what it's for. It is an idle threat, and an ignorant display confidence.

"Perhaps," Haram continues, "if we finish the job this time, old Vincent will get the message."

The other men nod in agreement, make vulgar comments and reach for their swords, each eager to be the first to strike. I watch silently, waiting for the right moment.

"A better idea," Haram says, "would be to hold you hostage until Vincent tells me how the jewel works. Then I will kill you. It must be pretty valuable, eh, boy? Or the old bastard wouldn't want it so bad."

"I don't know what you're talking about," Locke says. "I swear."

"You think I'm really stupid, don't you boy," Haram says, and the other men laugh.

Haram retracts the blade swiftly from Locke's throat and punches him square across the jaw. Locke absorbs the blow and falls over sideways to the ground, and another of the men wraps an arm around his throat from behind and lifts him to his feet.

He struggles for several minutes and the leader puts his face up close to Locke's, spitting as he talks.

"Ha!" the leader laughs. "You still haven't learned, have you boy? I suppose yet another round will do you good. What'll it take to make Vincent come out and play, I wonder? Has he suddenly caught on? He is not so confident against me as he once was?" He gestures toward the scar on his eye.

"Do you see this?" he asks Locke. "I owe him a favor. Perhaps he'll let you take the fall for him then?"

He backs away as if to strike again, but Locke reacts quickly. With all of his strength, Locke drives his elbow into the stomach of the man holding him, causing him to lose his grip. The man with the mustache doubles over in pain, releasing Locke. Now free, Locke turns quickly and kicks him square in the face. The man falls over, clutching his nose, which is now gushing blood.

At this point the two men with bandanas make a start for Locke. Locke grabs one by the shirt and, showing a phenomenal feat of strength, hoists him up over his head and slams him, back first, into the ground. Locke turns on a pivot and throws a hard punch at the other bandana-clad twin, knocking him right over backward. He then turns to face the leader of the group.

Locke takes a swing but the tall man catches his fist in his hand. Locke struggles to free himself for a few moments, until the two men in bandanas scramble to their feet and seize Locke by the arms, one on each side. The man with the mustache, still holding his bloody nose, kicks the backsides of Locke's knees, causing him to fall forward. He then grabs the back of Locke's hair and pulls his head back, revealing his bare neck.

Haram approaches Locke with his sword drawn. "I am going to enjoy removing your head," he says quietly. "Then I am going to tie it up from the mast of my ship like a flag, as we sail out of the port, so that Vincent and everyone else in this hellish village can see it."

The time for action has come.

Just as Haram raises his sword, I lift my palms from my position behind to crates. Luckily, Locke sees me out of the corner of his eye.

In an instant, Locke ducks his head as Haram swings his sword down, and a flash of bright light erupts from my hands. There is a loud crack and a bright flash that absorbs everything around us for a brief moment.

I stand immediately and Locke raises his head, a look of utter shock upon his young face.

All around his crouching body lay four deceased figures and some light rising smoke.

March 3rd, '39

On this day, I was working on a formula in my cabin. It was evening, quiet, and I was alone. I sat in my study, mixing two liquids together in a beaker: one, a luminous yellow color and the other, a vibrant orange. I lit a candle and placed it beneath the beaker to bring the concoction to a boil. I then sprinkled some gray powder into the mix, and the liquid bubbled and crackled as it turned a shade of blood red.

Just then, I heard a hearty knock at the door. Frustrated by this interruption, I grudgingly opened the door. A tall, dark, scrawny man entered. His hair was jet black and his skin was deeply tanned and scarred. He had a deep scar over his left eye, which was currently hidden by a black, tattered patch. The other eye was a dull yellow.

He was surely not welcome on this day, yet I expected him, having foreseen his appointment.

"Do you have the potion ready yet there, Vincent?" the man said. His accent was thick, of a Middle-Eastern tongue. He eyed me suspiciously, with his hand close to his side pocket. I already knew that he had come prepared for a fight and I wanted him to be sure that that dagger in his pocket was of no use to him.

"I am not going to do any harm to you, Mr. Haram. You will not need to remove your dagger from your jacket pocket."

Haram looked at me, amazed, embarrassed, and terrified. How could I possibly have known?

I returned to my workspace and removed a vial of vibrant orange liquid from a row of similar tubes. He lifted the patch over his left eye to reveal a shiny glass orb. Haram's yellow eye briefly brightened up as he held the vial up and examined it. I knew exactly what this was going to be used for, and yet I freely offered it to him anyway.

"We shall test it first, to be certain it works," I explained. At once I whistled and Vesta appeared with a squirming mouse clenched in her jaws. Much to Vesta's dismay, I removed the mouse from her mouth. I then placed a tiny droplet of the liquid into the mouse's mouth with a dropper. In an instant the mouse began to squeal; it screeched in my hand until finally its eyes turned black and its body went rigid, lying cold in my hand.

At the sight of this, Haram trembled slightly, but looked longingly at the vial. "Two drops should do," I added as I handed the vial to the Haram, and he secured it in the inside pocket of his jacket. Haram reached into a second pocket and pulled out a small black velvet pouch. He dropped it into my hand. As soon as the fabric touched my skin, my hand burned and sent chills up my arm and into my heart. The bag seemed to illuminate in my hand. Finally . . .

"You have no idea what I had to go through to get that," he said. I did not respond, but stared intently at the pouch clutched in my hand.

"And what of my other request?" I asked him.

"I have yet to find her," he replied. "Twice now I have pursued her and failed. I am planning another expedition next month. My ship leaves tomorrow and will return with a party a few weeks later."

"It has been a long time," I said. "You're time is running out. It seems that time has diluted the effect of my promise. Do not forget it."

Haram's expression faded. "I remember," he said.

"I expect I will be seeing you again soon, then," I said. "Good day, Haram."

"A pleasure . . . as always," he said as he backed out of the door.

I turned around and lit my pipe as the man closed the cabin door behind me.

"Liar," I said, and I turned back to my work.

VI

THE SHIP

Locke gets up and dusts off his cloak. He looks around at his attackers and then touches the slit on his neck, where the sword threatened him only minutes ago.

The back door to Olchabhar's tavern opens and the tavern-keeper sticks his head out.

"What the bloody hell is g-!" But his words are silenced when his eyes fall upon the sight of the bodies on the ground. The shock of the scene renders him speechless.

"Everything's fine," Locke says, breaking the awkward silence.

Olchabhar lingers for a moment more, then mumbles something similar to, "I sure hope he knows what he's getting himself into" as he disappears back behind the door.

I sit; my arms and hands are stinging from an intense, prickly pain that extends up to my shoulders. It is growing increasing more dangerous and wearisome for me to perform these acts. I must save my strength. I breathe deeply in an attempt to soothe the exalting pain.

Meanwhile, Locke rounds on me.

"You had to wait until they roughed me up a bit before you did anything?" he asks me angrily.

I don't answer. He walks over to the crates and begins kicking them, repeatedly, in an effort to vent his anger.

"Goddamn it!" he says, striking furiously at the helpless crates. "Son . . . of . . . a . . . BITCH!"

"Locke, your mouth."

"I DON'T GIVE A SHIT ABOUT MY LANGUAGE RIGHT NOW!" he screams in sheer indignation. He continues his relentless assault on the helpless crates. After he exhausts his energy, Locke stops and sits on one of the abused crates, putting his head in his hands. He is clearly handling this much worse than the incident with Ollam. His composure is beginning to break.

"I'm sorry, Locke," I say solemnly, enduring short flinches of pain. "I didn't want to act until I felt it was absolutely necessary."

"Well, thanks anyhow," he says sarcastically, his anger not yet subsided. "I needed to add a few more scrapes to my ever growing collection."

"Locke, I said I'm sorry."

Locke spits blood onto the ground and wipes his mouth. With what little strength I have left, I put my hand gently to his neck and the cut disappears. I pull my aching arm away.

Locke, completely oblivious to my suffering, gets up and turns from me to walk away down the road. He gets only a few feet before he stops abruptly and turns back towards me.

"Who were they?" he asks, rationality now setting in. "They said they knew you, and they said they knew me, but I've never seen them before in my life. Who were they?"

"Haram is an old acquaintance and, apparently, an enemy."

"Well, what the hell did you do to them? How do they know me? Where I have I seen them before?"

"I cannot be sure how they know you, Locke. Perhaps you came across them one night at the tavern. After a few drinks? You might not remember that."

I feel terribly for him, but I hesitate in revealing the truth. Locke suddenly fills with rage.

"THEY WANTED TO KILL ME!" he shouts back at me, his arms raised in frustration. "I've never been that drunk! It's because of you! What are you not telling me, Vincent? I cannot continue on in the dark like this!"

"They have something of mine, and I intend to get it back," I say. "I didn't want to have to kill him, because I have no idea where it is. That's why I allowed things to go on as long as I did. But he gave me no choice. It was him or you."

"Oh, well thanks!" Locke says sarcastically. 'What the hell could he possibly have that is so goddamn important that you had to wait until I was *nearly* dead?"

"I cannot reveal it to you now," I reply. Locke drops his arms by his side in frustration. He knows he will not get a straight answer out of me. It is for his own good.

I reach into my cloak for the familiar vial full of black powder, but I release it, realizing suddenly that I no longer have the strength or the heart.

"So what do we do now?" Locke asks, exasperated.

"As I have already told you, we must go to the ship in the harbor. I must retrieve what they have stolen."

"Oh are we going on a treasure hunt now," Locke says. "Wonderful! And how do you expect us to man a boat?"

"It must be on the ship," I say.

"Of course it is." Locke rolls his eyes and starts off towards the dock. Struggling on my own, I follow him, both annoyed at his behavior and relieved that he has not given up on me.

⎯⎯⎯►∘◄⎯⎯⎯

The ship is old, yet modest in size. A black flag hangs from the mast, its ominous symbol hidden within its folds. I lean over the side of the dock and gaze into the murky water below. Locke, having calmed down considerably, reaches out to grab hold of the rope tied from the dock to the ship and hoists himself aboard. He then assists me over the edge and onto the deck. Vesta jumps aboard with ease, and immediately begins to explore the new surroundings.

Once aboard, I cannot help but freeze as I take it all in: the wet, mossy wooden deck, the large, towering sails, the vast network of ropes and pulleys and capstans, the wheelhouse and poop deck. I walk up the helm and gently rest my hands on the large, wooden projections of the wheel. I grasp them tightly and close my eyes. I breathe the sea air in deeply.

I see him, standing before me, looking tall and important, his hands on his hips in a proud gesture. He shouts orders imperiously at the men before him who rush about frantically, obediently, like a pack of dogs eager to please their beloved master.

I look up at him, admiringly, longingly. To me, he is everything.

He looks right through me. To him, I barely exist.

I feel a gentle touch on my shoulder.

"Everything alright?" Locke asks.

"Fine," I reply.

"Shall we press on?" he asks. I nod in agreement and, hesitantly, release my grip from the large wooden wheel.

The boat rocks mildly back and forth as we make our way to the lower quarters.

"What exactly is it that we are looking for?" Locke asks. His breath is visible in the night air; it is about fifteen degrees colder on the water.

"Perhaps you will recognize it when you see it," is all that I reply.

I lead Locke down into the hull of the ship. We descend the stairs, which shift and creak under our feet. The interior of the ship is dark; I dust my fingers with yellow powder, sparking a fire between then, and light a lantern on the wall. Locke takes it down and we proceed, myself in the lead, while Locke reluctantly follows behind me.

The floor, like the deck above, is mossy and slimy, as if it hasn't been scrubbed in weeks. The crew was obviously quite slovenly, or perhaps that is a better analysis of the ship's captain.

Layers of cobwebs drape across the ceiling and walls.

A mouse skitters across the floor, and Vesta takes off after it.

We first pass by a row of barred cells. One contains the remains of a man who seems to have been deceased for months. His corpse sits propped up against the wall and large bits of rotting flesh linger upon the emerging bones.

.Three more cells follow, and though they are empty of persons, they smell of death and decay. Skulls and other bones litter the floor and blood splatters cake the walls. There are ropes and shackles hanging from the ceiling. The sight is too much for Locke, who vomits in the corner of the room.

A few feet further down there is a passageway that leads into a dining hall. There is a long table in the center of the room, covered with filth and scraps of food. There are dirty plates and goblets scattered upon the table and floor. It is clear that these barbarians never cleaned up after themselves. A large chandelier hangs from the ceiling, and upon it, are a dozen lit candles, waning slowly and dripping hot wax.

I step inside and walk to the chair at the head of the table. I rest my hand on the grainy wood, and take another deep breath.

A sudden feeling of movement washes over me as the inside of a ship materializes in my subconscious. There are about twenty-five men sitting around a long, rectangular table. The table is littered with plates of half-eaten food, goblets of wine, and knives and forks.

The room smells of beer and mold and meat.

The men eat and drink, slopping food and beer all over themselves, the table, and the floor.

They laugh boisterously at obscene jokes and crude remarks about recent rendezvous with loose women.

Two men at one end of the table get into a heated argument, and one punches the other.

The entire table erupts in laughter as the two men wrestle on the ground.

At the far end of the table, the captain sits. He sits, deep in anxious thought, as he surveys the grotesque scene before him.

"This is difficult for you, isn't it?"

I open my eyes. Locke stands in the doorway.

"I'm just trying to remember what I saw in my nightmare," I lie. I quickly exit the room.

A series of doors lines the far wall, leading, assumedly, to various sleeping quarters and cargo holds. Locke opens each door slowly and illuminates the rooms, one by one, with the lantern. Each room is as bare and empty as the next, containing only two cots apiece, as well as a chest at the end of each bed. Locke searches each chest and begins rifling through coins and jewels.

"Your efforts are wasted, Locke." I tell him. "I doubt what we are looking for was a possession of any of the crewmen. It is much too important. Its possessor could be none other but the captain, since none of his crew managed to slit his throat yet."

"Though no doubt they were certainly planning to," I say to myself.

Eventually, we come upon and enter the captain's quarters. The room is double the size of the others, with a large bed and desk in the corner. Vesta jumps up onto the bed and curls up into a ball to rest.

There is a handsome chandelier hanging from the ceiling, as well as a painted portrait of Haram on the wall at the head of the bed. In the portrait, his glass orb of an eye glows.

There is a large wooden chest at the foot of his bed as well. Unfortunately, there is a lock on it. Locke searches the desk for the key while I look under his bed.

With no other option, Locke, with all of his strength, lifts the desk chair and smashes it over the top of the chest. Vesta jumps up in alarm. The effect is minimal, which leaves the task up to me. I raise my hand and, with a flash of light, crack the chest in two. An array of gold and silver, jewels, and other effects spill from the chest. Locke sifts through them as I watch behind him. I see nothing of interest to me. I turn my head away in anger and look once more about the room. I look once more at the portrait above the bed. Haram's yellow eye pierces through me, and I wonder . . . .

I walk up to the portrait and raise a hand. Suddenly, the portrait swings slowly open. There is a hole in the wall behind it. On the ledge is a small box. Locke removes the box and sets it on the bed. Nervously, I open it, revealing several curious objects: a glass eye—which looks like an alternative one –, a brass key, a tiny animal skull, and a smoky, silvery white jewel. I pick up the jewel and it begins to glow, radiant silver, and I can hardly contain my excitement: I have it back at last.

"What is that?" Locke asks me.

"Something I lost a long time ago," I reply, "and have waited many long years to recover. I sent Haram on a mission to find it for me; I think perhaps he learned of its value and intended to keep it for himself. I knew he had it. I saw him acquire it[8]. Yet he tried to keep it from me. Funny, how things have a way of finding their way back to their rightful place."

---

[8] Nightmare #604

"If you knew he had it, why did you wait so long to get it back?" I blink my sparkling violet eyes. I've tried, many times, but Locke wouldn't remember.

"He is a sailor, Locke," I say. "It is not often that he makes port in this part of the country. In fact, he is usually gone for several years at a time." Locke nods in agreement.

"Also," I continue, "I wasn't quite sure until recently where it was hidden. It is like I said, I did not know where it was and, therefore, he was no use to me dead. I do believe that until very recently it was being hidden elsewhere." This was only partially true. I didn't want to go after it myself unless I was sure of its location, but also in case Haram had discovered its power, which he may have. He must have gotten close to figuring out how to make use of it, and so that is why he brought it back.

"It's quite beautiful," Locke remarks.

"Yes," I say, "but its true value for me holds a little more weight than any amount of gold."

I take the jewel and place it safely inside my cloak. Locke picks up the eye and holds it up to the light, studying it closely. He seems to be enthralled by it, as it shines like nothing he has ever seen before.

I take it from him quickly and put that too inside my cloak.

"The key is useless to us now," he says, glancing back at the destroyed remains of the chest. "How about we start the ship on fire, eh, Vincent? We haven't done anything fanatical in about half an hour, and that would be quite dramatic, wouldn't it?"

"It would also draw quite a bit of attention, Locke," I say to him, annoyed. "Let us move quickly on."

November 12th, '37

Locke, with tears in his eyes and blood running down his cheek, looked up at me in horror. Anger and rage filled my head and my chest. I didn't mean for that to happen. Sometimes, my impulses get the best of me. I took a moment to gather myself, and then I scooped the boy up in my arms and carried him back into the woods.

I apologized profusely the whole way home; Locke lay crying in my arms. He was merely seven years old. And yet I was responsible for the bruises and cuts on his chest and face.

As I walked, I pondered what had happened in the last few hours. I had sent Locke out into the village on an errand for me. I gave food and shelter in return for his assistance. I knew it was dangerous, but I didn't care. These things are easily remedied when something goes wrong. Besides, what else could life for a boy like this, whom no one loves and no one cares for, be like? He enjoys what he does for me, what he remembers of it.

I sent Locke to the streets to collect some materials for me. Hours went by without his return, so I set out after him. I found the boy in the alleyway behind the farmer's market. He was shivering in the cold of the winter. When he saw me, he looked up, frightened. I noticed a fresh red bruise beneath his right eye.

"What has happened here?" I said to him. I don't know why I even asked, I had already seen what had happened in a nightmare, yet I sent the boy out anyway[9]. I wondered how badly he had been beaten. Yet, I hoped he had managed to get what I needed. "Well?" I hissed at him.

Without speaking, Locke held out his small hand toward me and dropped a vial of black liquid, a long white animal fang, and few gold coins into my palm. He then turned and looked back down at his feet, ashamed and deeply saddened. This was not everything.

---

[9]   Nightmare #606

My veins filled with fire and rage. I raised my right hand and made a swift, swooping motion. A jet of bright white flew from my palm and slashed Locke across the face. He toppled over backward and landed on his back on the ground. And that was the end of it.

I carried Locke into my cabin and lay him on the floor. He shivered and his heart was racing.

"Close your eyes," I whispered, and he did so as tears still flowed from them. I placed my hands, palms down, above the small child's face. I whispered a few words and a dim light emanated from my palms. Within minutes, Locke's face glowed softly and the cuts and bruises slowly disappeared.

I then took my left hand and placed it on Locke's tiny forehead. I reached into my pocket and retrieved a vial of scintillating black dust which I sprinkled over Locke's eyes. As I did this, Locke slipped into a deep sleep.

"I did not harm you, Locke," I whisper. "You have no recollection of what I have done. I saved you." I picked the boy up and placed him in my bed.

A few hours later, Locke woke up and cried for me. I knelt down beside him and gave him water to drink.

"Am I alright?" he asked me nervously.

"Yes, Locke, you're fine. Luckily I got there in time to ward off those villains."

"Thank you, Mr. Vincent," he said softly. "You are always here to help me." I quickly washed Locke's face, fed him supper, and read to him his favorite poem. ("The one with the funny words!" he said excitedly. "When the little boy slays the dragon!")

Once he was happy and content and very much relieved of any possible unpleasant memory, I sent him on his way. I told him I would need his services again the following week. He agreed to come back. I watched the young boy scuttle out the door and a little piece of my stale, icy heart broke.

March 2nd, '37

I stood in the darkness at the edge of the wood, an ominous figure shrouded in my bluish-black cloak. The cold air swirled about me as I stared enviously at the ship in the distance, floating effortlessly atop the placid water, lights ablaze within it. I imagined the men aboard were drinking and eating a hearty meal, enjoying a respite from a long voyage at sea.

A dark figure approached. He had two luminous yellow eyes.

"Vincent," he said.

"Haram," I replied.

"I found it quite interesting that you wanted to do business with me," Haram said. "I thought you might have sworn off association with our kind. I guess you just couldn't keep away."

"Don't flatter yourself!" I exclaimed. "I wouldn't associate myself with you or those heathen you call a crew if it wasn't absolutely imperative. Unfortunately for me, I do not have the time, so I must resort to employing your services. I think you'll find yourself handsomely rewarded if you serve me well."

"You can bet your ass that it will come with a heavy price," Haram said. "What is that you want?"

"There is a jewel," I began, "that is an iridescent, smoky-white. It glows radiant silver when clutched in your hand. It was a possession of my father's; he came upon it during his travels when I was a boy. I want it back."

"Aww," Haram spat sarcastically. "Is the mighty Vincent feeling sentimental?"

"Can you get it?" I asked, ignoring his juvenile taunts.

"Any idea where I might find it?"

"As far as I know, it is in the possession of an aged woman, a woman with shimmering pink eyes."

"And where might I find her?"

"I believe she might come looking for you, actually."

"What?"

I reached inside my cloak and extracted a small, shimmering pink gem. Haram's yellow eyes bulged greedily at the sight of it.

"Offer her this," I said, "in exchange for the jewel I desire."

Haram reached out anxiously and grasped the gem from my hand. He held it close, lost momentarily in its luminescence.

Then he asked, "Why don't you just do it yourself?"

"As I have already told you," I reply, "I do not have the time. I am busy with other matters. And, I am not so sure she would want me to have it."

"Why wouldn't she want you to have it?"

"Why do you ask so many questions that are not of your concern? Are you going to help me or not?"

"What's in it for me?" Haram asked, his eyes never wavering from the gem.

"In addition to a generous sum of gold," I said. "You are aware of my profession Haram?"

"Who isn't," he replied.

"Whatever of my personal services you may be in need of. You know that is not an offer many others receive?"

Haram looked up at me and, for the first time, smiled.

"Consider it done," he said confidently.

"You might want to start by sailing up to the northern border," I said. "There is a thick wood there. Here is an advance for your troubles." I handed him a small satchel. Haram accepted it happily and gave it a shake, content with the weighty jingle of the coinage concealed inside.

He then turned back in the direction of the ship.

"Oh, and Haram," I said.

As he turned around, he met a flash of white light and fell to the ground. He clasped his face in anguish and writhed in the dirt. Blood trickled from between his fingers.

I bent down to him and pulled his hands away, revealing a black, bloody hole where his right eye had been only a moment ago, a long, jagged cut dissecting it vertically.

"Let that be a warning should you try and deceive me," I said. "I hope it will deter you from trying to keep my little trinket for yourself. Oh, and there is one other thing I hoped you could procure for me amid you travels." I leaned in close to him and whispered into his ear.

Haram opened his mouth to speak, but before he could respond, I was gone.

———◆———

As I made my way back through the dense forest, I pondered how best to acquire the stone from Haram once he retrieves it. I know he will find it and, once he learns of its power, will want to keep it for himself. As I approached my cabin, I saw a faint light coming from inside. My stomach lurched at the thought of the child within. Would he never leave me be?

I opened the cabin door and saw him, his back towards me, sitting in front of the hearth, gently stroking Vesta's soft fur as innocently as could be. I walked up behind him, and he sat unknowingly. A cursed thought streaked through my mind: how easy it would be to rid myself of this burden.

The fire crackled and Vesta purred loudly at the touch of his tiny fingers.

He turned around suddenly and looked up at me.

And he smiled at me.

It was at that moment that the idea hit me.

Perhaps this boy will be of use after all.

VII

THE FOREST

Locke and I move swiftly away from the ship, back towards the forest. I can tell that he is very tired, and we need a place to rest. It has become icy cold, and I notice Locke shivering. His hands are purplish and rigid.

I grasp his palms in mine and hold them for a few moments. I close my eyes and wait; Locke does the same. Suddenly, warmth emits from my hands and his relax. The iciness subsides and a warm pink color returns to his flesh.

We continue to make our way towards the forest and reach the edge of it. Before entering, I turn around and take one last, longing glance at the ship in the harbor. How easy it would be to climb aboard, to sail away, Locke and I, and leave this place. I wonder if the two of us could manage it, with the help of my gifts of course. I wonder, in my old age, if I could muster the strength to steer the ship off into the horizon and never return. I close my eyes, picturing the bright orange glow as the setting sun sinks slowly into an abyss of blue water, and me at the bow, soaking in the light ocean breeze and the salty sea air, my sparkling purple eyes open once again to all the tranquility that the vast ocean has to offer. I am lost in the reverie.

Locke calls to me, interrupting my fantasy, "Vincent?"

I open my eyes. "Come, Locke," I say to him walking into the forest ahead of him. "We must go visit the sisters. It isn't too far, we need to backtrack through the woods a stretch; they live in a cabin on the outer edge of the forest. If we move quickly, we should be there in a few hours or so."

"Who are they?" he asks curiously. "And what do you want with them?"

"They are old friends of mine."—I use the term 'friends' very loosely—"They will give us a place to stay for the night, so we can get some rest and replenish our strength. Also, I have some unfinished business with the eldest."

"What business is that, sir?"

"You shall see," I reply. "But I suppose, I should forewarn you, Medea, the eldest, is quite a vicious creature."

"Really?" Locke sighs. "As if we don't need to encounter any more foul characters tonight. What makes this woman particularly nasty?"

"Well, Locke," I reply. "Since we have quite a way to go, I might as well tell you their story." As we walk through the darkness, I recount the story of the three sisters to Locke, who listens intently to my tale.

"Many years ago, there lived a kind, decent woman of magical ability, who learned that she was pregnant. Because she so feared anything immoral or evil in the world, she created a magical potion, drank it, and prayed to the gods that she might give birth to a child who would be ignorant of all malice in the world. She begged that her child never glimpse a wretched sight, hear a vicious sound, or speak a wicked word.

"However, to the surprise of the woman, she did not bear one, but three children, born one after the other, and her prayer and magical abilities were divided amongst them. It seems that her honest life and diligent prayer pleased the gods, and it appeared that they granted her wish, though spitefully.

"Her first daughter was born blind. Thus, she would never glimpse a wretched sight. Her middle child was born deaf, so that she may never hear a vicious sound, and her youngest daughter was born mute, so that she may never speak a wicked word.

"The three sisters, though very beautiful indeed and magically gifted, could not have been more different.

"The youngest of the sisters grew to be very kind and humble. Because she could not speak, she used her mind and her delicate countenance to communicate with confidence. She used her magic to help and to heal, and to bring merriment to those with affliction.

"The middle of the sisters grew to be very frightened and meek. Her inability to hear caused her to be very self conscious, always feeling that people were whispering things about her. Because she spent most of her time hidden, her magic was weak and undeveloped, and thus grew feeble and worthless.

"And the eldest of the sisters grew to be very wicked and envious. She did not understand true beauty, because she could not see it, and grew to be very jealous and bitter towards those who did. In her envy, she grew to be quite wicked, preying on those less fortunate than herself. She used her magic for personal gain only, and it was therefore, like she herself, tainted and cruel."

"Great," Locke says sarcastically when I finish my recitation of the old tale. "I can't wait to meet them."

⟶•◆•⟵

Locke and I continue our trek through the dense forest. If the night seemed black before, the forest is even darker. I hear a howling sound in the distance and am reminded of my fate. I look up into the sky, the moon is nearly full. Only a night or two left to go.

Locke walks a few paces ahead of me, trying his best to clear a path for me over fallen branches and through thick, unforgiving vines. I stumble several times, though Locke is quick to lift me back upon my feet. I cannot help but wonder what I would have done had he not been so insistent on accompanying me. He is clearly a necessity, and I selfishly accepted, knowing what the ultimate cost may be for him.

The trek is an arduous one. We walk for several hours before fatigue really starts to take over. Locke sits down for a moment, and I next to him. Locke takes in a few deep breaths and wrinkles his nose in disgust.

"Do you smell that?" he asks.

"What?" I say, unable to sense anything displeasing. Locke stands and begins walking off in a different direction. Disgruntled, I stand, though wavering, and follow.

As we walk in this new direction, Locke on the trail like a Bassett hound, a pungent odor fills the air, a smell of ash and smoke. Upon further travel, the air becomes so thick that it becomes difficult to breathe, visibility begins to diminish. Locke coughs several times, holding his arm up to cover his mouth and nose with his sleeve.

Visibility becomes increasingly more strained as a thick smoke-fog fills the air around us, stinging my eyes and causing them to tear up. I can see the violet shine from my eyes in the smoky air ahead.

After a few more minutes, we approach the culprit. A huge pile of ash and embers lay in a clearing ahead: my cabin, burned to the ground.

I choke back immense emotion, and anger wells within me. I knew that this happened. I watched Roman and his men break down my door and set fire to my home as Locke, Vesta, and I made a dramatic yet narrow escape. But actually seeing my beloved cabin burnt to the ground, with all of my hard work reduced to a pile of smoldering ashes, ignites a fury within me.

I feel my palms turn white-hot and I lift them high into the air. A burst of light erupts and streaks upward into the night sky. The sound of the blast sends shock waves echoing through the trees, which is immediately followed by a cacophony of falling branches and leaves.

Locke steps back.

I hold my hands upward for a few moments, allowing all of the anger and exasperation to surge from them, before I lower them gently and look at the bright glow that resonates from my wrinkled palms. This was foolish of me. With all the energy I released upon Haram and his cronies, I knew it I should have reserved my strength. I was helpless now, until I had time to rest.

Locke, now sure that he is safe from my wrath, walks closer to the remains of the pyre. He kicks around a few pots and bits of wood. What he is looking for, I cannot guess. I don't care to know. He looks back at me hopelessly, with sympathetic eyes. This too, was his home, off and on, for many years. Vesta rubs her soft fur back and forth against my cloak, as if to say that she, too, is sorry. I bend down and pick her up, allowing her to nuzzle gentle against my cheek. We all stand in silence, reflecting on the years and memories that are now a heap of burning rubbish on the forest floor.

"When this is all over," Locke says with hope, "we'll come back here and rebuild it. It'll be just like new again, I promise."

I nod, wondering if I would be around to see it.

Suddenly, in the distance, shouts are heard. Locke rushes back towards me, grabbing me by the shoulders. We quickly take cover behind the thick of some trees and brush. We squat down low to the ground, and I close the hood of my cloak over my eyes, so that the glow from them does not give us away.

"What do you see?" I ask Locke, in a whisper.

"A group of men," Locke replies. "Must be members of the league."

They were waiting for us to return. A few weaker ones left behind to keep watch and to alert the others if we came back. My violent outburst must have signaled them.

"How many?" I ask him.

"I don't know," Locke says, his voice growing more hushed as the men approach. "It's so dark and foggy. It looks like just two or three. No real threat there. And, wait, a girl."

"A girl?" I ask, puzzled.

"They have a girl with them."

I look at Locke. He stares, transfixed, at the group ahead. I pull my cloak back and look out at the group. Though each of the men look familiar, there is indeed, a young woman with them, one that I am sure I have never seen her before, even in a nightmare. She looks to be much younger than the men, probably about Locke's age, if I were to guess correctly. She is quite pretty, with long dark brown hair that is pulled back into a braid that rests over her left shoulder. She is lean, medium height, with smooth, tan skin. She has soft, pale grey eyes, perfectly round and surrounded by a coat of long, full eyelashes. She carries a bow and a quiver of arrows strapped to her back. She is dressed as the men are, in pants and a shirt, with the sleeves rolled up, a cloak tied about her shoulders.

"Who is she?" Locke asks, his eyes widening a little.

"I don't know," I say, "I've never seen her before."

"I'm going to get a closer look. Stay here."

"Locke, no!" But before he can hear me, he has crept away. I sit, still as a statue, and watch the group of men search about them.

"There's no one here," one of them men says, annoyed. "I'm going back to sleep."

"A flash of light," the girl says eagerly. "I saw it, I swear!"

"You're always seeing things," says another of the men, "that aren't really there. Stop trying to be a hero." The three men laugh.

"Didn't you hear the blast?" she asked. "Or were you too deep into your drunken stupor to notice?"

"Vincent's not coming back here," the third man says. "Don't you understand? We are just sitting here because we're not considered useful anywhere else."

"Speak for yourself," the girl says angrily.

"You want to stay here and look around for this imaginary light you saw," the first man says, "be my guest. I'm going back to bed." The three men laugh and walk off in the direction from which they came, leaving the girl behind them.

She kicks angrily at a burnt cauldron and it goes sailing off into the trees.

"Evander would have never just left me behind like this!" she shouts in protest. "He trusted me, and he believed in me. Worthless drunken idiots. I'll show them!"

She begins looking around the clearing. She looks in my direction and stops. I quickly cover my eyes, but it is too late. She proceeds to take a few steps towards me, moving as slowly and agilely as a lion ready to pounce upon its prey, when her attention is diverted by a snap of branches echoing from the opposite side of the clearing.

The girl reaches back and pulls an arrow from the quiver strapped to her back. She sets her bow, without breaking her gaze from the direction of the sound of the snapping branch, and begins walking slowly towards it.

Suddenly, a mewing noise is heard off in the distance. The girl spins around, arrow cocked, her breathing now fast and fearful. The mewing sound comes again, louder now than before and constant.

Vesta. My pet. She is saving us. She is toying with the girl, the way she toyed with the spider. The shouts of the other men are heard—they must also have been roused by Vesta's mewing—and the rustling of branches as they chase after her.

"Oh you heard that did you, you fools!" the girl shouts. She then takes off into the trees.

Locke emerges from behind a tree on the opposite side of the clearing. He looks in my direction and holds a finger to his lips. I sit, unsure of what he is up to.

Then, quick as a flash, an arrow streaks across the clearing and pierces through Locke's shirt, just above his right shoulder, pinning him up against a tree.

Out of the woods walks the girl, another arrow at the ready, and she draws near to Locke.

"Who are you?" she demands, feigning intimidation and authority. She edges closer, but maintains a safe distance.

Locke remains silent, but struggles to pull the arrow from his shirt. Blood soaks the fabric and his hands.

"Lilia! C'mon!" a voice shouts from the distance.

"Just a moment!" she shouts back, without breaking her observation of Locke. She assesses him carefully before building up the confidence to proceed.

"Who are you?" the girl, Lilia, asks.

Locke doesn't respond, but continues to struggle helplessly. The girl approaches Locke, arrow and bow readily aimed, and looks into his innocent, pale blue eyes. He stops and assumes defeat, panting against the tree. His pain seems to recede momentarily, as he stands captivated by her beauty and mystery. The girl begins to lower her bow, seemingly convinced of Locke's innocence. They stare, for a long moment, completely submersed in each other's pale eyes.

I have minimal time to act. I reach into my cloak and remove a vial of glittering black dust. I grip it tightly in my fist. *This is all I have. But what's done it done.* I throw the vial into the clearing; it smashes onto the ground and erupts in a cloud of thick black fog.

There is coughing and screaming on the part of the girl. I find my way to Locke quickly and, in a joint effort, break him free from the tree. We run, as fast as we can, away from the clearing and deeper into the dense wood. More shouts erupt from the scene behind us. Locke turns to look back, but a grab him and push him onward.

"You brainless boy!" I shout at him once we are at a safe distance. "You could have been killed!"

"Vincent," Locke says, stumbling over his apology. "I'm sorry. I don't know what came over me. I-"

"Enough!" I say, silencing him at once. "Do not ever wander away from me again! Do you understand? Or I may kill you myself!"

I storm past Locke in a rage. He knows he has disappointed me.

"She could have killed me," Locke calls after me. "But she didn't. Why?"

"Forget about her," I say, not bothering to turn around. "Because once that fog subsides, she surely won't remember you."

I welled up with fury at the news, my insides seething with fire. How could this happen? A league? What league? Where and when? How could this be possible?

But it was possible. And apparently, Evander set it into play several years ago.

"A League of Heroes," Janus said. I leered at him, not wanting to hear any more. "Sworn to hide and protect the twins until they are of age. Then they will come for you." I was in disbelief. It was true, I had not been able to locate the twins in the past year, but I did not anticipate this. I threw my hand in a tyrannous rage and the pot of boiling brew in the hearth across the room exploded.

"Show me!" I demanded.

We crept stealthily out into the night. We walked for several hours until we came upon a tall, brick building. I put one hand on the wall but Janus pulled me in another direction. Around the back of the building, shouts could be heard. A fire was blazing nearby and we crept up behind a tall oak. I peered around and looked on ahead. There were seven or eight men. And two boys.

They were talking quite loudly. I scrutinized each one. Looking for signs.

One man was very dark of skin, with bulging muscles curved in such sculpted formation and proportion it could make Michelangelo's David crumble. He had a large black tattoo that curved down his right arm, spiraling tightly around his muscles as if to keep them held in place. He had large, dark brown eyes and a ring in his left nostril. When he spoke, his voice was so deep and thick that the ground trembled. In one hand he held a large axe, with a large curved blade.

The second was man was less muscular but still well-built, with tanned skin. His toned arms were matted with thick, dark hair. He was tall, with long hair that was pulled back into a braided ponytail at his neck. He wore a bandana tied around his forehead, which conveniently collected the sweat that was beading up upon his brow, though some of it trickled down the side of his face. He was strapped with a sheath that contained a long sword. Its metallic handle glinted in the light of the fire.

The third man was short yet stocky. He was strapped with a quiver of arrows and a bow. I wondered if those thick, muscular arms allowed for a quick set and release of those deadly arrows.

One, I noticed, did not seem to fit in with the rest. He had pale white skin, like ash, and sunken, glowing green eyes. He appeared light, fragile, and, although thin, he looked incredibly strong.

I stared at him intently, enthralled by the sheer inexplicability of his appearance. He seemed annoyed by the gaieties in which he was being forced to take part and seemed to be transfixed by something.

After watching him a moment, it seemed evident that he was not looking, but listening, perhaps smelling, for something. He cocked his head to the side, as a dog would, and then he lifted his nose to the air and sniffed. None of the other men seemed to notice this odd behavior.

He turned his head slowly, discreetly, in my direction. In a moment of terror, his eerie, glowing green eyes locked with mine. I felt a cold rush flow through me, as if his icy pupils were enveloping me in their gaze. Then, he smiled, licked his lips, and returned his attention to the rest of the party.

"Jesus Christ, Vincent," Janus said in sudden alarm. "Do you suppose he saw us?"

I did not answer, forcing my own fearful assessment of the incident out of my mind. If he did in fact see us, he chose not to act upon it, and that made matters much more frightening.

I continued to evaluate the members of the group. The rest of the men were equally built and strapped. They all, with the exception of the pale, ghostly one, looked more like Roman gladiators than men. They each also bore, upon the chest, an emblem. It was a silver disc with two Rs with a sword in between them. The first letter was backward so that it faced the other, and they connected with the sword in the middle. The hilt of the sword was set upwards. Curving along the bottom edge of the disc were the words, 'ANIMOS USQUE AS MORTEM.'

"Courage until death," I whispered distastefully.

I then espied the two boys, who sat, huddled together, enjoying a meal. They were identical, though one is slightly larger in both physique and confidence than the other. They looked completely at ease.

My brain seethed as I turned to Janus.

"How long have you known!" I spat at him in an angry whisper.

"Vincent, I only just discovered!" he replied fearfully, though I doubted his sincerity. "Honestly, I was having a drink last night and this old hag of woman came in. She was drunk as day and rambling about a slew of strapping young men waltzing about the country, two young boys in tow. I inquired a bit further as to their whereabouts and came to you straight away."

I frowned at him.

"What are you afraid of?" he went on foolishly.

"Don't you see," I replied. "Evander knew what he was doing. He knew I wouldn't touch them if they were protected."

I looked back upon the group of men, watching them closely. How happy they all were. Fools.

"Well, do you want to know what I think?" Janus asked. "I think that what you should do is go in there and blast the whole lot to pieces."

"Silence yourself," I snapped. "I do not have that kind of power." I turned and glared in the direction of the hulking men. "Not yet . . . ."

VIII
THE THREE SISTERS

The trees begin to thin out and a faint glow becomes visible in the distance. We come to the forest edge and approach a small, wooden cabin with a hay thatched roof. There is smoke coming from the chimney, and a warm glow emits from the windows, though the curtains are drawn. Locke, who hasn't spoken a word since the incident in the forest, looks excitedly at the inviting abode, though I know his longing is in vain.

Just as I raise my hand to knock at the door it swings open, and an all-too-familiar figure stands in the doorway.

"Vincent . . ." She smirks. "How good of you to drop by."

She has long gray hair and smooth, colorless skin. Her eyes, though big and shimmering pink, are surrounded by faint scars. She smiles a crooked smile, with pointed teeth and blood red lips. She is wearing a long black dress with a pink striped bodice; the lace, which extends all the way down to her wrists, is ripped and ragged, scarcely veiling the pallid color of her arms. Her nails are long, black and bejeweled. Silver rings adorn each of her slender fingers. The skirt of her dress hangs low to the ground, revealing beneath it black, pointed shoes. Standing before us, with arms folded in mock protest at our imposition, she has the perfect look of an old woman and beautiful young maid in one.

102

This is a woman who learned long ago of the captivating power of feminine beauty and its manipulative benefits on the ignorant man, and she has not been shy about utilizing that power all her life. It has brought her great confidence and arrogance, knowing she can manage to obtain anything she desires through use of her body and feminine charms. She is the type that gives a poor name to other beauties who uphold modesty and class.

I have known her for many years, not in the traditional, perverted implications of the word 'known'—though *she* would prefer the relationship that way—but in that I have been inescapably tied to her through other means. She is a horrible human being, as hypocritical as it is for me to say so. It both humbles and pains me greatly to have to rely on her help. I would rather see her dead.

"Medea," I say, bitterly, "I hope I may find refuge with you for a few hours. Locke and I are in chase. He needs nourishment and rest, and you and I need to talk."

"Oh, Vincent," she replies with an air of mutual innocence and sarcasm, "you know I do not harbor criminals." She glances over at Locke, who is shivering before her, and she smiles. "But how might I turn away such a young, handsome man. Come in."

We enter the cabin, which is warm and inviting. A fire is blazing in the hearth and a kettle is boiling, with emanating smells that fill the entire room. The cabin, though dusty and ridden with cobwebs, is neat and quaint.

I take a seat at the large dining table in the center of the room and remove my cloak. Medea retreats into the kitchen area, begins preparing cups for tea, and puts a kettle of water on the fire to boil. Locke takes it upon himself to look around.

Candles are lit everywhere, illuminating the many odd artifacts scattered about the house. The aura of such romantic lighting and captivating objects gives the room an air of enchantment.

There is a huge painting on the wall, that of a young woman and three beautiful little girls in her lap. Beneath the painting is an ornate oak chest with many drawers, each with its own brass handle. Atop the chest rests a wooden clock and a gold statue of a ram with large curled horns. Next to the statue is a candelabrum that holds three brightly burning candles.

In the far side of the room is a huge, handsome wardrobe. A large looking-glass stands next to it. Interestingly enough, the reflection in the mirror turns the room and our own selves upside down. Locke stood, studying his inverted reflection for several minutes.

Near the fire are several small kettles and cauldrons, each of which is rusted and dirty. Along the far wall is a row of paintings: three young women, all of whom are strikingly beautiful. The portraits depict the women at different stages of their lives, and, while walking along them, one becomes engulfed in the illusion of watching them grow up. Locke inspects each of these closely. Another painting of a rather large woman covers the far wall, one curious enough in itself for, if you look at long enough or at the right moment, you might think you saw her smile or wink at you. I cannot help but chuckle as Locke does a double take at the portrait himself. Another painting, this one much more gruesome than the rest, hangs next to the portrait of the large woman. This portrait depicts a beautiful young man but has long slash marks ripping through the canvas.

Locke scrutinizes this portrait thoughtfully. Then, his eyes fall upon a huddled mass in the corner and Locke stares, frightened. An old woman sits in the corner, she is draped in a moss green cloak, and her hair is white and sparse upon her head. She clutches at her knees and is rocking slightly back and forth on the floor. One can hear her mumbling to herself.

"Is she alright?" Locke asks, concerned.

Locke approaches her curiously, and rests his hand on her shoulder. The woman lifts her head suddenly and Locke falls back in terror. Her face is white and covered with scars and wrinkles. She lifts up her hands towards him, which are black, as if they had been set on fire, and are now covered with soot. Most frighteningly of all are the hollow, black sockets where her eyes used to be, which are covered about the corners with deep, seeping scabs and thick scars.

The woman begins to scream and howl. Locke backs away, mortified at the sight of her. I rise to stop him from falling to the floor. I, unfortunately, am unmoved by the woman, as I have seen her pathetic face before.

"Millicent!" Medea rushes over to the woman in agony and embraces her. Medea rocks Millicent delicately and shushes her, like a child.

"Shhhh . . ." Medea coaxes, patting her hair and rocking her gently. "There, there, my sweet. Everything is alright." Millicent whimpers and quiets down and Medea lets her go. The old woman on the floor then puts her head back between her knees and resumes rocking and mumbling to herself.

"E-e-e-eyes," Locke stutters uncontrollably.

"Everything's alright," Medea says, getting to her feet. As she rises, she dusts off her skirt and fixes her hair in proper fashion.

"E-eyes . . . eyes . . . her eyes," Locke continues to repeat.

"You gave her quite a fright," Medea says gently, ignoring Locke's disturbed utterances.

"Me?" Locke says, still in shock. "I gave *her* a fright? Her eyes, she has no eyes!"

"Yes, and she cannot hear either," Medea says, her tone now angry. "So you can imagine how terrified she must be with an unknown hand touching her like that! Poor ignorant creature."

"Medea, he didn't mean to scare her" I say.

"Indeed!" she replies.

"I'm so sorry," Locke says in earnest apology. "I only meant to see if she was alright."

"Of course she is alright!" Medea says, affronted. "Do you not think I take care of my younger sister?"

"*Younger* sister?" Locke mutters, confused.

"Medea, Locke meant no harm, his intentions are only honest and good. He is tired and wary. It's been nearly twenty-four hours since he's slept and he's surely famished. Why don't you fix him a proper meal and give him a place to rest? Then you and I can speak privately, and Locke can regain his wits."

Medea turns sharply on her heel and stalks off towards the kitchen. Once she is gone, Locke turns to me in earnest.

"Vincent," he says. "I am so sorry. I did not mean to insult anyone!"

"Don't you dare apologize for insults made to *her*," I say angrily. "Not when the fault lies in her. It is because of her that Millicent cannot see, and Medea knows that!"

With this, Medea returns to the room, eyeing me suspiciously, a tray of food in her hands. "I do hope you do not speak ill of me in front of my new guest."

"I do no such thing," I reply. Medea gestures towards the table with a nod of her head, and we all sit down. She sets down a pot of tea and teacups, a bowl of sugar, milk, tableware, a cauldron of hot stew, a tray of biscuits, and several small sandwiches. She pours out three cups of tea, and distributes the plates and silverware. Locke fills his plate, but he eats slowly, his plaguing hunger abated by guilt he still feels from disturbing Millicent on the floor. Though he eats slowly, he finishes everything on his plate and fills it again. When he is satiated, Medea shows him to a room where he may lay down to rest. She is gone for a few minutes, then returns to sit with me at the table.

"How dare you accuse him of disturbing her, Medea!" I say bitterly. "He meant no harm. It is because of your own wickedness that your sister cannot see!"

"Wickedness?" she says with a cackle. "Millicent did not deserve those eyes! They did her no good! She was always cowering and hiding them. Why may I not deserve to see? Especially when I make good use of them!"

"Because look at her now! Deaf and blind. While you walk around with all of your senses about you. You are a vile woman, Medea."

"Then why are you here, Vincent? If I may be such a horrid woman?"

"Who else may I seek refuge with now?"

"So the only time I am good enough for you is when you need help?" she says curtly. I ignore her comment.

"The league is after me," I say. "And I am not sure how much longer I can evade them. I must make it to the oracle before they catch me; I must know what else I can counsel with her one last time." Medea looks at me in disgust.

"You are going to try to defeat Roman?" she asks in disbelief.

"I have found the jewel. I think, with it, I might be able to defeat him." Medea shifts uncomfortably in her seat.

"Do you not realize that your purpose is lost?" she says. "Look at you, Vincent, you are old, you are tired, you are growing weaker. You have forgotten who you once were, and you have forgotten, in your greed and wickedness, your purpose, a purpose which has corrupted you. What else are you trying to accomplish? If you do kill Roman, what will you do next? The league will not stop until they have rid the world of you. Perhaps it is time for you to give up."

"I cannot."

"And what of Locke?" she asks. "Are you going to continue to risk his life as well? How many more people must die so that you might get what you want! You are a selfish old man!

"You have been using that poor boy since he was small; his whole life is a wretch because of you. When are you going to let him go? And give him a chance at a life of his own? He lives to serve you! And you couldn't care less for him!"

"You hold your tongue!" I snap. She has struck a nerve with me. "You will speak nothing of Locke! You do not know anything of my concern for him. And don't you dare try to assume that you do!"

Medea smirks as if she has won some silent battle.

"Do you mean to say," she says spitefully, "that even through all your years of loathing and anger, you have actually grown to *love* the boy?"

The words sting.

"I will defeat Roman," I say, ignoring her question. "Locke and I will flee the country. I will right my wrongs with him. I wish to repent myself for all of my evils before I am gone."

At this Medea cackles loudly. "Oh Vincent," she says sarcastically. "It would take you ten lifetimes to repent all of your evils."

She gets up and begins cleaning Locke's used dishes. She then turns and looks at me with a malicious grin.

"You are going to tell him," she says. "Are you not?"

"That is for me to decide."

"Decide carefully. I am not so sure Locke would not turn on you, if he were to find out. But I think you at least owe him that."

"I owe him a lot more than that," I say softly. But no one hears me save for my own guilty conscience.

August 26ᵗʰ, '34

It was near nightfall and I was walking home from the market. Well, when I say night, I am merely referring to the time of day, rather than the idea that night actually 'falls' these days, for it seems it is always night or nearly so.

I was dressed in my usual thick wool cloak, as there was a rigid chill in the air. I made my way through the dense trees and brush that keep my cabin hidden in the thick of the forest. One can never be too careful these days, especially with the days growing darker and the nights more perilous still. I could not help but smile, for this age has been brought on by my own hands, leapt from the very hell that exists within my heart.

As I approached my cabin door, I pondered the events of the day that has set itself behind me. So deep in thought was I, and with my hood up covering nearly all of my face, that I barely noticed him: a young boy, sitting on the front steps of my cabin.

I stopped dead in my tracks and looked about me suspiciously. The boy did not move; he did not stir; he merely looked up at me, as innocent as could be. He was very small, perhaps four or five, he had soft brown hair and pale blue eyes. He was dressed in new trousers and shirt, as if someone had prettied him up to be dropped off on my doorstep.

"Who the devil are you?" I hissed at the small boy. It was quite clear that I had frightened him, for he now looked shaken. My anger rose with his silence. "Are you deaf? Who are you? How dare you come to my home!" I found myself yelling at this point. "Get out of here!" With that, I walked up and kicked the boy off of my doorstep. I went into the house and slammed the door behind me.

August 27th, '34

When I awoke this morning, I set out for a stroll in the woods. Upon my return, who should I find sitting on my doorstep but the same boy, dressed just as neatly as the day before and staring just as innocently up at me. This time, without a word, I simply walked past him and shut the door, not caring whether he was still sitting there or not.

August 28ᵗʰ, '34

This morning, when I awoke, I opened the front door to find him, like a statue, still sitting, and waiting.

"Well, come on then," I said with disgust, and the little boy scrambled to his feet and came inside. He was shivering and wet, for it must have rained in the night. I gave him a blanket and laid his sopping clothes by the hearth. To my surprise, Vesta, my young kitten, seemed to be fond of the boy. She curled up in his lap and allowed him to stroke her soft fur. He seemed to enjoy it himself, for he sat, smiling, gently petting the tiny beast without a word while I fixed him something to eat.

I set a plate of food down in front of him and he sat still. He looked at the plate and then up at me.

"Well go on and eat it then," I said, annoyed. "Before it gets cold." The boy smiled jubilantly and began to consume his meal with his bare hands, completely disregarding the fork and napkin I had set beside the plate. I watched in complete disgust as he devoured his food, making an utter mess of himself. Children, I thought, nasty little things.

When the boy finished, he drank heartily from the goblet of water I had also provided him with. He then proceeded to wipe his face in his sleeve.

We sat together for some time before I finally decided to speak to him. "What is your name then, boy?" I asked, really uninterested in his reply.

The boy did not reply. Instead, he looked down at the floor. He took his index finger and dipped it into a bit of ash that had blown off from the fire. He then scrawled, barely legibly, the letters L-O-C-K-E on the wooden floor in front of him. When he finished, the boy dusted off his hands, smiling, as if he was quite pleased with himself for what he had done.

"Well then, Locke, do you know how old you are?" The little boy held his up his right hand extending four tiny fingers. With his left hand he pointed to each one, as if recounting to double check, yet he still did not utter a single word.

I continued with my interrogation. "And where did you come from? Meaning, to whom shall I be returning you?" At this the boy lowered his eyes to the floor and a small *tear left his eye and trickled delicately down his cheek. It was apparent to me that this boy had no one to go home to. But then, how did he get here? Who had raised him to this point? Who named him? And told him how old he was? He couldn't possibly have been alone.*

I leaned back in my chair and let out a heavy sigh. I scrutinized him, and noticed, though I believed my eyes were deceiving me, the faintest trace of a glittering black dust in the corner of his eye. I stared at him, gravely. I leaned forward and looked at him more closely. He looked up at me and wiped the tears away.

The boy reached into his pocket. He pulled out his hand and unfolded it. There, in the middle of his hand, lay a tiny, blue piece of lace. The lace burned through my eyes and my skull as I filled with rage.

"Get out!" I screamed instantly. Get out of here! I don't know who you are or where you came from, but you are not welcome here!" The young boy looked up at me in disbelief, tears welling in his pale blue eyes. "GET OUT!" I bellowed.

The boy scrambled to his feet and ran out the door as fast as he possibly could.

My heart racing, I slammed the door after him. Then I returned to my chair, put my head in my hands, and cried.

September 4ᵗʰ, '34

I haven't seen her in years, but I didn't know who else to turn to, so I went to see Medea for help. She's looking much older these days, as if her own sins have been catching up with her.

She and I sat at the table together, across from each other, while the boy played on the floor. I stared down at my teacup, the contents of which had yet to be touched.

"Where did he come from?" she asked.

"I don't know," I replied. "It's as I have already told you, I came home and he was there, waiting for me."

"Does he remember anything?" she asks.

"No. He's so young."

"But surely he knows who brought him."

"I believe all of his previous memories have been erased.

"And you have no inkling as to whom he belongs?" she asked, almost sarcastically.

"I know who he is." I said, choking a little on the reality of it. "He's the one from my nightmares[10]."

Medea sat back and stared at him.

"Interesting," she said.

"What shall I do?" I asked her.

Medea got up from the table and walked around the table, over to where I was sitting. She knelt down next to me and looked me gravely in the eyes. She rested her hand on top of my knee.

"We could raise him," she said, "together."

I turned away from her.

---

[10]   Nightmare #512

"Vincent, think of how happy we could be," she insisted. She turned to look at the boy and smiled. "He would never have to know he was an orphan. A real family; isn't that what you've wanted all of this time? It's right here, right in front of you."

I stood, and she did as well, facing me, her eyes watery with hope.

"Not with you," I said. I grabbed the boy by the arm and walked him towards the door.

"That dream died a long time ago."

"Vincent," she said, quietly, desperately. I paused for a moment with my hand on the doorknob, but I did not turn to face her. "Am I not beautiful enough for you?"

"Love looks not with the eye, but with the mind," I said, and I opened the door, leaving her behind me.

As I walked away from her cabin, I heard the sound of broken glass and what I thought was gentle sobbing.

IX

THE SEARCH

Medea and I sit up for several hours into the early morning, giving Locke ample time to rest. Sleep eludes me, as my mind is a swell of chaotic thoughts. Medea stays up to keep me company.

I light a pipe to smoke and ease my head. She gazes intently at the rings of purple smoke I release from my lips. I wonder what she is thinking and wish desperately for some insight. We sit in silence; Medea watches me effortlessly, while I ponder my own thoughts as well as hers.

"You feel an overwhelming sense of guilt. It fuels your anger. You need to wash your hands of it."

"All of the water in the ocean could not wash the guilt from my hands," I say.

"You need to try."

"What would you have me do, Medea?" I ask her, now that I am somewhat subdued.

"Stay here," she replies frankly. "We may be able to buy some time and then depart for the countryside.

"You wish to accompany me?"

"I do not wish for you to go off and put yourself and others in danger. There is nothing left for me here, save for that pathetic sister of mine."

I turn around to look at the creature huddled in the corner, staring blankly at the ceiling with hollow eyes, and rocking slightly back and forth. She moves her mouth but no words come out, instead, just saliva and foam.

"I could be of help to you," she continues, leaning forward to rest a delicate hand on my own. "It has been a long time for you, Vincent. I am sure you wish to have some sort of companionship other than that of a young boy. Some female companionship, perhaps?"

I do not respond to this but gently pull my hand away, and the room grows quiet again. Medea sits back and looks out the window uncomfortably.

She has once again left me bemused. For what purpose would Medea want to join us on this impossible quest? Is her purpose self-gratifying or does she truly have our interests at heart? I have known Medea for many years, and still have not the slightest grasp on her, her motives, her desires. Why does she feel so strongly against my attempt to defeat Roman, I wonder? Could it be possible that she actually fears for Locke's life? For my own?

My thoughts are interrupted when the smirk on Medea's face fades into a countenance of sudden fear. She is staring out the window, and I read both the expression of her face and the reflection of fire in eyes: the League.

There is a powerful knock at the door.

"Quickly," Medea says at once, jumping up from her seat at the table. I follow her hastily as she walks over to the wardrobe.

There is another loud knock, this time with much emphasis.

"Just a minute!" Medea shouts in mock aggravation. She opens the door of the wardrobe and motions to me.

"In here," she says.

"What of Locke?" I ask as I step inside.

"I'll take care of it," she says and shuts the door. She leaves it open just enough so I may peer out into the room.

I watch Medea glance into the looking glass as she ruffles up her hair and loosens the top strings of her corset, revealing more curved flesh. There is another ferociously loud bang on the door. Medea stalks over and swings the door open.

"Can a woman have time to make herself decent," she says flirtatiously, "before she answers to a crowd of unruly men!"

"My apologies, Medea," says a gruff voice. "But we are in somewhat of a hurry. May I?" Medea stands aside and makes a gesture with her right arm as if to welcome them in.

A tall, burly man steps inside the door. He is well-built with dirty blond hair and pale hazel eyes. He is followed in by several other men of similar stature and demeanor.

"Well, well, well," Medea says as they file in past her. "It must be my lucky night, Brogan, to have both you and such young, handsome men come knocking at my door." She walks over and caresses the arm of one of them, and he jerks away from her.

"Forgive me," she says. "I can't help myself."

"Search the rooms," says Brogan, the lead man, ignoring her.

"If you'll excuse me," Medea interrupts sternly, as if suddenly offended by their presence. "But it is first thing in the morning and you are barging into my house, and I am alone and unable to defend myself, and I do believe I have a right to know what is going on here!"

"What's going here, woman," Brogan replies, "is that we have reason to suspect that Vincent may be or may have been here."

"Oh really," she says, annoyed, "and what gives you that impression?"

"Come now, Medea. Do not try to fool me. We both know that you have some affiliation with Vincent."

"I do not deny 'some affiliation with Vincent', sir," she says in a derisive tone. "But, if I may rephrase the question to fit your capacity for intellectual understanding: what gives you the impression he would come here *now*?"

Brogan glares at her threateningly, but Medea ignores this.

"Vincent is in hiding, he has not been seen for months. Why would he jeopardize himself by wandering about? Unless, of course," she says, returning to her coquettish tone, "you're saying that a visit with me is worth mortal peril?"

"Don't flatter yourself," Brogan says in disgust. "Vincent is on the run; we discovered the whereabouts of his home and burned it to the ground two nights ago. Unfortunately, he was not inside."

"Really? Slippery old man, isn't he?" Medea states amusingly.

"What's more," Brogan continues, "the schoolmaster is missing and a group of sailors were found dead in an alleyway."

"So he was in the village."

"Just yesterday, we believe. Our men have been searching the forest and village and he is nowhere to be found. There is no way he could have gotten very far, unless of course, he is being helped, but we don't believe he is; we killed his only ally. So he must be hiding somewhere."

"Well, he certainly hasn't been here. Regrettably, I am not harboring any strange men at the moment." From inside the wardrobe, I cannot help but chuckle at Medea's sarcastic yet alluring charm.

Brogan, however, is not amused. He simply scoffs at her and begins to peruse the room. His gaze circumvents the room and he walks towards me. My nerves tense and my heart skips a beat, but I relax as Brogan turns his attention to the looking-glass.

"What sort of trickery is this?" he says, confused by his inverted reflection. "Why does it reflect things the wrong way?"

"The wrong way? Whatever do you mean?"

"Don't be foolish. Everything is upside down!"

"Well," says Medea, "perhaps it is not a reflection of our world of us upside down, but right-side up. Did you ever think of that?"

"Nonsense," he replies. Brogan backs away from the mirror and then stops, staring in my direction. He has obviously just discovered not merely the wardrobe, but the curious fact that it cracked open just slightly, or possibly he caught a glimpse of my sparkling violet eyes.

I close my eyes and back up nervously into the darkness of the wardrobe, which seemed slightly deeper than I expected. I hold my breath as he approaches and know that my time has come. I rack my brain for what I could do to defend myself. Should I kill him here? And risk putting Medea in danger? Surely the league would come after her. And what if the other men escape? They would know I have been here and would track me much more easily. Perhaps I could blind him with light and slip away undetected, but would Medea think quickly enough to explain the phenomenon of the glowing wardrobe?

I have no more time to think. As Brogan reaches for the door, I raise my palms and brace myself . . .

"Brogan," a voice calls. He stops and turns away.

At that moment, two of the men from the league emerge from the bedroom with Locke in their grasp. He is struggling, though unsuccessfully, to free himself. He is only partially dressed, clearly roused from sleep, both confused and frightened.

"And who might this be?" Brogan asks angrily. "I thought you weren't harboring any strange men?"

"Oops," Medea says, gliding her fingers daintily through her hair. "I guess you caught me. I met this young lad up at the pub last night;

he needed a warm meal and good night's rest. Couldn't help myself, I'm afraid." With that, she winks at Locke, who looks more confused than ever.

"You dirty tramp," Brogan says, with a smirk. "You never cease to amaze me." Medea purses her lip and narrows her eyes with a look of ire.

"You don't seem to complain about that when it's your turn," she says.

"What's your name, boy?" Brogan says to Locke, seemingly amused at the situation. Behind his back, Medea gives Locke a grave look, and he reads her expression.

"N-names Marlo," he says. "Not from around here, I'm afraid. I'm a seaman. Just pulled into port last night and the crew's going to dock for a day or two. Who are you? Her husband? I'm so terribly sorry, I-"

"Ha!" Brogan laughs heartily and the other men chuckle as well, letting Locke go. "Luckily for you boy, I sure as hell am no husband of hers. I don't think a soul in the world is foolish enough to try to tie this one down." Medea frowns, insulted.

"I suggest you be careful of the company you keep, lad," Brogan says referring to Medea. "A few of your mates turned up dead yesterday." Brogan then turns to Medea and says, "You really are something else you know that? This boy's barely of age."

Medea smirks and raises her finely crafted eyebrows. "Why don't you go dress yourself, dear-y, while I finish up with these men, then I'll make you some breakfast." She kisses him on the check. Locke is all too eager to go back to the room and out of sight.

"You want to be next?" Medea asks Brogan with a smirk.

A couple of the other men laugh, though their eager eyes suggest that they hope to be extended the same offer. Medea notices and smiles, obviously quite amused with herself.

"You're mad, you know that?" Brogan says.

"Well, we're all a bit mad here, aren't we?" Medea replies, chuckling lightly.

Brogan shakes his head at Medea in disgust, and, as he does so, notices the crumpled mass of gray hair and black wool in the corner.

"And what is this?" he says, suddenly excited, as if catching her in a lie. He storms over to the corner and reaches down to put a hand on the woman's shoulder.

At his touch, Millicent raises her head and begins her bloodcurdling howl, her black, empty sockets twitching around as if she is desperately trying to distinguish who it is that threatens her.

Brogan leaps backward and draws his sword from his side. Sensing the danger, Medea grabs him by the arm that wields his sword and pulls him away from her.

"OUT!" she screams at the other men, pointing towards the door. "All of you get out!"

The men look stunned and wait for direction from Brogan, who nods in ascent. All the other men hurry out of the door, and Brogan waits while Medea kneels down beside her sister and rocks her back and forth in an attempt to soothe her. As she does so, she looks viciously up at Brogan.

"How dare you!" she says, angered by his ignorance. "How dare you disrupt my poor delicate sister! You tyrant! You fiend!"

"I thought maybe it was-"

"Vincent? I told you he has not been here!"

At these words, I suddenly remember my apparent danger and gently pull the wardrobe door so that it is nearly closed.

"Shh," Medea whispers, soothingly, rocking her sister back and forth. "It's alright." Millicent's scream subsides and she whimpers softly.

"I will be waiting outside," Brogan says, and before turning to leave he grabs Medea by the waist and pulls her up to her feet, and then in close to him. He grabs her by the face.

For the first time, there is a note of fear in Medea's pink eyes.

"He would kill you, you know," Brogan says softly. "Without a second thought." He turns her face away to expose the soft flesh of her neck. "One bite, right here." Medea takes in a quick breath, tears forming in her eyes.

Brogan, ignoring her distress, whispers in her ear, "He would rip the sweet flesh right off the bone. And there is nothing your witch magic could do to save you." He then leans in as if to bite, but instead kisses her neck gently.

After the weight of the sentiment has sunk in, Brogan releases Medea's face, but keeps his grasp upon her waist. Pulling her in once more and kissing her roughly, with not a sense of love and affection, but with cruel bestial lust, and he gropes her body with his large, paw-like hands.

"Next time there better not already be a man in your bed," Brogan says, and he releases her. He then turns and moves out of my field of vision.

The sound of his footsteps tells me that he has left Medea to calm her sister and walked out the door.

Medea gathers her composure and looks over towards me, as if for the first time aware that I am also in the room. She stalks towards me and slams the wardrobe door shut. I then hear her pronounced footsteps as she returns to Millicent, who has all the while been whimpering and rocking back and forth on the floor. I hear her soft whispers, an effort not only to soothe her frightened sister, but herself as well.

In a few minutes Millicent is calm again and I hear Medea's footsteps as she walks towards the door and closes the door behind her, joining Brogan outside. I press my ear to the wardrobe door and strain to hear the muffled sounds. I hear them speaking wildly to each other, though, through the walls of the house and wardrobe, I cannot decipher their words.

I back away from the door, defeated, and resolve myself to waiting for Medea's return. I look around and consider my surroundings for a moment, as well as the events that I know will take place in the future. I reach inside my cloak and remove the small, silver key that I was sure to tuck safely inside before my departure from the cabin. I place the key on the floor, tucking it safely into a back corner. Then I sit in silence, and I wait.

In the quiet of the dark wardrobe, I close my eyes and Medea's words replay in my mind.

Do you mean to say that, even through all your years of loathing and anger, you have actually grown to love the boy?

I breathe deeply. Is it true?

. . . you have actually grown to love the boy?

Is it possible?

. . . to love the boy?

Suddenly, I begin to feel very lightheaded. The words repeat themselves and I dissolve into another trance. My head swirls with a sudden memory.

A ten year old Locke is sitting out on the front steps of my cabin. I see him through the open window picking twigs up off of the ground, snapping them into pieces, and throwing the pieces out in front of him. I sense that he is frustrated.

I attempt to ignore him, but then, after a time, I see a small tear slip down his cheek.

"Locke?" The boy hastily wipes away the tear.

I sit down next to him uncomfortably.

"What . . . I mean . . . is there," I stutter. I swallow as I try not to sound awkward. I take deep breath and gain my composure. "Is there something the matter?"

He looks up at me with swollen, watery eyes.

"Mr. Vincent," he says. "Are you my dad?"

The question renders me speechless. I look into his anxious face and try to choose my words carefully.

"No," I say, barely able to get the word out.

"*Do you know what happened to him?*" My stomach sinks.

"*I do not.*"

Locke turns his face away from mine and another tear falls.

"*A boy at school today made fun of me,*" *he says,* "*And he told me that I was an orphan and that nobody cared about me. I told him he was wrong, but he just laughed at me. I pushed him down and ran, but he continued to laugh at me as I ran away.*"

"*You should not care what other people think about you, Locke,*" *I say. Locke sits silently without another word.*

"*I guess you're right,*" *he finally says.*

Unable to stand the tension any longer, I get up to go back into the house.

"*Mr. Vincent?*"

"*Yes, Locke?*" *I slowly turn to face him; he is still sitting down on the steps.*

"*Do you . . . I mean, I know you're not my father, but . . . I kind of feel like you are sometimes . . . and even if you're not, which I understand that you're not, and I won't be upset if you don't but,*" *he hesitates, it is obviously very difficult for him to say,* "*I just wondered . . . if maybe . . . well . . . do . . . do you love me?*"

The question sends a shock through my body. I stand and stare back at him, speechless.

"*It's ok,*" *Locke says, getting to his feet.* "*You don't have to answer.*" *And he turns and walks away down the path into the woods.*

I shake my head in an attempt to clear the memory, but the stress is immense, and I notice that my face is wet. Is it sweat? Or possibly . . . tears?

I become increasingly dizzy and I sense, fear, that something is now behind me. I turn around and see, as I have feared, deep in the back of the wardrobe, a bright, white light floating toward me, calling me out of the darkness. I back up against the door of the wardrobe, but it is closed and I am trapped inside with the iridescent light. My head fills with fog and my body goes numb. As the light draws closer I hear the muffled sound of Medea's voice.

"Vincent?"

Then the light approaches me. Everything goes black as the door of the wardrobe is pulled open and I collapse out onto the floor.

I knew the timing was not right, but my irrational eagerness and thwarting paranoia would not allow me to deter this any longer. I needed to dispose of them, and needed to do it now. I did not wait until a vision enlightened me with possible complexities; I did not thoroughly execute a proper plan. In essence: I have been very foolish.

I waited, earnestly, outside the door for the pleasantries to abate. The night was darker than usual, with thick clouds overhead, blocking the moon and stars, the perfect night for the actions ahead: dark, ominous, foreboding. Raucous laughter from the gentlemen inside signified their complete ignorance of the bloodshed to come.

After some time of waiting patiently on my behalf, the revelry began to subside. Several men bravely exited out the door beside which I sat, but in their intoxicated state, they failed to glimpse the shadow blending into the wall. Many stayed behind, and I sat until the last twinkling candlelight diminished and the final drunken misfit stumbled off to slumber. Then I waited ever still, until the gentle snores drifted into the night air.

Despite the new, pristine stillness, I heard their whispers up above, two stories or so. I heard them, quite shaken yet excited at the same time: young, ignorant voices, regaling each other of heroic tales of their own futures. What rubbish, what complete deception.

A wicked grin crept across my face as I scaled the brick wall and peered through the open window. There they were: two young lads, each sitting up in his own bed, with a candle lit on the bedside table between them, an open book resting upon it. They both had dusty brown hair and pale brown eyes. They looked just a bit older than the last time I saw them, though still quite identical, though it was easy to discern which was which, as the slightly smaller brother wore that same uneasy countenance that rivaled the look of sheer bravery typical of his brother.

I watched them for some time, as they poured over the book between them. I could not quite see its contents, but it appeared to be a map which adorned the open pages. I strained to listen to their words. The larger brother spoke valiantly to the other.

"You see, brother, we will chase him up through the mountains, upon the tallest peak, and we shall slit his throat, rip out his heart, and hold it high for the world to see! Then all of the world will praise us for our bravery!"

"Is it necessary to kill him, brother?" said the other, looking concerned. "Why can we not just chase him up into the mountains and threaten him that if he should ever return, then we will slit his throat?"

"Don't you understand?" said the other, annoyed. "He killed our mother! And he continues to kill innocent people. It is our destiny, brother. It is up to us to make the world right again." The smaller brother looked down at his comforter, and a tear slipped down his cheek.

"I'm sorry, Roman," he said. "I just don't think I can." The larger brother, Roman, left his bed and joined his brother in his, hugging him.

"Don't worry, Remy," he said, consoling. "You have nothing to fear. We will be brave, and we will avenge our mother's death. It is the right thing to do. He is a wicked man. He killed our mother; he deserves this fate."

That was as much as I could bear. I deserved my fate? After what she did . . . .

With that final thought, my body twisted with a maniacal rage and the glass of the window through which I was spying shattered, spraying shards of glass in all directions. The boys jerked around and looked in my direction. With the black of night, I can't imagine they saw anything but the burning of my sparkling violet eyes.

The larger brother, Roman, stood on the bed, shielding the younger as I slinked in through the now open window.

"What exactly was it that you were saying about fate?" I said curtly as I stood up. The boys trembled in fear. The younger brother, Remy, let out a scream and I, with a flick of my wrist, silenced him. He grasped at his throat as he choked.

"Stop it!" cried Roman. "Please, stop! Stop! Remy!" He fought to help his brother, trying to pry Remy's hands away from his throat, though his efforts were futile.

I raised my hands towards the struggling boys and my head jerked back and twisted about as I whispered under my breath. The heat in my hands burned like fire and they began to glow. The power in my palms charged, and the glow got brighter. I pulled my arms back, ready to release the hellish fury building within me, when suddenly, there was a large slam across the door, and it cracked in two. The noise broke my concentration and I inadvertently let Remy go. He gasped for air. Roman grabbed his brother tightly around the waist and pulled him away, off of the bed, and the two rolled underneath it as another loud bang splintered the wooden door. The pent-up energy needed to be released before it exploded within me, so I sent two large blasts of light in the direction of the intruder, and the door burst in two. The boys screamed from beneath the bed and clutched each other in fear.

Before a face materialized from the smoke, an arrow zipped through the doorway and whipped just past my left ear. In an attempt to avoid it, I turned sideways and fell to the floor.

A tall man, slightly older but with a strong build, skulked through the doorway. His hair was completely white, and his eyes were pale green. He already had another arrow set in the bow as he moved toward me.

"Vincent," he said in a husky voice. "I never, in my wildest dreams, thought I'd be the one to kill you. Here I was, training these lads to save the world, and it seems that I can take that burden away from them."

I stayed, still on the ground, facedown.

"Do not be foolish, old man," I said. "You do not wish to interfere with the prophecy, do you?"

"It appears you already had that in mind," he replied. He moved closer to me, pointing to tip of the arrow at the back of my head.

"Come now, Evander," I said in disgust. "Do you really plan to take my life as I lay helpless on the ground? Is that a heroic action? Why not let me up, to face you, man to man, and make this a fair exchange?"

"You never were one for fighting fair," said Evander. "And you certainly are not a man. You are a monster." I listened as he pulled the bow back, ready to release. I held my breath and looked straight ahead. I could see the boys, under the bed, and they were looking straight into my eyes. I winked at them. At that moment, Evander let go, the boys screamed, and I disappeared, leaving nothing but an arrow sticking out of the ground where my head should have been.

Evander looked around helplessly. He could not see me, he could not hear me, and he could not feel me as I grabbed him by the back of the neck and sunk one of his own arrows into his side. He dropped to his knees, and blood dripped from the corner of his mouth. He looked over to the boys and mouthed the word, "Run." The boys scrambled to their feet and ran. I made a feeble attempt to pursue, which was halted when Evander grabbed my arm in protest. I shook him off me, but did not chase after the boys. The shouts of men downstairs led me to believe that would be unwise. And besides, I had loose ends to tie up here.

I circled around Evander and faced him. He glared at me but did not speak. I wiped the smear of blood off of his chin and bent down towards him. I leaned in very close and grabbed his chin in my hand, which, coincidentally, was still quite hot. Evander screamed as his flesh burned against mine. He then went very quiet and looked up at me, as his face shook in my palm.

"Another time," I said. "Those boys are mine."

"The league will protect them," he whispered, barely audible.

I could not help but scoff at his presumption.

And with that he seemed to go limp in my grasp and I let go of him. Evander fell, face first, to the floor, and did not get up.

———◆◆◆———

As I made my way home, the most peculiar and curious event occurred: a brief vision flashed before my mind. Usually I do not experience visions while awake. It was brief, but the point was made. I caught a glimpse of four large men, in the very room where these past events took place. They were standing in a circle, around what were, no doubt, Evander's remains. One man turned away in disgust and, once the circle was broken, revealed a rather disturbing sight.

The two young boys kneeling beside the fallen Evander, their nightgowns stained slightly with his blood. One brother, looking immensely enraged, yet saddened. The other, crying openly and burying his head in Evander's idle chest.

You can imagine my frustration at not successfully disposing of the boys. I did not anticipate Evander's arrival. Foolish. I also have an affinity for dramatic effect, which is why I chose to stay and see Evander's death rather than chase after the boys and take my chances with the other men. I may have failed this time, but their protector is gone, and the next time we meet, the boys will not be so lucky. Perhaps I should try a new approach, picking them off one at a time. I think I shall start with the smaller one, Remy.

I detect an air of insecurity in that one.

X

THE COLD SIDE OF THE MOUNTAIN

I awake on a soft bed, with layers of warm quilts over me. I sit in complete warmth and comfort. as a gentle hand wipes my head with a cool cloth. My head aches and my senses are quite blurred from the trauma in the wardrobe. A fragrant candle burns delicately beside me, and the soft aroma entices me to open my eyes. I see the vague image of a woman. She smiles at me and touches my forehead softly, moving the hair out of my eyes. Her voice is muffled but sweet.

"Vincent?" she says gently.

Suddenly, my heart aches and I yearn to answer her. *Madeline?* I feel a sudden rush all over my body. I reach up and touch the gentle hand that caresses my face. The skin is not smooth and warm as I anticipated, but wrinkled and cold.

I strain to revive my senses and the vision ahead of me clears. I see not the brilliant blue eyes I expect, but the shimmering pink ones belonging to Medea, who is standing over me, and my stomach drops, diminishing the comfort and desire and replacing it with harsh reality.

I push her hand away, disgusted.

"Vincent, are you alright?" Medea asks, retracting her hand dejectedly. "You were shaking."

"I'm alright," I reply. "I just had a nightmare, that's all."

"A vision?" Locke's voice, questioning, concerned.

"No, a true nightmare," I say reluctantly. "I thought for a moment I saw—" Then consciousness floods back into my brain and I remember where I am.

"I'm alright."

"Locke," Medea says. "Why don't you go into the kitchen and I'll be right in to fix you some breakfast. You'll need your strength. I'll tend to Vincent."

Locke looks at me for approval, and I nod. He gets up reluctantly and goes out the door, closing it behind him.

Medea sits down on the bed next to me. She pours a cup of tea and hands it to me. I accept and sip it carefully.

"You need looking after," she says. She takes her hand and begins to caress the side of my cheek affectionately as she did before. And, as before, I quickly push it away.

"How long?" I ask her.

"How long what?" she replies.

"How long have you been sleeping with Brogan?" I demand, sitting up, and setting the teacup on the nightstand.

Medea stands, offended. "Excuse me?" she says, shocked at my blunt question.

"He is trying to kill me and you're going to bed with him!" I shout. "How much does he know! How could you do this?"

"For your information," she says angrily, "it's all I can do to keep him from cutting my throat. He'll have me either way, so I might as well go willingly!"

"You can't defend yourself?" I ask.

"Not everyone's magic is as powerful as yours!" she says, as she folds her arms across her chest.

"Maybe if you spent less energy on your looks, it could be!" I snap back at her.

Medea brushes her hair from her eyes, clearly insulted.

"How much does he know?" I say again.

"Very little," she says. "I have been feeding him false information about you. He knows nothing of the boy . . . obviously. Even Ollam kept his mouth shut about that piece of information."

Ollam? Brogan had mentioned the schoolmaster was missing. Was he working for league as well? I knew I'd recognized those glowing green eyes.

"Although," Medea continued, "I think his motives for keeping that secret were quite personal; he may have been hoping to have Locke to himself. A little midnight snack, if you know what I mean." With that she gets up and goes out the door.

Medea leaves me to rest for a few more hours. In the early evening, Locke wakes me and we ready ourselves for our departure. Medea is nowhere to be found, hiding somewhere out of shame for my frank exposure of her recent fraternizations with Brogan.

Locke is very quiet this evening, obviously still shaken and distressed from the previous night's events. This is so hard on him, and my heart aches with guilt and sympathy for the poor boy. He begins filling his satchel with some sandwiches and biscuits.

"She told me I could take whatever we needed," Locke says awkwardly, as if he feels the need to justify his actions.

As I tie my cloak around my neck, Medea emerges from the other room. She looks quite distressed, as though she has been crying. Her cheeks are stained from tears and her shimmering pick eyes are puffy, with dark circles under them.

"You're really going through with this, are you?" she asks coldly, her arms crossed in front of her.

"Medea, the choice has been made," I reply.

"And you, Locke," she says, directing her question to him. "You also wish to continue to try and fight a losing battle?"

"Vincent has always been there for me," he says assertively. "And I shall always be there for him."

"Ha!" Medea laughs, and then adds sarcastically, "We shall see about that!"

With anger building inside me, I grab what few provisions we have made and head out the door, Locke just in front of me. Just as I attempt to step out the door, Medea grabs my arm and pulls me back inside.

"Don't do this," she says. "I need you here with me." She seems to have abandoned all the previous confidence and wit she displayed the night before, and for the first time, seems desperate and vulnerable. I pull my arm from her grasp and turn away, without another word or glance back at the pitiful woman. She does not reach for me again, but sinks back, allowing me to walk away from her once again. Locke nods to her, with a mixture of gratitude and sympathy, and follows me, closing the door behind him.

As we make our way from the cabin, Medea hangs her head out of the door and calls after us, "You will be sorry, Vincent! You will not prevail!"

Locke gives me a sideways glance as we ignore her final call.

"She is mad," I say finally, burning with anger and disgust.

"Well, I can certainly see that," Locke replies. "Sad, that one's completely mental and the other is completely senseless. It's a wonder how they get along by themselves."

I do not reply to this, which allows Locke a few short minutes to dwell on that matter further.

"But Vincent," Locke says, suddenly confused. "I thought you said that there were three sisters? There were only two, what happened to the third?"

"She died," I respond bitterly. And that is the end of the conversation.

<hr>

It must have been obvious to Locke that my temper is quite short, for he does not speak again for several hours as we make our way through the countryside into the mountainous region to the north. As the elevation climbs, the temperature drops, and the ground becomes frozen. The brown of the dirt and grass becomes blanketed by ice and snow. The mountains are the only place where snow does exist, though it doesn't fall and glisten in soft piles upon the ground; it is hard, and icy, and unforgiving. The wind blows it about fiercely and the piercing hail slices at my skin like razors.

I pull my hood far down over my face and Locke does the same, following behind me blindly, as I brave the storm in the lead. As we walk, the snow crunches under our footsteps, and, in areas, the slippery ice cause us to lose our footing. We trek about a mile into the icy abyss when the side of the mountain begins to steepen immensely.

Locke and I travel for several more hours and the fatigue sets in hard. The mountainside is quite steep but is destined to become ever more challenging. Locke must use all of his strength to grasp the rocks and pull both him and me up further and further. After a time, his hands are so frozen and raw that the skin has rubbed away, and they are bleeding. The sleet and wind are so powerful that it is impossible to hear one another speak. I decide that perhaps we should stop to rest for a while. The idea is further justified as I look up at Locke, whose eyes seem to have turned to ice.

Up ahead is a small nook in the mountainside, so I motion to that spot, and Locke nods in agreement. We climb a bit further and, finally, Locke pulls me up, teetering, onto the ledge. I realize almost immediately that the nook is not as deep as desired. There is barely space for the two of us to sit down. Locke looks frightfully over the edge and down at the threateningly jagged rocks below.

I conjure up a little light and, after anointing my hands with a vibrant orange elixir, raise my palms towards the solid wall of rock. Locke ducks his head down as I blast a bit of the wall apart, pieces of solid, frozen rocks fly off and tumble down the mountainside. The alcove is now increased to a comfortable depth, and we sidle into it. Locke begins to construct a small fire. Unfortunately, there isn't much timber in the rocky hills, so we must improvise. Locke gathers a few measly branches lying nearby. I tear a few pages from the end of my manuscript. I knew these would be needed.

I rub my hands together and allow them a few minutes to heat; then, after dusting them with my luminous yellow powder, I hold my palms over the kindling. A fire erupts, and the alcove begins to warm.

"Nice," Locke says, holding his hands over the feeble fire to warm them. "But, it's not going to last. I better go out and find some more wood. There were a few dead trees on the way up. I'm sure I could break off a few branches."

"Locke, no," I begin in protest, but Locke insists.

"We're not going to sit up here and freeze all night," he says. "Don't worry, Vincent." He rests a hand on my shoulder. "I'll be right back."

Locke removes his satchel and sets it down next to me, then carefully lowers himself down the side of the ledge. I sit, shivering nervously in the frigid night.

Sitting alone, I look about me, paranoid, trying not to think or lose focus. My eyes dart back and forth feverishly with each crackling of the fire, each whisper of the wind. My nerves are causing my hands to twitch worse than the unbearable cold. Then, out of the corner of my eye, I see a beam of white light. I sit in stunned silence.

The light does not move, does not brighten with intensity, it just gleams down from above. I get slowly to my feet and, cautiously, move towards the opening of the alcove. I look out into the night air and notice, to my great relief, that it is not the fateful white light which has been haunting me, but the glow of the moon, which is a sliver away from being full. It shines brightly, a great iridescent bulb in the thick blackness of the night sky. A single beam of light cascades down to the side of the mountain, as if to taunt me, to remind me, of what is to come. I hear faintly, though I think it may be my own imagination taunting me, a howling noise in the distance.

But that is not the only sound I hear, for a thump and a crack echoes in from the distance. My heart drops.

Locke.

I fling myself down onto the ledge and look over the side. I see nothing but the snowy, desolate mountainside below, illuminated by the bright moonlight.

I feel suddenly helpless.

"Locke?" I whisper. My heart starts to race and I look around frantically.

"Locke," I say again, louder this time. No answer. I get to my feet and start pacing around anxiously, looking out in all direction, my eyes darting from one direction to another in manic pursuit.

My hands begin to tremble and I hear noises all around me. I tread close to the edge of the cliff, looking over, teetering on my toes, threatening to fall.

I clutch at the sides of my head and scream, "LOCKE!"

"Vincent?" A gentle voice calls to me. I turn around and there is Locke, standing with a small pile of branches in his hands.

The noises and anxiety disappear instantly. I walk back towards the fire and I sit down quietly, ignoring Locke's questioning visage.

February 13ᵗʰ, '31

I would be lying if I said I was not nervous, creeping down into that dank, dark basement, slinking, like a snake, against the stone wall. I hear voices, shouts of excited yet frightened men. I reach the bottom and slide up against the wall adjacent to the doorway, out of which comes a bright light from lit torches and the choir of impatient questions.

"Evander, are you mad?"

"What's the meaning of this, man?"

"Why are these children chained?"

"Unhinge them, Evander, you tyrant; they're merely boys!"

"Stand back! All of you!" said the raspy voice of the one that must be Evander. "You must wait, be patient, you must see."

I poked my head around the doorway and looked in on the backs of five or six men. They were staring at something in front of them, which remained hidden behind their surly backs. A slight crackle and the men turned abruptly. In the same instant, I pulled back from the doorway. One of them men walked slowly toward the doorway by which I was hiding, and I became a shadow. He looked out into the hall and, by no surprise, noticed nothing.

I slunk down from my position above the doorway and peered once more into the room. From this higher level, I could see what so disturbed the men.

Two young boys, perhaps nine or ten in age, were chained hand and foot to the opposite wall. These boys were almost identical; they were similar in stature, short and stocky, though one just slightly shorter and leaner than the other. They shared the same dusty brown hair and the same brown eyes. Chained to the wall, they both wore the same look of fear on their faces, though the smaller one was crying slightly.

Though they looked so innocent, my insides boiled with rage at the sight of them.

These twins will grow fast and strong. They will hunt for the evil wizard.

The thought makes me cringe.

The one they call Evander walked up to the crying boy and wiped the tears from his cheek.

"Nothing to fear, little one," he said. The boy sniffled. His crying stopped, as if he was trying to be brave, like his brother.

Evander looked up at the ceiling to a lone window high above on the far wall. The nightfall was darkening and showed promise of full moon.

"Any moment now," Evander said, looking grim. "You will see the salvation that has been sent to us. These two young boys possess a dark secret, a secret that enables them to fulfill the prophecy. They must be trained, they must be informed, and they will end our suffering. We must keep them safe, we must help them find and defeat the sorcerer."

My mind began to race as I watched intently to see what great secret he withheld.

Through the window, it was evident that moon was beginning to rise in the night sky. The small boy began to tremble, and his twin breathed in deeply, as if bracing himself. Then, the moon broke out of the darkness outside and the bright, luminescent rays streaked through the glass panes and shone down upon the boys.

Simultaneously, the boys froze. Their eyes turned black and their skin white; they began to writhe and shake. The men backed several feet away from them and looked upon the boys, shocked by what was happening before their eyes.

I watched in silent horror as they screamed and convulsed, their muscles tensed and their skin became dark. I moved in to get a closer look and gasped involuntarily at the sight of the gruesome boys. At that moment Evander spun around and I had only a moment to vanish, leaving behind the shouts of frightened men and the faint howl of a frightened beast.

XI

THE SPARK

"Vincent," Locke says, setting down the branches, "what's the matter?"

"I had a brief fright," I say calmly. "That is all."

I sit in front of the fire, staring at my hands, which are still shaking slightly, and glowing with my heightened emotion. I turn them towards the fire and release the pent-up energy by re-igniting the dwindling flames. Locke sits down next to me. He opens his satchel and takes out a few of the biscuits from Medea's. He passes one to me, but I shake my head. I still cannot eat. Locke chews quietly.

After a few minutes of silence, Locke finally speaks.

"How do you do it?" he asks.

"Do what?"

"The light, the fire, everything. How?" I wonder why it has taken him so many years to ask. When he was a boy, Locke was quite curious about my 'abilities,' but he always assumed they were natural, and that it was *he* who was different. I think that once he realized that my qualities were unique, he became fearful and neglected to ever question them. Like everything else that I chose to conceal from him, he just accepted. But it seems now, in the face of our eminent danger, he is not about to hold back any longer.

"I mean, it is clear that Medea possess some magical qualities," he goes on, "but you're different, obviously quite powerful. But how? Where did you learn to do that? What makes you so special?"

"It is not so much something that is *learned*," I say. "But something that is *developed*."

"Developed?"

"Locke, I am old, and have been developing my abilities for many, many years. It takes time, it takes concentration and control, it takes patience, it takes, yes, some outside influence, but most of all, it takes passion."

"Passion?"

"Regular people, people with bland emotion, dull intelligence, no concentration, no motivation, no perception, they have no drive, no passion, and so, they are magic-less."

"You have passion?"

"As impossible as it sounds, yes. I was once very passionate. But passion can come in many forms."

"Like evil?"

"Like anger." *And jealousy,* I think to myself, *and guilt and sorrow. All of them.*

Locke sits back, no doubt, embarrassed at his assumption. I myself have never referred to myself as *evil*; that was reserved for the 'good.'

"When you have too much pent up anger," I say, "it can be very hard to contain. You may have noticed that sometimes I can control it, and sometimes, unfortunately, I can't."

"Like in the forest?" Locke asks.

"Yes," I say, embarrassed. While I have reacted out of anger many times, Locke has never seen me lose control quite like that before.

"Is it something that everyone can do?" he asks finally.

"If they have the spark." At this, Locke looks extremely puzzled. I hold out my hand and a miniscule flame erupts from my palm.

"A spark," I say, "Something to light to fire. Then, a fire needs fuel: passion, concentration, emotion." With that the flame in my palm begins to grow. I then let it die out as I say, "Without fuel, the magic dies."

"How do you develop it?" Locke asks, now completely intrigued.

"I'm not so sure it is in our best interests for me to share this information with you."

"You still don't trust me," he says dejectedly.

"It's not that," I reply. "There is a very specific reason that I have not shared any of this with you before. It is obvious that over the years I have done more harm to myself and others than good, and I do not wish to send you down the same path."

Locke sits back against the stone wall, disappointed. I spend a few minutes debating the necessity of what I am about to tell him. Locke can be trusted, right? He deserves to know, doesn't he? Do I not owe him something? After a few more minutes of watching Locke's sulking I finally give in.

"Magical Energy is a four way connection," I begin. At this Locke perks back up and leans forward, listening intently to my every word.

"Eyes," I say, pointing to my own. "Mind." I indicate my own head. "Heart." I move my withered hand down over the area chest where my black heart thumps lightly. "Hands." I lift them up in front of me.

"Eyes, Mind, Heart and Hands," he repeats softly.

"Everything within your body," I continue, "must be in tune with the world around you. Eyes . . . you see and perceive, you find a reason *for* the magic. Why do you think my eyes burn so brightly? Because they are always watching, perceiving, taking the world in."

Locke frowns, no doubt at the thought of his own eyes, the pale blue almost completely lost in them. "Go on," he insists.

"Do not rush me," I snap, as if he should be ever patient and grateful that I am revealing such delicate information.

"Your mind," I say next, "intelligence, concentration; it signals the magic. Your heart . . . passion, motivation; it fuels the magic. And finally, the hands." I lift them up again, palms facing Locke. "Hands enact the magic."

Locke looks down at his own hands which are rough from years of work and still scraped and sore from the climb.

"It is a natural flow, in through your eyes, up to the brain, down through the heart, and out through the palms of your hands."

"What's the point of all the powders and potions then?" Locke asks.

"Some things are more of . . . aids . . . or triggers. They . . . encourage certain magical elements. They strengthen them. I have been working for many years, not only to strengthen my own energy, but to create these magical aides."

"But they're not entirely necessary?"

"Not necessary. No."

Locke points his palms at the fire, in a measly attempt at something, and I cannot help but laugh.

"I don't have a lot of anger," Locke says shyly.

You will. I think to myself.

"The emotions are not always the negative kind," I say. "Actually, there are more powerful emotions than anger."

"Like happiness?" Locke asks.

"Happiness, yes," I say, quietly, then add, "and love . . ."

Locke makes yet another face. No doubt because he clearly hasn't experienced much of that either.

"It takes years of focus," I tell him, "and you need the spark."

"How does one get a spark?" he asks.

"It is transferred."

"By whom?"

"By anyone who has it himself. It can be given, and it can also be taken away."

"For what purpose?"

"To further strengthen your own."

Locke considers this for a moment.

"Millicent, did you see her hands? How black they were?"

Locke nods, then asks, "She had the spark?"

"It was taken from her. You can probably guess by whom." Locke frowns at the thought. "It is true," I continue, "that Millicent's eyes were not the only thing that she had stolen from her from her wretched sister. I saw it happen[11]. Medea also took away Millicent's spark in order to make herself a more powerful witch." I often wondered what she hoped to gain in doing that, but have to remind myself that there may be little motive at all, save for satisfying Medea's greediness and jealousy of anyone who possesses qualities of similar or greater value than her own.

"She stole her sister's magic?" Locke asks. "How could she do such a thing? How is it that she came to be so horrible?"

I consider my answer, thinking back on the younger Medea and all that she had been through.

"Well," I say. "You remember how I said that Medea was born blind, so that she could not see evil?"

"Yes."

"And you remember that eyes are the first step in magical creation?"

"She couldn't use her magic?" Locke says, putting the puzzle together.

---

[11]   Nightmare #588

"Not really, no." I reply. Not only could she not see, but her magical gifts were useless because of it. This caused her great insecurity.

"Medea," I say, "like her sisters, had always been very beautiful, but she was not always so good at heart. She, like many young women at the time, had a man with whom she was completely infatuated. She lived and breathed for him. He pledged his love to her, told her he was going to marry her, promised her the world."

"And what happened?" Locke asks. "Did he die?"

"He left her."

"But why?"

"Because she gave herself to him entirely. And once he had her innocence, he no longer desired her. He found another, a younger, prettier, more virtuous woman, who did not allow him to conquer her so easily. He ended up marrying her, leaving Medea lonely and heartbroken."

"Wow," Locke says. "I actually feel sorry for her."

"There is something to be pitied in her, yes," I say. "She became obsessed with beauty, with men, and with herself. Her first step was to gain sight; that was when she stole her sister's eyes. Once she had them, she rendered her sister useless, but Medea was suddenly flooded with magical ability that was powerful and restless, after years of being pent up inside her. She finally had magic of her own, but she spent little developing it fully. Medea used the magic when she could, but focused mainly on trying to find secrets to maintaining her beauty. She has done well to keep her looks, but her heart, mind and magic have grown old and rotten. I believe at one point she realized the damage she had done to herself and attempted to reignite her magic by stealing it from her sister. It helped a little, but her sister's spark was also weakened once she was left deaf and blind."

"So once you have the spark," Locke says, "it must be used, or it dies."

"Exactl," I respond. "Magic is just like a fire. A fire needs fuel and tending to, or else it withers away and dies. Magic is a fire that burns inside you, and the spark is what ignites that fire."

"Who gave the spark to you?" Locke asks.

I feel a sudden sting in my chest as I think of the answer to Locke's painful question. Suddenly my head swirls with memory.

The warm sunlight on my face. The cool breeze. The scent of lilacs and cherry blossoms. The soft hands on my bare chest. Then, the magnetic pulse into my heart.

"Enough for now," I say to him.

May 20th, '31

I arrived home early this morning after my arduous journey, my head swimming with new information. I need someone else to do it for me. I know just the person, but he is away at sea, it may take several years for him to come back. No matter, she told me to wait.

I entered my cabin and shut the door tightly, barring it. I then snapped my fingers and the drapes in the windows closed themselves.

I climbed the rickety steps leading up into the loft. I walked over to my bookcase and removed a single thick black volume. I opened the front cover, revealing not printed pages but a hollow compartment. Inside the compartment lay a single, silver key.

I grasped the key tightly in my hands and proceeded to descend the steps back to the main floor. I brushed my hand aside through the air, and my great oak bed slid carefully in the same direction. Behind the bed, in the area where it previously rested, was a small latch in the floor. The latch was so inconspicuous that the naked eye could not see it if one did not already know it was there.

I pulled gently on the latch and a wooden plank opened forward, revealing a small hole in the floor. Reaching cautiously inside, I extracted a small, wooden box. I placed in delicately on the floor and inserted the silver key.

Inside the box lay a small, black pouch. I opened it and procured a shimmering pink stone. I grasped it tightly in my hand, feeling its weight, its utter smoothness, making sure it was still real.

She desires it. She will do anything for it.

And she will have it, in time. I put the jewel back inside the pouch and returned everything back to its proper place.

XII
THE SEER

After our conversation, Locke lies down to rest. I stay awake, alert, trying to think about whether I should have told him all those secrets. I decide, in the end, that it is for the best. I know that Locke can be trusted, and that, ultimately, he will make wise decisions.

As I watch him sleep I cannot help but feel a deep affection for this boy who has been loyal to me for so long. I think perhaps it is time.

I sneak quietly over to Locke, who is sleeping soundly, and gently put my hands on his chest. I close my eyes. I feel a pulse of energy materializing in my body. It is as small as a pea, spinning inside my heart. It swirls and grows and begins to spark, like a firecracker. It takes a moment or two to extend, increasing in pressure, and then, when I feel like my insides are about to explode, I release it. A charge emits quickly into Locke's body, sending a pulse like a mini bolt of lightning. At the moment of the release Locke jerks awake in a panic. He starts gasping for breath, clutching at his chest. He rips his cloak open and reveals a glowing red mark upon his chest.

"What the hell was that?" he says, frightened.

"I'm sorry, my dear Locke," I say apologetically. "You were shivering, and I attempted to warm you. I think I lost a little control in my own frigid state."

"You almost burned my goddamn skin off!" he shouts, rubbing the singed skin on his chest.

"Watch your tongue!" I snap back nastily, insulted by his insolence. "I was merely trying to help you, you ungrateful brat!"

Locke stands, chest heaving in anger. Then he storms off away from me. My own arms tingle, as if just being shocked by an electric volt. I sit uncomfortably, holding them out limply in front of me, waiting for the tingle to subside.

Locke comes back after several minutes and begins packing up our things. He extinguishes the fire by scooping up snow and dumping it onto the flames.

"We better get moving," he says. Without a word, I get to my feet and we continue our climb.

Locke's energy seems to have been replenished, or else his anger is fueling his new-found strength, because he climbs easily, while I trail, slowly but surely, behind him. As we ascend the mountainside, Locke is silent. I cannot help but wonder why he responded in such an outburst. Locke has never spoken to me that way before. He has been quite ruthless towards others, yes, but never, ever towards me. Perhaps he is frightened and the intensity of the state of affairs is taking a toll on him. Perhaps he has grown weary of my lack of information, and my constant demand that he risk his life for me. I do not blame him.

Luckily for us, we were much closer than I had thought. We reach the topmost ledge within an hour. Locke climbs up first and then pulls me up after him. The mouth of the cave is deep, black and empty. I look ahead into the cavern, remembering all too well what transpired on my last visit here. I drop to my knees and put my face to the ground in homage. Locke, not sure of what else to do, does the same. After a few seconds, an echo is heard from within the cave, a tiny, whisper of a voice.

"Vincent?" Although I know the voice comes from deep within, it presents itself with such clarity and volume that it seems as if the speaker is no more than a few feet away.

"I have come to seek council with you," I say. "If you'll have me."

"The boy?"

"He is my companion."

"He is not welcome inside." Locke looks at me disconcertedly. I was afraid of this. I turn to look at Locke, who is shivering, teeth chattering.

"I'll just wait out here," he says, with a blend both of sarcasm and bitterness.

I reach inside my cloak and dust my hands with a fiery red powder. I hold out my hands, palms downward, and grasp Locke by the shoulders. His skin thaws under my grip. Within seconds, he becomes wet with perspiration, his skin becoming as warm as my hands. The snow at his feet begins to melt away, revealing a dry circle around him.

"I think that'll do," I say. Locke's cheeks are flushed pink, and he wipes sweat away from his forehead.

"I won't be long," I reply. I revolve slowly, facing the mouth of the desolate cave, and brace myself to enter the abyss. I hesitate, then take a small step forward, but she stops me abruptly, her frail voice floating out delicately through the open air.

"Your eyes, Vincent. You know I do not like you to see."

Reluctantly, I tear a piece of fabric from my decaying cloak. I turn my head around towards Locke, who, for the first time, seems completely hurt that there is nothing he can do for me.

"It'll be alright," I assure him, though I lack the confidence myself. I tie the scrap of fabric about my head, blinding myself. I then take a slow breath and proceed into the cave.

Although I am submerged in pitch blackness, my other senses are keenly alert to the mystifying atmosphere of the cave. The cave is damp and, like everything else atop this mountain, exceedingly cold. It smells strongly of must and mold, wet rock, and ice. The eeriness of the surroundings sends a chill down my spine. A cacophony of sounds meets my ears: water, dripping steadily from what seems to be icicles hanging from the low ceiling; the gentle scurry of the miniscule feet of spiders, beetles, and other various insects along the floor; and the light whistling of the wind through hollow passageway. And, although I cannot see it, I can feel the frosty mist form from my breath.

After a few minutes of walking cautiously deep into the cave, the gentle crackling of a fire becomes audible. I near the fire eagerly and the air begins to warm, as the heat from the flames intensifies.

Though still thoroughly blinded, the light from the fire glows through the fabric covering my eyes, and I know I have walked close enough. I sense the other, ominous, yet familiar presence in the room. I bow slightly in the direction which my intuition suggests she might be.

I feel her approach, and then, the soft touch of skin grazes my face. She presses her hands softly upon my cheeks, as if assuring that I am real. She traces the lines of my cheeks, the wrinkles of my forehead, and the line of my jaw, and she runs her fingers through the tangled mess of my hair. Her warm touch is intense yet soothing.

"You have changed," she says delicately. "You are so unlike what you once were."

I take a deep breath. Her voice is euphoric, sensual.

"Sad," she whispers into my ear, "the way people change." I feel the warmth of her breath as it curls down my neck. I feel a familiar longing sensation rising within me.

"Sit," she breathes. I obey, though I stumble to find the ground. I can hear her moving about, though am ignorant of her actions. After a few light crackles of the fire, an array of scents fills the air. The space becomes heavy with a thick, perfumed smoke that enters my lungs and weighs heavily within them. As I breathe them in, my brain begins to fog and my muscles relax, though the process is habitual and welcome.

I wait a few minutes as my senses numb, and then she speaks, delicately, calmly.

"You are much troubled, Vincent," she says. "You are different."

"Yes," I reply.

"So sad," she says with genuine regret. "You were once so beautiful. This world has corrupted you as much as you have corrupted it. Your purpose, it has destroyed your soul."

"You say that as if it is not something you have seen before."

"I say it because it is so unfortunate." Her words sting. It is not very often that I think back to when I was young. To the kind of person I used to be. It was so long ago, and she is right; I was a different person then.

"Why have you come?" she asks, though I am sure she already knows the answer.

"I seek council with you," I say. "I have had visions of the possible future, and I am unsure of how to proceed."

"You cannot see as I see, Vincent. You see what others see."

"Madam, this vision was different. I did not see the unfortunate circumstances of another or the reiteration of my experiences. I saw future events unfold regarding my own position. I do not know how much of it will occur exactly as I have seen it, or what role my own choices play in the accuracy or certainty of the events."

She paused for a moment to consider my words. "You have come to ask me if your future is as you have seen it? I am insulted!" I feel her presence ebb away from me as she storms backward. It is apparent that over the years she has grown less patient with me and, no doubt, has become exhausted by my nagging questions.

"I do not wish to insult you," I say apologetically. "But what I say is true. I only wish to ask you how to proceed. I do not know if the fight with Roman is worth pursuing, or if I should give in." She does not answer me, and she does not move.

"Please," I beg. "I need your help."

The oracle, though I cannot see it, begins to move about again. She begins to whisper and I feel suddenly stiff and cold. The glare of the fire though my blindfold darkens, and then there is silence. My mind races with all of the possibilities she could reply with. I am both nervous and anxious, knowing that my future lies in her grasp.

When she speaks again, he voice is changed; it is deeper, flat, and grim.

"The choice is yours," she says at last. "The wolf will come to end the violence and suffering on these lands. He will try to triumph over the evil wizard, and The Age of Darkness will be over. However, the wizard may choose to fight back, and with the silver light and the help of his successor, he may prevail."

"And . . . and . . . what will become of them?" I ask.

"They will live on," she answers, now in her normal, gentle tone, "and continue to suffer in misery and bring sadness and corruption to the world. The outcome of the battle is uncertain." This was what I was afraid of. Even if I do succeed in killing Roman, what kind of life will I continue to lead? What kind of life will there be for Locke? What other choices do I have?

"How much longer can I possibly run?" I ask her.

"That remains to be seen," she says. "They will continue to hunt you until you are found. Remy's death has turned Roman maniacal with rage and vengeance. I do not believe he will stop until either you or he are dead. Though I do not believe you have the strength left to produce the necessary enchantments to defeat him. The time must be right and the power must be obtained."

"Seer, I have this," I say, and I reach into my cloak and extract the small, silvery white jewel that Locke and I abducted from Haram's secret chamber.

"Ahh," she says excitedly. "You have been successful." The Oracle reaches out and takes the jewel from my hand. She then begins moving about again quietly, though vigorously. There is a light *crack* and a grinding, then a swirling and a twinkling.

"Here," she says. I reach out and, after a few false grasps at the air, my hands close around a small, smooth vial. The glass is hot and I place it quickly back inside my robes.

"When the time is right and the moon is full and the tensions are at their highest," she recites, "drink the potion and the light will fill you."

"And I may be able to defeat Roman?" I ask.

"You may," she answers. "Though it is more likely now." A smile creeps across my face as I think about Roman lying dead and cold on the ground at my feet. Then, I think of Locke, who will have to play some part in this. And what if I fail? What will happen to him?

"What about the boy?"

"The boy's fate is in your hands, Vincent. He has served you for many years, and he has served you well. He lives to serve you, to live up to your expectations. But deep down inside, he has the heart of a hero; he is good and pure. It is time for the boy to make choices of his own. Locke will have to choose a side. Secrets will be revealed."

"Secrets," I say quietly. I ponder this for a moment. I have kept many secrets over the years. I cannot imagine what might occur if they were uncovered. And how? I ponder this for a moment. Then I ask, "What do you know of the possibility of betrayal?"

"Ah yes," she says, as if recalling some important memorandum. "The wolf with find you with aid. You will be betrayed, Vincent. There are those who know you better than you think and who you do not know as well you think. Your allies are growing thin." This last sentence stings my heart as I think of Locke. Is he as loyal as I think he is? I told myself I could trust him. Is that true? She said he will have to make choices of his own. What if those choices are to betray me? What if he has been working with me all along just to lead me into some kind of trap? Would I not have seen this? Is it possible that my own corrupt mind is working against me?

Sensing my uneasiness, the Oracle moves close to me and sets a hand on my shoulder.

"It is time to decide the fate of you and those close to you. You and you alone can seal the fate of the boy."

I get up and she takes my hand. She kisses my cheek. As it did before, my body aches with desire. Almost instinctively, I reach a wavering hand to the clasp on my cloak, and I gently pull it open. I remember the first time I came to her, how naïve I was and nobly I up held myself, but in the times since then, I had not been so strong to deny her. As she had said many years ago, I have withered.

"That will not be necessary this time," she says, confusing me. "As I have said before, you are a different person than you were then." I stop, embarrassed, and reaffix the clasp on my cloak. Could I possibly have changed that much for her to reject me like this?

"There is one more thing I have seen," she says. I wait in anticipation, what other puzzling news could she possibly have for me. "I have seen *her*. You have the final ingredient that you lacked many years ago? She is ready. She waits. She forgives you. When you are ready, she will be there." My stomach twists violently into a knot. I clasp my hand over the black velvet pouch around my neck.

She kisses me again and turns me around towards the mouth of the cave. She unties the cloth around my head, allowing it to fall gently to the floor, and gives me a soft nudge forward.

"Farewell, Vincent," she says. I begin to walk away slowly. The perfume scent in the air and the warmth are sucked away as I depart, and then, that cold, deep, ominous voice echoes out from far behind me.

"Fear the wolf, but beware the cat."

Had I known all along just how close she was, I would have gone to see her long ago. But after years of searching, the proper information finally procured, I knew it was time. It was a difficult journey up the cold, steep mountain, but there, in the mouth of the cave, the mysteries and suffering of my past seemed to absolve instantly. I knew she would have answers for me, though I did not expect that I would be sickened by them.

As I crept along the dank, desolate entranceway, I wondered whether she would see me at all. I could barely contain my nervousness as that delicate voice floated out of the abyss, and I heard her words for the first time.

"Bow," a voice said from within. Unsure of what to do, I bent myself forward in an awkward bow.

"Further," she said. I paused for a moment, upset that I had to degrade myself in such a way, but sure that it would be worth it. I got down to my knees and bowed my head and hands to the ground.

"Who?" she breathed.

"My name is Vincent," I replied. "I am here to seek your wisdom."

"I give wisdom to no one," she responded. "What do I owe you?"

"If you please, great oracle," I begged. "I have been searching for you for many years. I seek comfort, seek guidance."

"You are the one that has brought the darkness?"

I stopped. I never like to admit to this fact, of course. It is merely the assumptions of others, which I seem to have been designated responsible for. Nevertheless, it would be false for me to deny it. But before I had a chance to answer her, she beckoned for me.

"Come," she said. I got cautiously to my feet, breathed deeply in, and entered the alcove. I walked for several yards in the chilling blackness until it became warm, as there appeared to be a roaring fire in the distance.

"Stop," she commanded, though somewhat politely. "You must be blinded." I froze in my tracks. Blinded? Surely she did not mean to take my sight from me? I felt a breeze blow towards me and piece of silk blew across the stone floor and caught itself upon my shoe.

I bent down to pick it up and, without thinking, tied it around my eyes as a blindfold. I continued my procession towards the burning flames.

As I neared her my senses began to heighten. I felt extreme warmth all over my body; the smells from within were saccharine and delicious. My mouth could not help but water. I heard a soft, melodic humming and yearned to peek at her. My mind raced with thoughts of her beauty. I reached up towards my blindfold, but resisted the temptation, remembering the ghastly details from the prophecy.

When it had appeared that I had walked far enough she stopped me.

"Sit," she commanded, though, yet again, in an inviting manner. I obeyed but with some difficulty in my impaired state.

"You are here because you wish to know about the prophecy," she said. Was that a question or a statement? I wondered.

"I know who you are," she went on, "it was your great ancestor who first came to me, and to whom I recited the prophecy hundreds of years ago."

"It is how I knew you were here," I said.

"You may also be interested in knowing," she went on, "that I spoke with your father as well, many years ago."

I sat in silence. My father?

"I think it is no coincidence that you have found me here, all these years later, and seek my council."

"The prophecy is true then?" I asked her.

"I have much to offer you," she said. "What have you to offer me?"

"I have nothing," I said, ashamed.

I felt her approach me, and she touched my cheek delicately.

"That is untrue," she said softly in my ear. "It has been many ages since I have had a visitor. My body aches for companionship."

I knew immediately what she implied. I was instantaneously reminded of how much time had passed since I had the companionship of a woman myself. I had become so engrossed in my quest that thoughts of intimacy had escaped me for years. I suddenly felt a strong, wrenching urge of desire pulse through my body as it became instinctively cognizant of her closeness.

Slowly, mechanically, I nodded my head in agreement. She released her hand from my face and the rapture collapsed.

"The She-Wolf, she has wronged you?" she asked abruptly.

A surge of pain struck my heart at the question.

"She did," I said, in barely a whisper, as I choked out the words.

"You have killed her."

"I did."

"You did so in vain. The twins have already been born."

"I know of this. Forgive me; I have seen them[12]."

"Ah," she said, in a sarcastic tone, "but you have yet to see what gives them great power."

Another twinge in my heart. This time it is a mix of anger and fear at what I am still ignorant of. I loathe ignorance. It makes me feel vulnerable.

I continued, "And so, I fear, that the rest is true? The prophecy will come into fruition?"

"It will."

"What can I do?"

"There is little time," she said. "Your only chance is to dispose of them before they grow into men. But beware, they are well-protected. It will not be easy."

"Evander?" I laughed. "I do not fear him. He is no match for my power."

"Do not be foolish, Vincent. You already have been. You are a terrible man with great power. You must be careful with what you do with it."

"I beg your pardon," I said, suddenly confused and agitated by her trite remark. "But, how have I already been foolish?"

"The jewel," she said.

---

[12]   Nightmare #182

"Jewel?"

"The silver jewel. I believe you know what it truly was, of its power. And yet, you traded it away."

"Of its power? Do you mean . . . ?"

"Are you telling me that you did not suspect it? After all those years you spent traveling around with your father, looking for its brothers? You did not think . . ."

"The others have long since been lost."

"You lie. Not all of them."

"What difference would it make now? Besides, I was desperate . . . I needed the secret."

"You traded away the jewel for a dark secret, a secret which, as you have already discovered, was a lie. She did not give you all of the details of the spell. There is a missing piece. That is why the spell did not work completely. You traded the jewel for half a secret. And, it was that very jewel that may be essential for your triumph over the twins. You must retrieve it."

"But how? That was years ago."

"She still wanders, at the edge of the northern forest. You have something she desires, another stone—its sister—one of a shimmering pink hue. It possesses the ability to create beauty. She desires it. She will do anything for it."

"Then I shall set out at once!"

"You must send another. If she recognizes you, she will not relent to your request."

"I shall find someone else then."

"You must wait; it will be a few years yet. The signs of aging have begun to present themselves to her, and she has already begun to seek out ways to acquire youth, but you must wait until she becomes desperate."

"How long?"

"Five years, at least. That will give you ample time to wait for assistance. You will need to employ someone else to retrieve the stone for you. You must not go to her again yourself. She will not allow you to have it."

"What about the secret? You said the spell was not complete."

"Incomplete, yes," she said spitefully. "She wanders half in this world, half in the next, as you attempted to drag her from it. You can save her."

"You mean that there is still a chance? If I find the missing piece?"

"There is." She came close to me and whispered delicately in my ear. My heart fluttered with the news, and a thrilling sensation erupted inside me. This news excited me greatly, another chance! I thanked her profusely.

"It will be difficult," she said.

"I will do anything," I replied.

"And now," she said, as she approached me once more. "You may go, unless you wish to stay and fulfill our agreement."

With this she came close to me, gently pressing her body up against mine. I became intensely aware of her fragile frame; its closeness to mine, its delicate shape, its longing, and I again felt the surge of desire that possessed me before.

For the first time in many years I felt extremely vulnerable, but as she touched me, caressing my face and neck, all feelings of anxiety, anger, stress, and sadness dissolved when she touched me, and I didn't care.

For the first time in many years, I felt contentment.

Then, suddenly, a pair of brilliant blue, orbs appeared in my subconscious . . .

"I'm sorry," I said, pulling away from her, and simultaneously the state of ecstasy that flooded my body was quickly gone. I stood there, feeling, once again, immense pain.

"Another time," she breathed. "For it is certain that you will be back. And next time you will have withered. Now go." I didn't want to. I wanted to stay with her, to give myself to her, again and again, to forever rid myself of these feelings.

I turned to leave, but not before asking for permission to return. She agreed, and I felt relief. As I began my descent back into the narrow tunnel, her words stopped me dead in my tracks:

"You will be receiving a visitor soon, Vincent."

I turned abruptly. "What kind of visitor?"

"Someone has been watching you. They know what you have done, what you have tried, but failed to do. All actions have a consequence."

"But what . . . ?"

"That is all. Until we meet again, sorcerer."

She kissed me gently on the cheek. I sighed knowing that there was no resentment spawned from my inability to fulfill my end of the bargain. Perhaps it was a test to see if I would take advantage of a lonely woman, or perhaps this was sympathy for my emotional incompetence. But she said I would return and fulfill my obligations to her. That I would wither. How could I?

And with that I was dismissed, left to my own devices to ponder all of the words she has shared with me. Suddenly, the memory of what she had told me flooded back into my consciousness. Another chance! The spell was incomplete. Missing one piece. But how? And where to find it? Where to look?

I am afraid I am getting ahead of myself. I cannot let this distract me from my plans of attack on the twins. But still . . . another chance.

And still. The visitor? What did she mean? This is another puzzling piece of information, one that has been weighing heavily on my mind since I left the mountainside. Even now, as I sit in the darkness of my cabin, planning my attack of the twins, I cannot help but jump every time I hear a noise outside. When will this visitor come? Who could it be? And what will be in store for me when he arrives?

XIII

THE FLIGHT

These last words spoken by the Oracle pierce through my brain. What could she possibly have meant?

Fear the wolf, but beware the cat . . . Fear the wolf, but beware the cat.

Fear the wolf; this is obvious. Roman is coming for me and my fate is to be decided in battle. Beware the cat? This leads to confusion. And speaking of cats . . . I feel sudden remorse as I think of what has become of my dear sweet Vesta, who risked her life to save us back in the forest.

As I walk swiftly through to the opening of the cave, I am deeply concerned. The Oracle's words roll around my brain, they are heavy, confusing, and frightening.

When I approach the mouth of the cave, I see Locke sitting huddled on the ground, his head in his knees, with his back towards me. Without thinking, I suddenly feel a surge of suspicion.

It is time for the boy to make choices of his own. Locke will have to choose a side. Secrets will be revealed.

The boy will make a choice of his own. Could that mean that Locke will turn on me? *Secrets will be revealed* . . . the motive behind Locke's treachery? Is it possible that, after all of these years Locke's loyalty will be threatened? He seems so innocent, sitting there, trying to keep himself warm. But what thoughts pass through his mind at this very moment? The idea that he is, deep inside, a traitor . . . this would break me.

"Locke," I say with a tone of melancholy. The boy turns around and, upon seeing me, gets to his feet.

"All set then, Vincent?" he asks.

"It is time for us to depart."

"Is everything all right? You seem a bit distressed."

"Everything is as expected," I lie. "Although our next destination is uncertain."

"What did the oracle say?" he asks.

"That is for me to worry about," I reply. I take a few steps over the ledge and begin to lower myself down.

"Fine," Locke says. Then, he looks over the side of ledge. "I really am not looking forward to climbing back down this mountain. Though I'm sure down is a lot less strenuous than up."

"Indeed," I say so low it is almost a whisper.

It is time to decide the fate of you and those close to you. You and you alone can seal the fate of the boy.

I shook the thoughts away. Plenty of time for that later. A more immediate concern is how to get down this godforsaken mountain. I have little desire to spend hours, if not a day or two, climbing back down the side in the glacial snow.

I glance at Locke, who appears to be having the same thoughts as he looks down the mountain with a countenance of defeat. For a fleeting second, a horrible thought crosses my mind. I could leave him up here. Then he will never know, and never have the chance to turn on me. I stare at him, with a slight sense of loathing, as he looks down the side of the mountain, so innocently, contemplating how to get down.

What am I thinking? I push the idea of abandoning Locke from my mind. No, I can't do that to him. I have done enough. The mountainside is steep and threatening. Perhaps it is time for a little trickery to make this journey a bit easier. I hope I can spare the energy. I reach inside my cloak and extract a vial of vividly lucid liquid. It is so translucent in fact that it almost looks like air. I uncork the vial and swallow its contents. A sudden rush of wind flows through my veins. My palms become airy, light, and feel cool. I stretch out my arms and call to Locke.

"Hold on to my waist," I say urgently. Locke stares at me in disbelief.

"You're joking," Locke says.

"Have you ever known me to make light of a situation?" I say, annoyed. "Especially in such dire times."

"I must be crazy," he says. "What the hell?" Locke hesitates, but put his strong arms around my frail waist. I feel a twinge of apprehension at his touch.

With one swift movement, we are in the air. Not so much flying, as gliding, down steadily toward the earth below. I wonder what Locke is thinking, as his arms grip me tightly. The descent is slow and steady, and the air defogs my mind, and I relax, thinking. I allow my eyes to close. The strength of Locke's grip is comforting to me. Dependence. So close, yet not quite, a hug.

In my comfort, I slip yet again into a state of semi-consciousness and my mind fills with the memory.

I was sitting at my desk, my head in my hands, in sheer misery. Was I . . . crying? I had tried over the years, so hard to forget. I felt the tiny little hand tug on my cloak. I looked down and there sat Locke, looking up at me with his big, pale blue eyes. He looked sad.

"What?" I asked him angrily, trying to mask my own sorrow. He did not say a word but reached his tiny arms around my waist and pressed his head firmly against me.

A hug?

I sat, shocked, while the little boy displayed this innocent affection. At first, I was appalled by his touch, then after a few moments, relaxed and allowed a new sensation to wash over me.

Affection? Perhaps even . . . .

Locke released me and looked up at me, and then he smiled. He patted my hand and turned and trotted away.

Yes, I remember it fondly. That was the first, and only time, I ever felt such affection since . . .

She is ready. She waits. She forgives you. When you are ready, she will be there.

My trance grows deeper and I open my eyes, dazed. Up ahead, gliding towards me, is a bright, blinding white light. My whole body goes numb. My mind erases. I can no longer feel Locke's tight grip, can barely make out his muffled shouts as my eyes roll into the back of my head, and suddenly the only thing I can feel is the falling . . .

July 28th, '30

I haven't slept in days. I sit in front of her tombstone, alone, wondering why I have failed. I did everything right. I killed the wolf, I worked for ten long years to procure all of the necessary ingredients, completed every daunting and sinister task. And yet, I sit here, feeling more dejected than ever, I cannot help but dwell on my failure. Tears slip from my eyes at this very moment and wet the page upon which I write.

Twice now, I have failed her.

My insides rip into shreds, they scrape and writhe and my heart feels as though it is being crushed in a giant's grip.

What did I do wrong?

I walk by them every day, and they still lay there, lifeless. No one has found them; no one has moved them to a proper place. I look into their hollow eyes and see my own guilty countenance reflected back at me.

Why did this not work?

When will I receive salvation? When will I be purged of my suffering? I long to feel her gentle touch again. Is my soul to wander the earth, lost and broken for all eternity? Will it not stop until I kill every last living being, and the only life left to take is my own?

My mind grows feeble, and I ponder the point of it all. How quickly, and how easily, I could end my own suffering.

But no. They are the ones who deserve to suffer. Not I. And they will. They will. It is them who have done this to me. To us. I will not rest until they are in the ground. Reduced to bones and decaying flesh.

Ashes to ashes and dust to dust.

Those boys will suffer as I have suffered. Their hearts will bleed as mine have bled.

And then I will find that cursed, lying gypsy and squeeze her throat until every last ounce of oxygen expels from her lungs, unless she tells me what I did wrong, and how to fix it.

And then I will find a way.

I will not fail you.

XIV

THE CEMETERY

The next few events are a blur.

I feel the weight of my body hitting the ground. Hitting the ground . . . hard? No. Soft . . . as if floating. Light all around me. Footsteps, hands shaking me . . . then . . . sleep.

———◆———

I awaken suddenly. I'm lying on my back. My vision is blurred and my eyes burn. When I open them, I see nothing but blackness. I turn my head to the left and right.

"Locke?" I am alone.

"Locke!" I scream. I cannot move. I look about me frantically. Then I see it—*her*—a few yards away from me, sitting alone in the dark.

As I am.

My body floods with despair and I begin sobbing uncontrollably.

"No!" I scream. "Locke!"

"Vincent!" I hear him rushing up the side of the hill, and he flings himself down beside me. I close my eyes and fall back to sleep.

———➤◆◀———

When I awaken again, my vision has been restored. I am atop a small hill. It seems that this place alone kept a deep chill in the air and a dense fog that always lingered, even in the day. It is night now and even more cold than usual. A warm fire is blazing and Locke is preparing supper. He must have worked hard to light it on his own. I feel terrible. Suddenly, the memory of the flight rushes back into my brain.

"Locke . . . how?"

"I don't know," he interrupts coldly. "We were falling fast and then there was light everywhere and it was almost like someone caught us . . . and just carried us down." *Light?* I look around and realize where we are. A sudden pain bursts inside of me. I brought us here. Subconsciously? The Light? It carried us here? No. I *carried* us here. But how?

I know he cannot explain it any further, and so I let the matter drop. I sense a harsh tone in his voice, something is wrong.

There is a tension in the air; Locke does not speak to me throughout the meal and I can sense a discomfort in his demeanor. He does not ask how I am feeling; he wants to know what is happening, and why we are here. We sit in silence for half an hour, as I ponder what could be weighing on his mind. Finally, he speaks:

"Tell me about her." Locke stares at me through the fire, but I look sadly at the ground. His voice is sincere and welcoming. We sit in silence a few more moments while I absorb the night air. I shiver under by cloak. I have always hated this place. I hadn't been here in years, and I don't understand why I inadvertently decided to come here now. What would *she* do for me now? She hasn't offered any comfort in the past forty years, what *could* she do for me now? This was clearly a mistake.

"I can't." I say.

"Vincent?" Locke says, "Why must you keep everything from me?"

"Locke, I—"

"The spark, the jewel, the oracle, and now this," he interrupts. "Why will you not share things with me?"

"Locke, I surely don't know what you-"

"You think I am 'the betrayer,'" he states. "That is why." I cannot up help but be startled at this comment, as well Locke's assertion that it is true. Is this something that has been worrying Locke all along? Is this why he has been so eager to please me, to help me, to prove to me that he is not as treacherous as the others? I think back on everything that Locke and I have been through over the years, everything that I have put him through. I feel suddenly guilty that the thought ever crossed my mind before. How could I not trust him with every inch of my being? He has never done anything to make me think otherwise.

"Locke," I say, though it is difficult, "I do not think you will betray me. I trust you. I will not keep things from you any longer."

"Thank you," Locke says. He smiles, satisfied, but he still looks somewhat troubled. He looks over at the dark presence looming nearby.

"Tell me about her." Locke insists once more.

"What is it that you want to know?"

"Everything," he replies. "I never even knew about her, how could you keep such a secret from me?" He seems genuinely hurt that I never spoke of her before. But why should I? He would have never understood. He was just an orphaned boy who picked pockets and got into fist fights; he never knew anything about . . . .

"Please, Vincent."

I sigh. I look over at the headstone a few yards away, the one that caused me so much distress when I first awoke. It is quite different from the last time I had seen it. It is not as shiny and new, the weather has clearly eaten away at it. Weeds have sprung up from the ground where flowers had once been. A brownish green moss crept up the side and mushrooms clutter at the base. Despite its newly grotesque demeanor, the letters etched in the stone are still decipherable, clear enough to catch the eye of Locke as we passed it by, clear enough for him to question me now. *Tell me about her.* What could I tell? My memory of her is both as clear as if she were still her, yet slipping away from me somehow, after all of these years. I stare at each individual letter etched into the dark stone. A tear slips from my eye as I look upon the name.

M. A. VINCENT

"I didn't know you had a wife," Locke says quietly. "Why didn't you tell me?"

"It is something I have been dealing with for such a long time: her death. It is painful to speak about."

He responds derisively, "The great and powerful Vincent feels pain? Hah! I didn't think such a thing existed." I lower my head in shame and despair. My heart becomes overwhelmed with anxiety and grief as I think about my past, about Madeline.

After several quiet moments, I finally develop to ability to speak:

"I haven't always been this way. When I think back on the past forty years, what I have done, what I have become, I am ashamed. I have spent ten times as much time feeling anger and rage in her absence than I did feeling love and comfort in her arms. I know she would not want to see me like this. This is not what she would have wanted.

"I have been very selfish. I have been greedy. Greed is the root of evil, you know. It drives you mad. But the greed stems from something far worse: vengeance."

"Go on," Locke says calmly. He is completely attentive. Waiting for me to tell my story, but I can't. I continue on, but the details are scarce.

"I met Madeline when I was your age," I say with difficulty. "We fell in love and were married after a short courtship. She was everything to me. And she was taken from me."

"I don't understand," Locke says. "What about the greed? The vengeance?"

"I wasn't always like this. I was an innocent, ambitious, and respectful young man, and Madeline was the only person who saw it within me. She personified innocence and beauty. Together, we had a love so powerful not the strongest spell could break it. And trust me, there were those that tried." I think of Medea and the jealousy that plagued her for years. That still plagues her. She fought for a long time to win my affections. But even after all of these years, and back then, I failed to see any danger in it.

"I was blinded by that love," I say. "I failed to see the cruelty in the world once Madeline's divine light shone upon my heart. I became weak, and weakness paves way for destruction. Perhaps if I hadn't been so ignorant, perhaps if I had been more careful, I would have been able to protect her.

"Madeline's life was taken because of an ancient prophecy that meant nothing to me, and hadn't meant anything to anyone for centuries. Madeline was taken from me, and my world was shattered."

"Did you know about the prophecy then?" Locke asks, afraid of interrupting me.

"Yes," I whisper. "My father told it to me when I was very young. He thought it was about him. He worried about it. It drove him made with paranoia. But I didn't even think of it. I was young, and I was naïve. It wasn't until later that I revisited my father's writings and reread the details of the prophecy."

"What then?" Locke asked.

"Then?" I chuckled sarcastically. "Then, I became so enraged that I swore revenge on her murderer, and I would stop at nothing until every life that threatened hers was taken. The vengeance consumed me; it turned my heart black and blood to ice. I had the spark, and I had the passion. I developed my powers, through months of practice and study, and I used them in my licentious pursuits."

Locke swallowed, trepidation emanating from his eyes.

"It was then that The Age of Darkness began. Slowly, but surely, the sky began to darken and sun rose less and less."

"It was then," I continue, "that I began to realize the enormity of my power. In my youth, it seemed awesome, and exciting to think that I could change the world in such a way. With new-found confidence, I continued my pursuit of Madeline's slayer.

"I became a savage, an animal, hunting and killing all who stood in my way. And then, I found her, I killed her, and in doing so I took my revenge, but it did not satisfy me. I wanted to make others suffer as I had, and still suffered. And so my power continued to grow. I sought out dark secrets and potions, I befriended the shady and dealt in the corrupt, and the more power I acquired, the greedier I became to have more. All the while, the world grew darker, and colder.

"With the accumulation of power, came warped ideas. I thought, with the right materials, I could bring her back to life. But in order to bring back a life, you have to take many. I became obsessed with the idea of having my wife back. I learned, from a mysterious gypsy, that there was a ritual that could be performed, but it called for many pieces. The accumulation of these specific pieces would be dangerous and life-changing. I decided to try. I killed many for precious potions, dusts, magical knowledge, and for blood.

"It was during this time that the darkness really began to solidify. The worse I got, the more crimes I committed, the darker the world became, until finally, the sun went down indefinitely. I'll never forget that day." I think back on it, and the memory flawlessly materializes in my consciousness.

I stood up and looked at the crimson blood which soaked my burning hands. The body lay basked in a sea of sunlight, as if God were putting him under the spotlight to highlight my sin. He was mutilated, loose flaps of skin and open gashes that oozed blood. His vibrant orange eyes flickered delicately and went out like candles. He lay with his mouth open, and his last breaths expelled gently out of his lungs. I stare, transfixed, at his pitiful face. All I needed was a vial of liquid from his person. I could have threatened, I could have bartered, but instead, I murdered.

Curiously, the light that shone on his vacant face seeped slowly away, and shadow crept across him. I looked up, into the distance, and saw, the sun was abnormally red, burning, and it was slinking back into the horizon, and it was gone. A thick gray darkness enveloped me, and I felt an uncomfortable mixture of both excitement and fear as I stood there, fresh bloos still dripping from my hands.

"After many months of traveling, killing, and delving into the depths of sin and evil, I was ready to try to bring her back. I was missing one final piece, but I did not know it, and I went ahead. Needless to say, I failed. But that was many years ago, and it has gotten worse since then."

I dare not tell him about the light, the light that, since this horrible incident, has haunted my mind, body, and soul. That I believe it is *her*, stuck between death and resurrection, coming for me.

"It was during this terrible time," I continue, "That I reread the prophecy, and learned of its details: that Madeline was taken because of the foolishness of my ancestor, that I was merely following the path laid down for me by the seer, and that my dark reign would be challenged by the birth of two twins. I now had a new mission: to destroy them before they had the chance to destroy me."

Locke sat back uncomfortably, no doubt pondering what he would have done if such news was shared with him.

"I had already hunted and killed the she-wolf," I said. "But it was not enough, I was too late, the twins had already been born. I knew the only thing I could do was to work to destroy them, before they destroyed me.

"I tell you, Locke, I've become a very different person in the past forty years. Running, hiding, and old age have worn me weak and thin. Never have I been so dependent on another—you, my dear Locke, who I have known since your childhood.

"I was completely consumed by my emotions. I had no love, no soul, no care—not since she had gone. After I failed to bring her back my anger became so powerful, yet my motives were obfuscated. All I needed was to wield my craft, to gain power, to control. But why? After all of this time I have never clearly defined a purpose. I do not seek vengeance, I do not desire wealth or fame or glory. Why have I spent the last forty years of my life building a villainous reputation, and committing the most unnecessarily senseless acts of ill-nature? Why? What motive? All I have lived with and understood was anger . . . loneliness . . . sorrow . . . guilt. Look at me . . . what have I gained?

"I used to be happy once. I was young, and free. My ill-will has locked these chains around my wrists and ankles and my heavy heart has weighted me to the floor. My empty soul has left me hollow, emotionless, careless. What has that gotten me? Nothing. Where has it gotten me? Nowhere. What have I left to do but die alone: to reflect upon the one thing that caused me to let my life become a criminal ruin?

"The prophecy says that the twins would seek out to destroy me. Well I have taken care of one, but feel that I am no match for the other. Perhaps I should just let him take me."

"Vincent, no!" Locke protests. "How could you say that?"

I do not answer his question.

"You know, sometimes, I look at you, and you are just like I once was: young, handsome, smart, so full of love and concern for others; but also outcast, and that is because of me. You are the same age now that I was when I fell in love with Madeline. I wonder, *Why have you not had the chance to fall in love yourself?* It is because you have lived for me. I do not wish for you to live like this anymore. You have your whole life ahead of you, and I have destroyed what life you have lived thus far."

Locke sits, speechless for several minutes, reflecting on the life he has lived. It is evident in his eyes that he does have some longing, some yearning for love as I had.

He stares at the ground where Madeline's dead body lies buried beneath the earth; a minute tear rolls down his cheek. I can see that he is touched by my story, perhaps, even feels sorry for me. But I do not want him to think I am weak.

"You said you were missing a piece for the magic to bring to bring her back. What piece were you missing?" Locke asks.

I reach inside my pocket and pull out the black velvet pouch.

"This," I say. I look solemnly back at the grave and then put the satchel back into my cloak. "But I do not wish to try it now. It is pointless, with Roman so near."

"Do not worry about Roman," Locke says. "I will not let him harm you."

"Locke, you must not interfere with the prophecy, it is not your destiny to save me, or to kill Roman. 'They alone will duel, and the better of the two will decide the fate of the world.' *They alone,* Locke. You cannot get mixed up in what is foretold, you cannot change what is written. Trust me, I have tried." Locke sits quiet for another few moments.

"Then we will keep running," he says with confidence. "Until he has given up on you, because I will not."

These endearing words touch my soul, well, what is left of it. I wonder what he truly thinks of me after all that he has heard. I remember the seer's words. It is up to him; Locke must make the right decision, and I must tell him to do so.

"Locke, there will come a time when you must choose between what is truly right and what you *think* is right. I hope, despite your loyalty, that you will make the right choice, because, for many years, I have made a lot of the wrong choices. I have been suffering for a very long time; I have done many terrible things. I tried to bring her back, but it only made things worse for me. I am haunted, every day, by her memory, by the light. I have allowed my grief to turn me into something I never wished to be. I do not want you to turn out as I have."

I cannot bear to look at him, for I am filled with shame and regret. But Locke does not judge me. He seems to struggling with a confession of his own.

"I don't exactly know how it feels," Locke begins after several minutes, "to lose someone you love." I look at him in surprise as he gathers the strength to continue. "But, I do understand the emptiness you feel in your heart. I have never known my parents, but I have loved them, and mourned their loss for all twenty years of my life.

"I know that I have had you to look after me from time to time, and that you gave me special jobs to do, and allowed Ollam to teach me, and I have thought of you, as a father at times. But it has not been the same. I have never felt the warmth and love a mother's kiss, or the pride a father has in his son. I grew up in the streets, got into trouble, slept in alleyways and ditches, I never had a home to go to when it got cold and dark. I never had a chance to feel wanted, or even loved. What kind of person would I have become if I had?"

He stops for a moment, looking at me as if he is really struggling to admit something to me. "Sometimes, when I think about them, I cry. And my tears turn to anger, and I become so enraged I could murder someone, just as you have described. My parents were taken from me, as Madeline was taken from you, and if I ever knew how or why, I would probably have done the same for them as you have done."

My heart aches at this confession, and I hardly know what to say to him. "Locke, I let anger get the best of me. Do not let anger get the best of you." He takes a deep breath and closes his eyes.

I look at the tombstone and back at the boy.

She would have loved him. It is a realization that makes this all the more painful.

"Locke, I . . ." But there is no time for this now, for I am distracted by an image in the corner of my eye: off in the distance, a pair of shimmering pink eyes materializes out of thin air.

June 2nd, '34

The blood of two young lovers: it was the final thing I needed. I knew who they would be. I had seen them[13].

I had been watching them for months: walking back and forth everyday through the woods. He with his arm at her back, and she with her hands clasped gracefully around a basket of bread, or linens, or flowers; or whatever she may be bringing in from the village that day. He was handsome; tall and slender, with jet black hair and pale violet eyes. He wore a suit of gray. She was beautiful, with long wavy locks of golden brown hair that glinted in the moonlight, soft, rose colored skin and delicate arms. Her eyes were soft and pale blue, and her smile was graceful and kind. She wore a delicate dress of white with blue lace trim. They walked together so elegantly, and when they kissed, his hands gently held her soft cheeks, and her eyes lit up and sparkled like the stars in the night sky.

I watched them every day; I watched them in vain. Today was different, I knew they were coming, but they did not know I was coming for them. I waited in the brush as they approached. He was regaling her with a heroic story of his younger days, and she was laughing sweetly, admiring his face and gestures as he spoke. They neared me, his voice grew louder and her laugh more sincere, and my heart grew colder as a twinge of loathing grew in my chest. What gives them the right to be so happy? *I wondered.* What makes them so special? *I couldn't help but think of her, knowing how soon it would be before I could smell her hair again, touch her soft skin, feel her warmth, and taste her sweet breath as she kissed me after all of this time. My heart beat faster; a mix of rage and passion, longing and exhilaration. Then, they were upon me.*

I sprung from the bushes and they froze in their tracks. She screamed, clutching her basket to her chest. He stepped in front of her and fear radiated from his false bravery. He spoke to me, but I did not make out the words. My head was filled with thoughts and determination. I took a few steps closer and she turned to run. The man reached inside his

---

13   Nightmare #504

coat but my reaction was faster. Icy white flames flew at his chest and he fell over cold on the ground. In the distance, the woman was tiring. I flew, and within an instant I was in front of her. She stopped and turned, but I cut her off again. She froze. A look of sheer terror flushed her cheeks and drained the color from her delicate face. She clutched the basket to her chest. I grabbed at the parcel and she resisted, crying and pulling with all of her might, but I was stronger. I pulled the basket from her grip and through it aside. She was crying now, tears streaming down her cheeks and wetting the breast of her dress. She mouthed something to me, but I did not hear her soft words. I rolled up my sleeves, not breaking contact with her frightened eyes. She looked over to where the basket lay in the distance, then back at her husband's lifeless body, and then she turned her head slowly back at me. I raised my hands.

Within a few seconds, she was laying, ice cold, on the dirt path; a small trickle of blood fell from her lips. I took a vial from my cloak and allowed a few drops of blood to fill the vial. I stared for a moment at the pale blue lifeless eyes before me. I closed her eyes with my hands and walked over to her husband. He was not bleeding, so I took my nail and scratched at his skin, which immediately began to bleed. His blood filled a second vial. I placed the two dead lovers next to each other off in the trees and turned to leave. As I walk away from the scene, I hear a faint cry in the distance.

I fear it is only the cry of the deceased, echoing inside my tainted heart.

It only took several hours for the concoction to be just right. When it was, I filled a vial and proceeded to the cemetery. I found her. The moon shone brightly upon her atop the hill, alone. I walked slowly up and knelt down before her. I fumbled with my robes as I searched for the vial, my heart racing and my nerves more jittery and intense than they had ever been. I pulled the vial from my robes and kissed it gently. I then took a sip and poured the rest onto the earth.

I whispered the words gently under my breath. I waited. Within a few minutes the ground began to stir. Then a white light erupted from the ground and lit up the sky. My chest began to tighten and my heart pounded fiercely against my ribs. I gasped for breath as the light shone brighter and brighter. My head began to spin and I felt dizzy and sick. The light shone brighter and whiter and more terrifying. It illuminated the entire sky and swallowed me in its iridescence. Suddenly, my breathing stopped and all of my senses went numb.

Then everything was black.

XV
THE BETRAYER

I see a pair of shimmering pink eyes hovering in midair, and the outline of a small, dark shadow forms around them. The hovering apparition completes itself with the materialization of a thin, cat-like grin.

Out of darkness, Vesta begins climbing slowly up the hill towards us. She's alive. But she's changed. After all the years of having such a loving, adoring pet, I suddenly feel the worst discomfort. I should be feeling excitement and overwhelming joy at the sight of her, who I thought I lost, but my intuition fills me with warning. The look in her eyes is changed and the grin on her face is full of malice.

Vesta stops suddenly, her eyes still transfixed on mine, and a thin, pink mist begins to rise all about her tiny body, enveloping her. Her frail feline form dissolves into the smoke and slowly intensifies. Within a few seconds, the smoke rises, spiraling in rivulets. It then begins to take a new shape, and my stomach twists into knots.

I look at the misty form, stunned.

"This cannot be," I breathe. But surely it is. Medea: not quite a ghost, not quite human. Peculiarly, she looks more beautiful than I have ever seen her. She is wearing a new, black dress, and her hair is no longer gray, but jet black. Her shimmering pick eyes are shaped into perfect ovals, and the scars that were around them before are scarcely visible. Her pallid skin is rosy and smooth, all signs of aging diminished. Her lips are blood red and form a vindictive smile. I turn to Locke, who has stood and braced himself.

"Locke, go," I say sternly yet fearfully.

"No, Locke, love," says Medea mockingly. "Stay. You may learn some very interesting information."

Locke looks from Medea, to me, back and forth and in great confusion.

"GO!" I yell, with a rage Locke has never experienced before.

Without question, Locke obediently backs away, down towards the base of the hill.

"I will be here for you always, Vincent," he says, "I will not be far away." When Locke is at a safe distance, my conversation with Medea continues.

"How did you find us?" I ask her.

"Oh Vincent, you really are not as mysterious as you think. Your one weakness is, and has always been, Madeline. I knew the light would bring you here."

"The light . . ." I whisper.

"It is no figment of your imagination, Vincent," Medea says as she approaches me. "You thought that spell would bring her back, but you were wrong. You have fallen victim to a trick of my own design."

At these words, a series of images passes through my brain at rapid speed: the gypsy . . . those pink eyes . . . the jewel, I traded it for the spell . . . the spell, Madeline, bringing her back . . . the tracking, the gathering, the lying, the deceit, the death . . . the two young lovers . . . the bright light . . . the haunting of the light . . . those pink eyes . . . Vesta. My heart sank and my voice froze I realized the sudden truth.

Fear the wolf, but beware the cat.

Medea, the Betrayer, not just now, but all along.

December 29ᵗʰ, '22

I approached her cautiously, unsure of what to expect. I could not quite see her face. She was heavily shrouded in a long black cloak. She was quite tall, menacing. Only her eyes, grey and empty, emerged behind the shadow that hid her face, though for a brief moment, I caught a glimpse of her pallid wrinkled skin.

She held out a long, withered hand; each nail came to a sharp point.

"You have the jewel?"

My eyes were bloodshot, though, I could tell, glowing brilliantly. I have been very tired and hungry, having walked for days without food or rest. I have not slept in months. Not since that day. And in the months before, searching, hunting. My mind filling with rage, grief, and blood thirst . . . until I found her . . . .

She has been haunting me since, the weight of her concealed in the tiny artifact inside my cloak pocket. I am anxious to be rid of it. Rid of the memory.

I reached apprehensively inside my cloak and procured a smoky white gem. I turned it over in my palm, and it glowed radiant silver.

I reached out and dropped it into the skeleton hand outstretched towards me.

"What do you plan to do with it?" I asked.

"It is what I plan to not have done with it that matters more."

I stay silent, unsure and unconcerned with what she truly meant by that last remark.

"Tell me, Vincent," she said, as she tucked the gem safely away with the other, "Do you feel any satisfaction in killing the wolf?"

"I did at the time," I responded, sullen. "But I still feel emptiness. An emptiness that, thanks to you, shall soon be refilled. You have my request?"

She extracted a small piece of rolled parchment from her cloak and handed it to me. Hands shaking, heart pounding, I grabbed it quickly from her and stuffed it into my own garment.

"You have no idea what this means to me," I said. "Thank you."

"You have lot of work ahead of you," she said with a smirk. And with that, a quiet win swept her up and she was gone.

XVI

THE TRUTH

"That's right," Medea says, relishing in her triumph. "It was I who met you in the woods all those years ago. It was I who traded you the 'secret' to bringing Madeline back, knowing that you would not receive all of the necessary tools and that the silver stone was the key to your defeat of the twins." She reaches into the bodices of her dress, between her breasts, and extracts a shimmering pink gem. "Look familiar?"

The weight of this revelation hit me with such force, I felt as though the wind had been knocked out of me. She knew I had the jewel, and knew I needed it to defeat Roman. She deceived me, not once, but twice. I stand speechless as Medea continues her rant.

"I watched you gather and slave away to find everything you thought you needed," she said. "I watched you murder; I watched you fail in your attempt, and I saw that white light that erupted from her grave. I saw what it did to you, how it engulfed you in shock and horror. I knew what it meant, that she was stuck in between two worlds and that she'd be forced to watch her precious husband turn into a murderous fiend! I knew the guilt that light stirred within you. I knew I could use it to control you.

"I sent the light to you all those times: in the underground corridor, the pub, in the wardrobe, on the cliff, and all the other times before. It was me, taunting you, tempting you, haunting you."

My heart collapses with dejection. The bright light, not only a plaguing reminder of my guilt and suffering, but also a glimmer of hope, a chance . . . . I had seen it so many times, was haunted by it tirelessly in my nightmares[14], and yet . . . it was all a beguiling illusion. Then where was she really?

"Locke was a present from me too," she says. "Because I knew the memory of what you did to his parents would haunt you too." I couldn't believe it. It couldn't be true.

"You have underestimated me," she says. "The problem with you, Vincent, is that you have been so absorbed with one woman your entire life that you failed to recognize the strengths and abilities of others. You think all women are weak, and that is one of *your* cardinal weaknesses."

Medea raises her arms and, with a flash of pink, knocks me off my feet. "I am not as weak as you think," she says. I am immobile, unable to speak or move. My entire body heaves with pain.

"And thanks to my dear sister, Millicent, I have twice as much power as before."

Another flash of pink and my body is overcome with piercing pain. Locke, in an effort to come to my aid, rushes back up towards me, only to be met with another flash of pink. His body is instantly bound by phantom coils, and he struggles to free himself from his invisible restraints.

---

[14]   Nightmare #514

I look at Locke helplessly. Then as I look into Medea's eyes, I see her weakening. My only hope is that she wastes her energy on me. I know her magical strength cannot endure. The question is, can I?

"I wonder," Medea says, "Was he a substitute for the unborn child you lost when that wolf ripped your dear perfect wife to shreds?"

I lowered my eyes in overwhelming anguish.

"How could you do this to me?" I ask feebly.

"How could *I* do this to *you?*" Medea suddenly fills with rage. "HOW COULD I DO THIS TO *YOU?*" I winced at her aggressiveness. She stood still, boiling, and then, as if the flood gates had been opened, she unleashed her fury upon me.

"What about me, Vincent?" she screeched. "I was beautiful too! And I could talk back to you! Why wasn't I good enough for your affection? My delicate sister, with her beauty and her sparkle! What made her so much better? I was beautiful too! I couldn't even see you and I loved you! Did that not mean anything? I waited and waited. Even after she was dead you still did not want me!" She sends yet another flash of pink searing into my chest, and I scream in agony. She does not relent, but her breath becomes short. She stops and closes in on me. I close my eyes and brace myself for more pain, but instead, I feel the soft touch of her hands on my face, and she bends down and speaks softly to me.

"I thought you were different," she whispers, through gentle sobs, "different than Mason, different than all of those other men. The night that Mason left and you stayed with me all night, I thought that meant something. I thought there was more between us. Did you not see me falling in love with you before your very eyes?" I did not speak, for the sting of her words is more paralyzing than the sting of her magic. I close my eyes, and the scene which had faded from memory so long ago materializes.

Madeline and I approach Medea, who is sobbing with her head in her hands. Madeline places a soft hand on her shoulder, and Medea, without raising her head, lifts up her hand revealing a crumpled letter.

Madeline cannot comfort her sister with words, so I offer my services. After Madeline has gone to bed, Medea and I sit up long into the night, in front of a fire drinking tea, and I try my best to soothe her broken heart with kind words.

Though she cannot see me, she looks at me and listens intently.

"No one has ever been so kind to me before," she says.

"You are a beautiful woman, Medea," I say. "You are going to make some lucky man very happy one day."

She smiles and places a hand on mine. I wipe the tear that rolls delicately down her cheek. She rests her head on my shoulder and I hug her gently, feeling satisfied that I have helped to ease her pain.

Did you not see me falling in love with you before your very eyes? Medea's words resonate in my brain as I open my eyes. She stands up and turns away from me.

"No," she says, "You didn't see that. And so, I had to take measures into my own hands. It was foolish of me to trade away the silver jewel, I'll admit, as I understood the power, but I was blinded by jealousy and more-so, by desire. I traded away the stone for its sister, and I procured the key to everlasting beauty! I went through great lengths to stay as young and beautiful as you could ever imagine, while you withered away into an old man. And yet, you still reject me! I have remained beautiful, after all of these years! I have lived with absence and rejection in my heart. I laid in bed with all of those brutish men, looking for affection, looking for some sort of compassion, and even then all I thought of was you!"

I can't believe what I am hearing. I knew she longed to be with me, but I never realized the true weight of her feelings. Now her voice softens, and she sounds hurt rather than angry.

"I spent years aching as you have ached," she says, "longing as you have longed, loving as you have loved. I could have taken away all of your pain, and you mine, but you chose to cast me off like some worthless tramp! How could you do that to me? I was not good enough for you, Vincent. And you have cast me aside; you have scorned me, Vincent.

"It was I who led the she-wolf to your delicate wife. And then when you still rejected me, it was I who sought to destroy you. If I can't have you, then no one can. You will pay for the years of suffering I have been through on your account. You could have loved me! But you were selfish and chose to love the dead! We'll see how beautiful she is after years of rotting underground, while I remain alive and beautiful here on earth. You still choose to love her? Well, you can join her once and for all!"

At this she raises her hands and I close my eyes, still too weak to defend myself.

As she focuses her attention on me, the restraints around Locke relinquish their hold and he falls to his knees. He quickly gets to his feet, races back up towards us and steps in front of my paralyzed form.

Medea cackles and says, "Get out of the way, you stupid boy." Locke doesn't budge. Medea nears him, slowly, arms still outstretched, and she sneers at Locke viciously. "Do you really think that this man is worth dying for?" she asks. Her voice is seductive yet cold. She laughs slightly and continues nearer still to Locke. "This man, who has wronged you repeatedly since you were no more than a few months old!"

Locke winces a little, but maintains his stance. It is clear that he is starting to waver, wondering desperately what truth is hidden in her words. Medea begins to circle Locke while still speaking softly to him. I lay at their feet. I reach inside my cloak, grasping desperately for that familiar vial of glittering black dust, but it is in vain. The girl in the woods. I close my eyes. It's all gone. Once again, the Oracle's words echo inside me head.

Secrets will be revealed.

I close my eyes and brace myself for the inevitable.

"This man is no loyal companion to you, Locke," Medea says as she nudges my limp body with her black shoe. "He is a traitor; he has used you and abused you since you were just a baby." I watch in horror as Locke's face cracks. He looks at me with a pained expression. His pale blues eyes questioning me. I make no reply. Suddenly, Locke regains his courage. He turns violently to face Medea, and he grabs her by the throat with both hands. She crumples in his grasp, shrinking towards the ground, but he holds her upright. Medea chokes, her shimmering pink eyes now struck with a mild fear.

"Vincent is my friend," Locke says slowly. "He has raised me from a young boy! He took me in when I had nothing. He has always been there for me! My parents were killed and he saved me! I will die protecting him."

Medea, still in Locke's grasp, lets out a vicious, shrieking cackle. "You stupid boy! The only reason you have nothing is because of Vincent!" Locke lets her go suddenly and she collapses to the floor. She the lifts her head slowly and beneath the mess of tangled hair, that malicious grin creeps across her face.

"Oh, I suppose he failed to mention that little detail," she says vindictively.

Locke looks at me and then back at Medea as she rises to her feet. Tears begin to well in my eyes. I cannot stop Medea now, Locke must know the truth; it is time. But I never wanted it to come out like this.

"What are you talking about?" Locke asks painfully.

Medea stands up and regains her proud, flirtatious composure.

"Allow me to tell you a little story," she says cheerfully. "One fine evening, twenty years ago, I was walking through the forest when I heard strange sounds in the distance. It sounded like laughter, and fun. Such an odd occurrence for those times, you know? So I crept through the brush to satisfy my curiosity. I saw a couple, walking together, a young man and his lovely wife. She was beautiful, with a blue lace dress and golden brown hair. So beautiful, in fact, that she reminded me of my late, yet beloved sister. She carried a basket on her arm and he held her other.

"Within a few minutes I heard yet another sound; a figure rose out of the darkness and attacked the young man and his wife. I recognized the figure immediately: it was your dear friend, Vincent. He murdered that man and his beautiful wife in cold blood. Shortly after he was gone, I approached the dead bodies for a brief glimpse of the carnage and, not immediately caring at all, turned and began to walk away.

"Just then, I heard a faint cry in the bushes. I followed the sound, and came upon the young woman's basket. To my surprise, within the basket lay . . . an infant child . . ."

With these words Locke's composure collapses. Tears stream from his pale eyes, and his chest begins to heave. Medea walks closely to him, her face nearly touching his.

"Yes, an infant child," Medea continues smugly. "You." With this, she touches him playfully on the nose. She then takes a step back and waits a moment to let the weight of these words sink into Locke's breaking heart.

Once Medea is satisfied by his display of emotion, she continues her taunt.

"Naturally, because of my kind heart," she says, touching her heart sarcastically, "I took you home. I took care of you until you were old enough to move on. I could not care for you forever. I left you on Vincent's doorstep with a scrap of your mother's dress in your hand. Do you remember when he left you all alone all night long and would not take you in? That is because he knew who you were, and that you have come back to haunt him.

"He then did finally accept you, but only out of the plaguing guilt that must have been eating away at his blackened soul. Oh yes, he did take you in, and he used you. He taught you do lie, and to cheat, and to steal;

it was all for his own selfish, villainous ways. When you failed him, he beat you, and then erased your thoughts to rid you of the wretched memories.

"I know this, because I saw it all. You see, I also appeared one day on his doorstep: a rare breed of feline that had yet to be discovered in this part of the world, and therefore, a precious prize for our selfish wizard. Yes, he took me in too, much more willingly in fact, and he named me Vesta."

I absorbed these shocking words at once. Vesta . . . my beloved cat . . . all this time . . . Medea . . . the Betrayer . . .

Fear the wolf, but beware the cat . . .

When would it end?

"That's right, Vincent," she says to me. "I spent years by your side, disguised as your beloved pet. At least as a cat, I could be close to you. Feel your love, and your gentle touch. It was the only way I could procure your affection."

I wince, mortified at her trickery.

"He killed your parents," Medea says, speaking to Locke once more. She senses that he is weakening, and continues with confidence. "And then he took advantage of you! He has been using you, Locke, all along. Using you to carry out the immoral deeds his weakening body is no longer able to do. Just as he is using you now to help him escape. Do you know how many times he sent you out in search of the very stone which was the key to securing his triumph over Roman? And do you know how many times you came back bloodied, and he beat you further for failing him? But you wouldn't remember. He wiped all of that away so you would stay loyal to him.

"Do you think he could have made it on his own? He needed you. And he used you. Knowing full well where you came from, and not offering you a bit of remorse.

"Look at you, Locke, risking your life to save his. Do you think he really loves you? He doesn't have heart to love. He buried that part of himself the day he laid his wife in the ground.

"Do you know why he killed your mother and father?" At this, Locke looks solemnly up at Medea to hear her final, painful words. "Because he needed their blood to raise the soul of his dead wife, who also, coincidentally, happens to be my sister. He took your parents' lives to try to bring her back, and he failed miserably. Then he wasted your life trying to fix his mistake. My poor, innocent, sister. He let her die too, you know; he let that wolf suck every ounce of blood out of her."

At that moment my strength returns to me in the form of hatred and anger; I rise to my feet.

"You lying, treacherous, witch!" I scream, and I fly at Medea. Within that same instant, Locke grabs me out of the air with one strong arm and throws me back to the ground. Anger raging within him, he turns to Medea. He again grabs her by the throat, with one strong hand this time and, with all his strength, lifts her up into the air, leaving her feet dangling inches above the ground. Again, she chokes and wriggles about, grasping at his hand but failing, in his moment of emotion-driven strength, to free herself. No doubt the combination of panic and fatigue are preventing her from using magic. As she makes an attempt at an attack her hands merely emit meager sparks.

"You wretched bitch!" he screams. "Why did you send me to him! You should have left me to die!"

"Locke," Medea chokes, as she swings her dangling legs in the air, feeling for the ground. "I wanted to save you!"

"You wanted to use me to torture Vincent! You have no care for what happens to me!"

"Why do you think I have come? I am here to persuade you, to beg you to come over the good side! Do not be foolish, Locke. He has turned on you!"

194

Locke's will is clearly fading, and a mixture of emotions sweat out through his forehead. He maintains his grip on her but stares blankly ahead.

"Do you not know how I knew you'd be here?" Medea asks him. "Because despite all of the danger and all of the chaos, there is only one thing that Vincent keeps in the back of his mind always: his desires. How does that make you feel, Locke? That you have been used to bring him to the very place where he spilled your parents' blood all those years ago!"

This is more than he can handle, as Locke clenches Medea's throat in rage.

"You may have your vengeance still!" Medea croaks, gasping for air. "Defeat Vincent! You may still use your powers to do good, as I have done!"

In the distance, a sudden glow of torches appears and the shouts of men can be heard.

"The league?" Locke whispers.

"Locke" Medea continues. "Let me go, the league will defeat Vincent. You may come with me, and I will help you start a new life."

"The league" Locke whispers. "You led them here! You have betrayed us all!" With this, Locke takes a knife from his cloak pocket. He raises high in the air. "You will burn in hell!" he screams, and drives the blade deep into Medea's chest. She screams and writhes in his grasp as blood spills from her wound and up through her throat. She stops screaming and stares, in a shocked silence, deep into Locke's eyes. For a brief moment, I sense pity in him.

For a brief moment only, for Locke lets her drop the ground and she begins to shrivel and shake. Her body flops about like a ragdoll, and then begins a series of contortions.

Within a few seconds, Medea is gone, and the body of a cat lies lifeless at Locke's feet.

It was twilight, and I ran.

I ran as fast and hard as I could. She was ahead of me, running with all of her might, her long, black hair streaming like a banner behind her. She ran with the swiftness of a gazelle, and it was all I could do to stay on her tail. I could sense that the imminent moonlight gave her strength and motivation.

I used what little power I had to try to trip her up, to knock her down, but she tripped only slightly and kept going. I chased her through trees, through brush, and then I came to stop, as I could see her no more.

I looked up through the trees into the black night sky and saw the outline of the moon forming behind a thick band of clouds.

My heart began to race due to the emerging danger.

I heard a sound of rustling leaves to the right of me, and then a crackle of twigs to the back. She was circling me. Clever. I tried to show fearlessness, though my blood was pumping and my nerves were strangling my body, though it was nothing compared to my recent nightmares[15], which have been plaguing me since that fateful day. I could only hope they will surcease once I severed this beast's head from her body.

I looked about in all directions, but I could not see her behind the trees. The clouds parted above and thick rays of iridescent moonlight blanketed the forest below. I heard gasping, writhing, moans of pain in the bushes ahead. There was the rustling and commotion of a struggle for several seconds. Then it stopped.

I froze.

Straight ahead of me, peering out from behind the bushes, was a pair of glowing red eyes.

Those eyes. They pierced through my heart like cupid's arrow, though no love was attached, only hate and retribution. The eyes were soon followed by a snarling mouth, which

---

[15] Nightmare #82

revealed a set of sharp, jagged, pearly white teeth. The beast and I stood, staring dead-lock at each other, each waiting for the other to make the first move.

Through my peripheral, I could see the moonlight off to the left begin to diminish, and I knew I had my chance.

I made the first move, which offset a series of events that occurred in rapid order. As soon as the beast saw me flinch, she lunged. I lifted my hands and a burst of white light erupted from my palms. The blast knocked her to the ground as the force of the beam flung me in the other direction. I sat up quickly and watched her struggle to her feet. She bared her teeth and inched closer. She was wounded, but ready to strike again.

This time, I reached inside my cloak and grasped the handle of my silver blade. She lunged at me a second time, and, with this opportunity, I hastily unearthed my knife from my cloak and slashed at the figure which flew at me. There was a glimmer of radiant silver that slashed through the air and a splatter of crimson as the beast hit the ground.

At that same moment, the clouds above regrouped and masked the bright moonlight above. I approached her cautiously, as she was lying facedown, struggling to get up. I slipped the toe of my boot under her stomach and rolled her over onto her back revealing, not a wolf, but a beautiful, dark haired woman. I bent down and extracted my silver knife from her heaving chest. She stared up at me, the redness quickly fading and turning once more to a dull brown. She looked down at the front of her slender body, which spilled blood onto the ground below her.

"It's too late," she whispered through desperate, final breaths. "They are here."

With these words my eyes widened with rage and I stabbed at her four or five more times, expelling, with each fateful stab, all of the suppressed pain I had built up over the past eleven years. I stood up, short of breath, and contemplated what I had just done. I had chased her for years; stalking, hunting. I knew I had her.

I expected to feel relief, joy, and vindication all in the same instant, but instead, I felt empty, grief stricken, and broken. I stared at the beautiful creature at my feet in disgust. When the moonlight reappeared I noticed a slight glint at her throat. I reached down and pulled a tiny circular jewel from the chain around her neck. The jewel was a translucent, smoky white, almost silver, and it was heavy and cold. Engraved on the jewel were the letters

LVPERCA

I stood for a moment in awe, gazing down at the stone. Its weight—both physical and symbolic—heavy in my palm.

Could this really be the one?

In a moment, the jewel began to glow radiant silver. My eyes widened ravenously, and without another thought, I put the jewel in my pocket. I dusted a luminous yellow powder in my hands and I poised them over her lifeless body. I whispered under my breath, hoping this would work, as my power had not yet been trained and strengthened. After a few short sparks, her body ignited. I turned to walk home, leaving her bloody corpse to feed the hungry flames.

XVII

THE WOLF

Locke faces me, horror-stricken. I lift my hand out towards him, my fingers searching desperately for that familiar grasp, but, for the first time since I have known him, Locke does not reach out to help me. Instead he backs away from me slowly, looking just as pained by his actions as I am.

"Locke, please," I begin, but there is no time. The angry mob approaching grows louder. Locke looks behind us at the torch lights and then solemnly back at me, then his eyes avert to the ground. With tears swelling in his eyes, he shakes his head lightly, as though struggling within himself. Then, Locke turns his back on me. He walks away from me completely, leaving me alone, defenseless, abandoned, atop that desolate hill; standing there, waiting for fate to be delivered into my hands. I do not blame him.

The men make their way up the side of the hill and form a circle around me. Some of them I recognize, some faces are new. They are like a pack of hyenas, ravenous and rabid, encircling around a threatened prey, ready to strike. Twelve men or so; looking excited, angry, and hungry for revenge. They are all physically fit, strong, yet tired looking, as though they have travelled and endured many hardships to make it here.

The tall surly one, Brogan, speaks first.

"Vincent," he says. "Roman is coming. You see, he wanted to make sure that it was you before he came. Gavin, send the signal."

The man called Gavin lifts his pistol and shoots a flare into the air, which explodes into shower of red sparks in the dark sky.

"I see that our dear friend Medea was useful after all," Brogan says. "You see, she told us you were hiding in the wardrobe the night we searched her home, but promised to deliver you to us if we allowed her more time to wrap up some personal grievances of her own. She has kept her promise, though, judging by the sight of this,"—he kicked the dead cat with the tip of his boot—"I'd say things didn't work out so well for her. No matter, we intended to take care of her any way. So thanks for saving us the trouble."

The other men around Brogan laugh.

"I suppose you're wondering why she chose to betray you. Well, it seems that she had some strong feelings for you, Vincent. When you denied her, she became angry and vengeful. And when you married her sister, well, that just about killed her. She spent many years trying to gain enough power to destroy you, and working to bring you to your demise. When she couldn't do that, she turned to us. It seems her love and her envy has served to benefit us. Although, for some strange reason, I think she actually thought you'd survive and she'd have you in the end."

Although I have already heard these words from Medea herself, hearing someone else's interpretation of her motives cemented them in my brain, made them more real. How could I not have seen this before? That which was so obvious to everyone else? How could his words be true? Medea. But it all makes sense. I feel ashamed of myself for not understanding sooner.

Sensing my discomfort, Brogan comes very close to me, within an inch of my face, and whispers, "We are going to kill you Vincent. We have waited a long, long time for this." He moves backward and sees what the men have been waiting for.

"Ah," says Brogan, then, "and here is the man of the hour." The men then part a bit in the circle and I see him: Roman, making his way up the hill and joining the men in the circle around me. Though he is heavily cloaked, to avoid contact with the moon's rays, there is no mistaking him. I look into the night sky, the moon is full, and its iridescent rays cascade down upon us.

A million thoughts race through my brain as I try to decide what to do.

Twelve of them, twelve. Only Roman matters. And where is Locke?

Out of the corner of my eye, down the hill a ways, I see Locke sitting with his back to us, his face in his hands. With him out of harm's way, it is time to act. But the other men see him too.

I raise my hands quickly and send jets of light out at two men ahead of me. They are thrown backwards and the other men beside them dive out of the way. I then open my hands wide, in a swift motion, and blast two other men on either side of me back into the air. At that same moment I feel a heavy crack across my upper back. I am knocked forward but turn about quickly and send bursts of light out at my attacker. He drops to the ground, and another attempts an assault. As I send blasts desperately in all directions, they maim, but none of them are fatal. My power is weakening, though my pumping adrenaline fuels my body to evade fatigue. Gavin comes at me with a sword, but as he slashes forward, I raise my hand and it stops mid-swing. Gavin's muscles protrude from his arms as he attempts to push the blade of the sword toward me, but my invisible force pushes him back. The blade glows hot in his hands and he flings it away. He punches me hard across the face, but I turn around and blast him backward. His head hits a stone with a loud crack and his eyes roll into the back of his head.

The men continue to fight me, but Roman stands, cloaked, unmoving, like the grim reaper, watching the rest of the men struggle. Like the leader of a pack, he is waiting, hoping his other pack members will weaken me, and then he will move in for the kill.

"The boy!" I hear a man shout. I look to my left and see three men in pursuit of Locke. I send a blast in their direction, but only one is knocked to the ground.

Out of the corner of my eye I see Brogan raise his bow and shoot an arrow towards me. I raise my palm and the arrow stops, inches from my hand, and it quivers in the air before snapping and falling to ground. Brogan's eyes turn red in rage and he sends several more arrows in my direction at rapid speed. With several quick jerks of my arms all the arrows are deflected, one of which is repelled back from whence it came, piercing Brogan in the right shoulder. He screams in pain.

I send a blast of light which slams into Brogan's chest and knocks him to his back. He jerks back and forth for a second or two; then he is still.

Down at the foot of the hill, Locke is also fighting for his life. He has two men on him; he punches wildly, making contact with every blow. One man comes at him with a club, which Locke wrenches out of his hands and uses to smash the man across the face. He grabs the man by the shirt and tosses him to the side and then turns to deliver an upper cut to the jaw of his partner. This man stumbles back in a daze as the other man returns to his feet. Locke then kicks him powerfully in the chest, knocking the wind out of him. He returns with a full fist and hits Locke square in the face. His nose begins to spurt blood.

Locke does well to fend for himself, but he is just a boy and, however strong, no match for these fully grown men. After a few minutes of struggle, they tackle him and wrestle him to the ground, one clutching at each of his toned arms and holding him still.

"Leave him alone!" I shout as I send another blast towards a man coming at me from the side, with a club in his hand. I raise my hands towards the men holding Locke and then I hear Roman's husky voice, "Enough, Vincent."

I turn to face the cloaked figure standing alone behind me, his brown eyes staring intently ahead. The remaining men stop and stand still, watching. It is clear that it is coming down to this.

The evil wizard and the stronger son will meet in battle, they alone will duel, and the better of the two will decide the fate of the world.

"The Age of Darkness is over," he says. "You have murdered my brother, my mother, Evander, many of my allies, and dozens of other innocent people. You have succeeded in shadowing the world in evil and suffering long enough. I alone have the power to defeat you, and that is what I intend to do. I am going to end your life, Vincent, and that of anyone else who has chosen to fight with you."

With that I look to Locke, in the grip of the other men.

"Does this boy mean something to you, Vincent?" he asks.

"This boy has nothing to do with me," I reply. "You will let him go."

"We shall see where his loyalties lie," Roman says. "But first, I think it is time."

As we stand, face to face, moonlight streams down over us. Roman raises his hands to remove his hooded cloak and throws it aside. For a brief moment, his striking figure is revealed. He is tall, muscular, and dark. His paw-like hands and long arms display large, sculpted muscles. His face is lined and dark, and his jaw is square and set.

He stands, arms outstretched, basking in the glow of the moon, allowing his skin to drink in the soft blue rays. Roman's whole body stiffened, he began to scream in terrible agony. His entire body twists and turns and his eyes turn black. He screams in horror, and soon his scream is replaced by a high-pitch howl.

Ahead of me is no longer a man but a great brown wolf. His eyes are black and his teeth are large and deadly. He snarls and inches toward me. I can see the look of sheer terror on the faces of those around us.

I again glance at Locke, who is still being held captive. It is now or never. I raise my hands towards the beast, and they begin to warm, to burn, as if charging with energy.

Locke stands behind me, and though I cannot see it, I know that something very strange is beginning to happen to his hands too. I sense his agitation and my concentration weakens. The two men holding him let go of him in fear. The light from my palms ceases and my body begins to fall.

At that same instant the beast lunges at me and I am tackled to the ground. I feel a fierce ripping at my neck as the flesh is torn off by Roman's razor sharp teeth. As I lay on the ground, I feel the warmth of the blood. I lift a wavering hand and touch the wound; my hand is cloaked in crimson. The beast turns around and begins a second assault. With one hand clasped around my throat, I refocus my other, and send a half-hearted blast of white light out at the manic creature. He evades the blast with ease by leaping sideways and rolls across the ground. But he cannot escape the second which strikes him, with moderate force, right in the side. The beast yelps and rolls over on the ground. I take this moment of weakness to turn to the Locke.

"There isn't much time," I yell to him, choking on my own blood. "You must do what is right, Locke. You may not understand now, but you will. You have the power; you feel it."

At this, Locke looks down at his glowing hands.

"The spark, you have it; I have given it to you. Eyes, Mind, Heart, Hands, Locke." God knows, this boy has a lot of heart. "Remember, you must do what is right."

The beast lifts his head and gets slowly to its feet. This is my only chance.

When the time is right and the moon is full and the tensions are at their highest, drink the potion and the light will fill you.

I reach inside my cloak and pull out the vial that the Seer gave me, as well as the smoky, silvery white jewel, which seems to come alive as it glows and burns, white hot in my palms. I take the tiny gem and place in my mouth and swallow. It burns as it slides all the way down my throat, until finally I can feel the scalding flames in the pit of my stomach.

I uncork the vial and drain it. I feel a terrible wrenching sickness inside my body as my insides surge. I double over to the ground. When I raise my head, my eyes are glowing with a radiant, silver light. I raise my hands high above my head and tilt my head back, the exposed wound still bleeding. I close my eyes and I feel the weight of an intense energy coursing through my veins, like electricity has replaced my blood.

Slowly, my body begins to lift off of the ground. As I raise myself into the air I separate my hands and bring them down to the side, still outstretched but level with my shoulders, like a large human cross. The electricity inside me becomes so immense that my heart bursts, and jets of radiant silver light erupt from my hands. I look towards Roman, my eyes on fire. I know it is now or never. I can kill Roman, or I can let him kill me, or . . . .

The world spins around me. And at the same time I sense the heat rising behind me.

Now, I think to myself, *do it now.*

I pull my arms out in front of me and aim them at Roman, whose eyes are darting from me to a space on the ground behind me. I unite my palms at the base. My fingers extended away from each other, and the lights intertwine.

Now! Do it now!

And then, I feel the blast, as if a cannon shot through my back, and the electricity within me explodes. My entire body goes cold and my senses go numb, and my eyes go black.

And I drop, with an enormous *crack!*, to the ground.

May 4ᵗʰ, '11

We awoke early this morning and decided to take a walk along the forest path, as we usually do on spring mornings. The sun was bright and hot, and the birds were chirping wildly with the promise of summer. Standing in the doorway, Madeline looked so beautiful, smiling, resting her delicate hands on the slight bump in her belly. I kissed her and we were off.

We walked all morning through the forest, up to the lake, and had our lunch by the water. We talked about our plans for the near future, what we would do, what would become of us. Madeline took my hands in hers and turned them to face upwards. She sprinkled a brilliant blue dust into my palms and stars and sparkles sprung delicately from my hands. Her unique gift was one that made her all the more attractive.

I held her face in my hands and kissed her softly on the lips.

As we walked through the forest at twilight, we were both completely at ease, when suddenly, the air changed. The sun faded from the sky and the air turned cold. A chilly breeze blew across our backs. There was a rustling in the trees and we began to walk a little faster. The sound seemed to follow us and we moved more and more quickly until we broke out into a run. The thing was now behind us. Madeline didn't dare turn to look for fear of losing her step, but I glanced behind me. In the distance, a pair of enormous shining black eyes and a black mass of body were bounding towards us. I grasped Madeline's hand to pull her along faster.

We ran with all of our strength. I yelled for Madeline to keep up, but she was too weak. In an instant her hand slipped from mine, and before I could turn around she was gone. I saw the black wolf, its eyes a fire with yellow flame, and hanging from its neck, a smoky, silvery white jewel glinted in the moonlight. The creature dragged the hysterical, screaming girl into the dense tress as she clutched frantically at the ground, digging her fingers futilely in to the dirt.

"Madeline!" I yelled as I looked about frantically. "MADELINE!" Tears streamed down my face and my heart raced. I turned and ran back as fast as I could. I was too late. The creature took one look at me and darted away, leaving Madeline lying breathless

and bloody on the ground. I knelt down beside her and lifted her head in my lap, I felt the warmth of her blood as is smothered my hands. She stared up at me with blank eyes; their brilliant blue shone brightly, then flickered in staccato and went dark, returning to a pale, lifeless blue. I told her I loved her, but it was too late.

She was gone.

XVIII

THE LIGHT

I open my eyes to see that sky has begun, for the first time in decades, to lighten, as if the sun is only minutes away from breaking over the horizon. Roman, in human form, stands back several feet watching. The rest of the league is at his side. One man threatens to move forward, but Roman lifts and arm in a gentle but restraining gesture.

Locke is bent over me, looking shocked and hurt. I cannot help but notice that his eyes have abandoned the pale blue that has dominated them for the past twenty years and have instead, been overcome by a bright, brilliant blue.

I can feel the residual warmth from the blast from his hands as they enclosed around me, and he scoops me up into his lap. At the same time, a searing pain rips through my back and engulfs my entire body. My spine is cracked in two, and my entire back burns from the blast. Though the pain from it is much less noticeable, the jagged gash in my neck hangs open like a flap, and blood seeps out of it.

Locke cradles me like a child. I know what he has done is killing him inside.

"What have I meant to you?" Locke asks bravely with tears slipping steadily from his tired eyes. To see this boy cry is one of the most painful experiences I have lived through in my life.

I lay in his arms, motionless, unable to speak. I long to answer him: to ease his anguish. I look into his newly acquired, brilliant blue eyes, and I try to speak with mine. But mine are no longer sparkling violet, full of life and magic. They are dead and hollow; they say nothing. His face is bruised and broken and looking for answers.

"All this time," he continues through heavy tears, his voice angry now, "I have looked up to you, I have been there for you, and I have risked my goddamned life for you! And all you have done is use me to do your dirty work. Am I nothing but a puppet to you? Am I anything more than an instrument, a machine that carries out the ill-wills that you cannot?"

I close my eyes and breathe in. My breath is slow, staggered. I can tell he comprehends how ashamed I am. At that moment, his voice softens.

"I looked up to you," he said. "You were a like a father to me." His tone turns from anger to grief. "I loved you; I idolized you!"

My heart aches and grows heavier; the weight of his words burdening my soul.

"I'm so sorry," he sobs. "You told me to do the right thing. Was this the right thing?" He is not asking me, but looking up into the sky, and asking whoever can hear. "What have I done? What have I done?" The men around us stir uncomfortably, astonished, each trying to make sense of the scene unfolding before them.

"Tell me this was the right thing, Vincent!" Locke continues. "Please! Tell me I did the right thing!" Even after all he has been through, all he has learned, and all that I have done to him, he still seeks my approval.

With all the strength I have left I reach my hand up and point to the satchel strapped around Locke's chest. He opens it, and extracts the small, leather bound volume that contains, written in my own ornate script, the tales of my past as well as this very adventure. I nod to Locke. He turns it over in his hand and looks confusedly from the book, to me, then drops it carelessly onto the ground.

"Please . . . tell me," Locke continues, pleading now, "that all of these years, after all we have been through, that I have meant something more to you."

I lift my withering hand up to touch his soft, bloodstained cheek. I try to speak to him with my gaze, I use all of my strength to nod my head shamefully, but that is all I can do. My eyes grow tired as my heart grows weaker.

"You can go," he says, crying heavier now. "I forgive you. I forgive you for everything. I don't have anything but you. I have never had anything but you." Locke breaks down completely and buries his head into my chest, sobbing. I want to hug him, to tell him everything I am feeling at this moment. I am actually feeling something—something that isn't anger or vengeance—something real and deeper than that. It is at this moment that I realize that I have been wrong all of these years. I have had more feeling inside of my heart than I have realized. I know now what it is: love. Love for him. Even after all of these years of suffering, and anger, of cruelty, and wrath, I have been feeling something good. I have loved him. Loved and cared for him as if he were my own son—like the son Madeline and I did not have the chance to have together.

As I think these words he stares into my eyes. He holds me closer and kisses my forehead. At this very moment I feel warmth, completeness. I lean over and look at the headstone just a few feet away. *Madeline.* I feel a pulsing, not in my heart, but over it, the black velvet satchel that hangs over my chest, it comes alive. I clutch it in my grip. I close my eyes and breathe for a moment. My heartbeat weakens and my breathing ceases.

I slip, willingly this time, into that familiar semi-unconsciousness as not one, but several memories flood my brain.

I see her, walking with me among a bed of lilies. She twirls and her soft curls dance in the wind . . . .

. . . Then, we are sitting together in front of a warm fire, her head leaning against mine. She looks into my eyes, and she kisses me gently . . . .

. . . Next we are lying in bed. She is propped up against the pillows and I lay beside her, my head resting on her chest, as she strokes my hair. I can feel heartbeat, her steady breathing . . . .

. . . I follow them through the dark woods. I see him, holding her hand, she smiles at him, kisses his cheek, and I fill with anger and jealousy . . . .

. . . I am sitting alone in my cabin, overwhelmed with loss and grief. I see him, sitting by the fire, playing with Vesta. A small boy. The cat curls up into his lap and he strokes her soft fur. He turns to look back at me, and he smiles at me . . . .

. . . I am sitting at my desk, crying. The boy approaches, he puts his tiny arms around my waist and hugs me . . . .

. . . I hold the bleeding boy in my arms. He looks up at me, thankful . . . .

. . . We are alone in my cabin, the boy sitting beside me on the floor, staring admiringly up at me as I read him his favorite poem . . . .

. . . The boy, now a man, places a loving hand on mine. "I will do whatever it takes . . . ."

And now, here, he cradles me, he longs for me to say the words that he has said to me "You were like a father to me, I loved you . . . ."

In one final attempt to see Locke's face before I go, I open my eyes again, and suddenly, I am blinded by a luminously white shining light.

In the distance, I see two brilliant blue eyes sparkling and shimmering brighter than the most precious stone. As the blue orbs near my broken body, I notice delicate features form around them. The white misty apparition reaches out a gentle hand. After all of these years, I recognize that face, I recognize those eyes, and that smile.

I reach out my frail hand and grasp hers. She pulls me close to her. She smiles as she looks at me, and my entire being fills with light.

She touches my face, which instantly feels full of life. My skin softens and warms under her gentle hands. My body feels less tired, less pained, younger, and stronger than it has ever been. I look down at my hands, which are no longer scarred and bloody, but youthful, glowing, and smooth.

I turn and look at Locke, who is still holding my frail, lifeless body. I wish I could say something to him, though I know he would not hear me. Instead I just smile, and I turn away with her, and I go.

She is the most beautiful creature I have ever seen. She has long, shiny brown hair that falls about her back and shoulders in soft ringlets. Her eyes are a brilliant blue, and they sparkle like the sun on the lake. Her face is warm, soft and gentle. She is an angel.

I had been in town this morning, wheeling my cart from the ship to the market, hoping to make a greater sale than usual, as my employer's patience with me has been growing ever thinner and his annoyance greater.

It was a chance moment that I saw her, as I rarely look up the usual path which I walk, avoiding, in my nervousness, the disapproving glances from others in the town. I have been here three months yet, and they can find nothing about me that is acceptable. From my torn and ragged clothes, to my dirty face and tousled hair, who could ever accept a poor boy from the sea? "Sea-rat," they call me, and "bastard-child," "street-trash," though they think I do not hear them. And so, I walk, every day, with my head hung, so as to avoid such disgusted looks.

And yet, today, for some reason, I looked up. And there she was.

She had been walking through the town square, accompanied by two sisters. They were walking together, with something odd yet extraordinary about them. All three matched each other in beauty, but it was the aura about them that differed. Hers is like an angelic radiance. She is no taller than either of her two sisters, yet seems to tower over them in grace, probity, and gentility.

I was struck immediately.

May 12ᵗʰ, '08

I had returned, once again, to town today, as I have done many times in the past few weeks. I just had to get a glimpse of her.

Every afternoon, after the schoolmaster's lessons have ended, they walk past. The three sisters. Equal is beauty but far different in eloquence and grace.

I sat back and watched her in silence, my heart yearning to tell her of my adoration for her elegance, her beauty, her loving smile. But I also sat in fear, and intimidation, for I know that such a highly esteemed young woman could never turn an adoring eye a lad like me, a ragamuffin, a sea rat, who has no money or status to speak of.

Surely she longs to discuss literature, and music, and language with a man of intelligence, not to hear stories of thievery and shipwrecks and storms.

What could I ever offer someone like her?

May 13th, '08

Today, a chance event occurred.

As the sisters exited the schoolhouse and descended the stone street, a small book fell out of her bag. I ran up to retrieve it and, excited with the opportunity to approach her, made my way through the crowd.

But they were lost, and I had stood in the center of the crowded street, her book in my hand. The binding was torn and the pages worn, it must have been a personal favorite.

I opened at glanced at the first few lines of verse within it and was immediately entranced by the words that spoke of a young love that was torn apart.

How well-versed she must be. And how well-versed I shall become.

May 26ᵗʰ, '08

I waited outside the schoolhouse today to speak to the professor. As the pupils exited the building, I could not help but become overcome with anxiety and nerves. She walked past, without a glance. Again, her sisters were on either side of her. As she strode past, she turned and, I thought, gave me a quick glance. And as she raised a delicate hand to wave, my heart sank. Just as I opened my mouth to speak, a boy pushed past me. Alas, I am too bold, 'tis not to me she speaks.

He was quite handsome and most definitely wealthy. He walked right up to the sisters and offered his arm. Arm in arm, the four of them walked on together.

I turned away, dejected, and returned to my original purpose: I hoped to ask the schoolmaster to allow me to begin attending his lessons.

Although the schoolmaster turned me away without a second's hesitation, he agreed to lend me several books: works on mythology, science, and philosophy, great plays and novels on love, war, greed, and heroism.

I will devour them. I will study them from front to back. I will not let her down.

August 28th, '08

It has been quite some time since I have written, and only because the most miraculous turn of events has occurred, events that the written word does not seem to do justice, and many an entry has been written and crumpled.

Several months ago, shortly after my last writing, fate reared her beautiful head. As I was delivering a shipment to the inn, the dog-cart I had been pulling struck a rock in the road, and the wheel instantly shattered. I was awe-stuck. Never, in all my time, had I ever seen a wheel splinter so easily and so completely from contact with a mere rock. It was fantastic. I cursed the cart in anger as well as embarrassment, as the sisters were just passing.

Then she stopped and approached me. She put her hand on my shoulder and looked sweetly into my eyes, as if she was trying to speak with them. Then she knelt down and placed a palm to the wheel, and behold! It was whole again! I stood dumbstruck at what I had just witnessed, and could think of nothing but to thank her profusely and offer her and her two sisters a ride home.

As I dropped them off at the gate, she kissed my sweetly on cheek.

It was there that it began. We spent hours together, and I would ramble on about my adventures sailing and traveling in my early adolescent years, and she would listen, and nod, and laugh, but she had no stories of her own to tell.

Instead, she gave me books to read. She was flattered by my interest, and when I bashfully admitted my desire to learn in order to hold conversations with her. She laughed at the irony of at all, for she could not speak. Most might find this troublesome, but I utterly taken in. I can read to her, and talk to her, and she listens, and she cares. She does not judge me for where I come from, but for who I am.

Now, we walk through the dirt roads of the forest holding hands and enjoying each other's company. Once in a while, she shows me the beautiful charms she had learned in her youth: how to create dancing sparkles in her hands or ripen apples on the trees.

One evening, Madeline did the most curious thing. I was watching, as always, she enthralled me with the little charms she made in her hands. The expression of sheer pleasure and interest no doubt adorned my face. She lifted her gentle hands and placed them on my chest. I felt a slight warming sensation, as I gazed into her eyes, waiting what was to come.

She smiled at me, and winked. Suddenly, I felt a surge of heat surge into my chest. It hurt slightly, like a spark. But I suddenly felt lighter, felt an aura I had never experienced before. It was like a new found life was sent into me, it was like a trace of a jolt of lightening; it was like . . . a spark.

Since that day I have never felt more alive. With every graceful move, I have fallen more and more in love with her. I know one day, I am going to make her my wife.

She accepts my flaws, and my rugged past. She does not expect me to be smart, to be brave, or to be strong. Never have I felt more at home, more complete.

I worry though, that the older sister may be envious of our love, for though she has had many suitors, and charms men with her beauty and lustful ways, there is little to desire about her inner nature. She cannot see, but she hears and senses all. Often I catch her turning her ear slightly in our direction, with envy on her face, whenever Madeline gives me a soft kiss, a gentle touch. I will have to beware of that one.

XIX

THE END OF AN AGE

The scene subsequent to my departure is obfuscated. I have just a dismal glimpse of the remaining members of the league surrounding Locke as he clings to my inert corpse. They are both shocked and amazed at what they have just witnessed, and I believe they, too, finally understand.

Roman kneels down beside Locke and rests a hand delicately on his shoulder. Locke looks up at him, and recognizes that what's done is done. He places my body down next to Madeline's grave. Roman reaches for Locke's hand and pulls him to his feet.

Then, looking down at the ground beside my body, he notices my journal, picks it up, and places it reluctantly in his back pocket. Finally, with the comfort of his fellow men, he turns and walks away, leaving me and all our painful memories behind him.

What will become of Locke following my departure is not for me to say, for it is here that my nightmare has ended. I cannot explain how his life will continue on without me, but I know that he will be strong, and he will become the man that I, in all my years, could never have been.

That is the point of it all, in the end. I know what will become of me; I know that I will die. And I do not intend to change that.

It is time to decide the fate of you and those close to you. You and you alone can seal the fate of the boy.

This entire adventure is for Locke, for him to learn, to make wise decisions, and for him to finally realize the truth. I know that he will choose good over evil in the end, and that he will prove himself a noble man. I do not wish to interfere with that.

I wrote this in order to assuage his resentment towards me. I hope that he will, one day, accept that I am not a cruel and evil man, but one who has allowed my own torment and grievances to overtake me. I can only hope that when all this is done, if my adventures play out as I have seen them, Locke will learn from the mistakes that I have made, that he will understand my appreciation and affection for him, and that he will forgive me.

Above all else, I hope that Locke can one day learn how to love. I believe the story of my life proves that, whether it be for a man or woman, a parent or a child, a friend or an enemy, one thing is true: love is the most powerful magic of all.

I would like to say more, but I must hurry and finish this manuscript. This vial of sparking black dust that sits ominously beside me is waiting patiently to be put to use. If I am to change one thing about this adventure, it will be this: after I make the final notes in my manuscript, and as Locke is distracted by the preparations for our departure, I will uncork the bottle, and sprinkle an adequate amount of this into my eyes.

I will feel the fateful burn as the memories of this cursed nightmare drift slowly and silently from my consciousness.

I do not wish to go into this adventure with any insight as to how will play out; for fear that I will do something to change it.

But now is the time to put my pen to rest, as I believe—if my sight does not mistake me—that that is my dear Locke knocking on my door and it is time for our final adventure to begin.

NIGHTMARE APPENDIX

Nightmare #1: 2 am, June 28th, '06

I am lying on the bed as the ship rocks back and forth,

I am deep in sleep,

Then, horrific visions and illusions engulf me.

I am wrapped within them like a blanket.

My skin burns, and a pain shoots from my head to me feet, my entire body on fire.

I feel it, the fire, trying to pry its way out.

I scratch at my face, and feel blood trickling down my fingertips,

My nails break as they scrape against the bones of my jaw.

The pain is intense, unbearable,

Sweat seeps through my clothes and soaks sheets beneath me,

I twist and turn and kick,

And I scream,

And scream,

And sweat,

And twist,

And scratch,

And scream.

Repeated June 30th, '06
Repeated July 4th, '06
Repeated September 14th, '06

L. M. Mendolia

Repeated March 16th, '07
Repeated August 8th, '07
Repeated November 28th, '07
Repeated February 10th,'08

#82: Midnight, May 5th, '11

The woods. Twilight. A cold breeze, a full moon. Heart pounding, racing through the nights. I can smell her fear. I can smell my own. We run, time and place flying by so fast, so fast, the world around us spinning as her delicate hand slips from mine. Then . . . .

Those eyes, red and fiery, those sharp teeth, blood dripping from her malicious mouth. I sit, crying like a baby. I cradle the lifeless figure in my arms. Pressing her beautiful face into my chest as I rock myself and her back and forth, tears streaming down my dirt and blood streaked face. I scream and scream.

I want to rip my hair out of my skull.

I want to scratch the skin off of my own face.

The horrible agony.

The pain is too great. It pulses through my veins like a sickness. It boils inside me, ready to burst through me.

I cannot bear it any longer.

And then,

I awake in a cold sweat, I cannot breathe.

This horrible, horrid, nightmare.

It haunts me. It plagues me. It is death knocking down my door.

The emptiness is eating me from the inside out. My heart that pumps cold blood and lungs that breathe cold air.

I will find her. I am going to tear every limb from her body.

Repeated May 6th, '11

Repeated May 12th, '11

Repeated May 24th, '11

Repeated May 25th, '11

Repeated May 28th, '11

Repeated June 5th, '11

Repeated June 9th, '11

Repeated June 11th, '11

Repeated June 20th, '11

Repeated June 27th, '11

Repeated July 1st, '11

Repeated July 2nd, '11

Repeated July 4th, '11

Repeated July 18th, '11

Repeated July 22nd, '11

Repeated July 26th, '11

Repeated July 30th, '11

Repeated August 2nd, '11

Repeated August 13th, '11

Repeated August 15th, '11

Repeated September 4th, '11

Repeated September 17th, '11

Repeated September 23rd, '11

Repeated September 26th, '11

Repeated September 30th, '11

Repeated October 10th, '11

Repeated October 14th, '11

Repeated October 21st, '11

Repeated October 25th, '11

Repeated November 1st, '11

Repeated November 7th, '11

Repeated November 14th, '11

Repeated December 6th, '11

Repeated December 12th, '11

Repeated December 27th, '11

Repeated January 8th, '12

Repeated January 16th, '12

Repeated January 31st, '12

Repeated February 11th, '12

Repeated February 21st, '12

Repeated February 23rd, '12

Repeated March 26th, '12

Repeated April 3rd, '12

Repeated April 9th, '12

Repeated April 10th, '12

Repeated April 11th, '12

Repeated April 12th, '12

Repeated May 4th, '12

Repeated May 5th, '12

Repeated May 6th, '12

Repeated October 16th, '12

Repeated October 21st, '12

Repeated March 4th, '13

Repeated March 8th, '13

Repeated March 11th, '13

Repeated March 12th, '13

Repeated March 13th, '13

Repeated March 14th, '13

Repeated March 15th, '13

Repeated March 20th, '13

Repeated April 18th, '13

Repeated May 1st, '13

Repeated May 2nd, '13

Repeated May 3rd, '13

Repeated May 4th, '13

Repeated May 5th, '13

Repeated May 6th, '13

Repeated May 7th, '13

Repeated June 29th, '13

Repeated July 27th, '13

Repeated August 12th, '13

Repeated September 15th, '13

Repeated October 25th, '13

Repeated November 18th, '13

Repeated November 22nd, '13

Repeated November 26th, '13

Repeated December 9th, '13

Repeated December 13th, '13

Repeated January 14th, '14

Repeated February 8th, '14

Repeated February 11th, '14

Repeated May 4th, '14

Repeated May 6th, '14

Repeated May 9th, '14

Repeated June 19th, '14

Repeated July 2nd, '14

Repeated August 10th, '14

Repeated October 31st, '14

Repeated November 4th, '14

Repeated November 5th, '14

Repeated November 13th, '14

Repeated November 23rd, '14

Repeated November 30th, '14

Repeated January 5th, '15

Repeated May 4th, '15

Repeated May 5th, '15

Repeated May 7th, '15

Repeated May 8th, '15

Repeated May 13th, '15

Repeated July 17th, '15

Repeated September 20th, '15

Repeated October 4th, '15

Repeated October 30th, '15

Repeated November 14th, '15

Repeated November 23rd, '15

Repeated February 12th, '16

Repeated April 10th, '16

Repeated April 13th, '16

Repeated May 3rd, '16

Repeated May 4th, '16

Repeated May 5th, '16

Repeated May 12th, '16

Repeated June 1st, '16

Repeated June 2nd, '16

Repeated August 28th, '16

Repeated August 29th, '16

Repeated September 2nd, '16

Repeated October 12th, '16

Repeated December 1st, '16

Repeated December 5th, '16

Repeated December 7th, '16

Repeated January 16th, '17

Repeated May 4th, '17

Repeated May 5th, '17

Repeated May 6th, '17

Repeated May 7th, '17

Repeated May 8th '17

Repeated May 9th, '17

Repeated May 10th, '17

Repeated May 14th, '17

Repeated May 15th, '17

Repeated November 26th, '17

Repeated November 28th, '17

Repeated May 1st, '18

Repeated May 3rd, '18

Repeated May 4th, '18

Repeated May 5th, '18

Repeated May 17th, '18

Repeated May 21st, '18

Repeated August 31st, '18

Repeated May 3rd, '19

Repeated May 4th, '19

Repeated May 8th, '19

Repeated December 3rd, '19

Repeated December 6th, '19

Repeated December 15th, '19

Repeated January 16th, '20

Repeated February 10th, '20

Repeated February 13th, '20

Repeated February 24th, '20

Repeated March 9th, '20

Repeated April 18th, '20

Repeated May 2nd, '20

Repeated May 4th, '20

Repeated May 7th, '20

Repeated June 6th, '20

Repeated July 13th, '20

Repeated July 14th, '20

Repeated September 9th, '20

Repeated September 12th, '20

Repeated September 18th, '20

Repeated November 10th, '20

Repeated November 15th, '20

Repeated January 2nd, '21

Repeated January 15th, '21

Repeated January 23rd, '21

Repeated January 26th '21

Repeated February 9th, '21

Repeated February 28th, '21

Repeated March 7th, '21

Repeated May 3rd, '21

Repeated May 4th, '21

Repeated May 8th, '21

Repeated May 14th, '21

Repeated May 22nd, '21

Repeated June 8th, '21

Repeated June 15th, '21

Repeated July 9th, '21

Repeated July 17th, '21

Repeated September 8th, '21

Repeated September 22nd, '21

Repeated October 7th, '21

Repeated October 11th, '21

Repeated January 10th, '22

Repeated January 11th, '22

Repeated January 13th, '22

Repeated February 16th, '22

Repeated April 2nd, '22

Repeated April 11th, '22

Repeated April 19th, '22

Repeated April 30th, '22

Repeated May 1st, '22

Repeated May 2nd, '22

Repeated May 3rd, '22

Repeated May 4th, '22

Repeated May 4th, '22

Repeated May 6th, '22

Repeated May 9th, '22

Repeated May 12th, '22

Repeated May 13th, '22

Repeated May 17th, '22

Repeated May 20th, '22

Repeated May 25th, '22

Repeated June 13th, '22

Repeated June 17th, '22

Repeated June 20th, '22

Repeated June 25th, '22

Repeated June 28th, '22

Repeated July 1st, '22

Repeated July 6th, '22

Repeated July 11th, '22

Repeated July 18th, '22

Repeated July 31st, '22

Repeated August 4th, '22

Repeated August 7th, '22

Repeated August 11th, '22

Repeated August 13th, '22

Repeated August 15th, '22

Repeated August 18th, '22

Repeated August 23rd, '22

Repeated August 26th, '22

Repeated September 1st, '22

Repeated September 3rd, '22

Repeated September 4th, '22

Repeated September 5th, '22

Repeated September 7th, '22

Repeated September 9th, '22

Repeated September 10th, '22

Repeated September 13th, '22

Repeated September 16th, '22

Repeated September 17th, '22

Repeated September 19th, '22

Repeated September 23rd, '22

Repeated September 25th, '22

Repeated September 26th, '22

Repeated September 27th, '22

Repeated September 28th, '22

Repeated September 29th, '22

Repeated September 30th, '22

Repeated October 1st,'22

Repeated October 2ⁿᵈ,'22

Repeated October 3ʳᵈ,'22

Repeated October 4ᵗʰ,'22

Repeated October 5ᵗʰ,'22

Repeated October 6ᵗʰ,'22

Repeated May 4ᵗʰ, '23

Repeated May 4ᵗʰ, '24

Repeated May 4ᵗʰ, '25

Repeated May 4ᵗʰ, '26

Repeated May 4ᵗʰ, '27

Repeated May 4ᵗʰ, '28

Repeated May 4ᵗʰ, '29

Repeated May 4ᵗʰ, '30

Repeated May 4ᵗʰ, '31

Repeated May 4ᵗʰ, '32

Repeated May 4ᵗʰ, '33

Repeated May 4ᵗʰ, '34

Repeated May 4ᵗʰ, '35

Repeated May 4ᵗʰ, '36

Repeated May 4ᵗʰ, '37

Repeated May 4ᵗʰ, '38

Repeated May 4ᵗʰ, '39

Repeated May 4ᵗʰ, '40

Repeated May 4ᵗʰ, '41

Repeated May 4ᵗʰ, '42

Repeated May 4ᵗʰ, '43

Repeated May 4ᵗʰ, '44

Repeated May 4ᵗʰ, '45

Repeated May 4ᵗʰ, '46

Repeated May 4ᵗʰ, '47

Repeated May 4ᵗʰ, '48

Repeated May 4ᵗʰ, '49

Repeated May 4ᵗʰ, '50

Repeated May 4ᵗʰ, '51

Repeated May 4ᵗʰ, '52

Repeated May 4ᵗʰ, '53

Repeated May 4ᵗʰ, '54

#182: June 28th, '22

There are trees everywhere.

A woman, swollen with child, stumbles across the path.

She is saturated with sweat.

She falls to the ground and lies on her back.

She screams, and cries,

But no one hears her.

She digs her nails deep into the ground.

She arches her back up and down in agony.

Then, she pushes

And pushes

And pushes

And pushes

And screams

And pushes

And a little mess of flesh and blood escapes her womb.

But she doesn't stop.

She pushes more

And more

And screams

L. M. Mendolia

And cries
And the baby cries
And then another.

I awaken, drenched in sweat and feeling intense pain in my own abdomen.

#504: 3 pm, March 11th, '30

They walk hand in hand down a dirt path in the dense forest.
The sky is darkened,
But they smile as they look into each other's eyes.
They stop.
He wraps his arms around her and pulls her in close.
He kisses her passionately.
He moves a strand of hair out of her eye and gently caresses her cheek with the tip of his index finger.
He kisses her again.
They walk away and she rests her head on his shoulder,
Her hand on her swollen stomach.

#512: 11 pm, June 3rd, '30

A cool wind.
The rustling of leaves and branches.
The stillness.
The silence.
Then,
A faint crying.

Repeated April 1ˢᵗ, '31
Repeated July 9ᵗʰ, '31
Repeated August 23ʳᵈ, '31
Repeated February 16ᵗʰ, '32
Repeated March 2ⁿᵈ, '32
Repeated June 21ˢᵗ, '32
Repeated September 15ᵗʰ, '32
Repeated October 8ᵗʰ, '32
Repeated December 25ᵗʰ, '32
Repeated January 4ᵗʰ, '33
Repeated May 19ᵗʰ, '33
Repeated July 9ᵗʰ, '33
Repeated September 17ᵗʰ, '33
Repeated December 4ᵗʰ, '33
Repeated February 22ⁿᵈ, '33

Repeated March 25th, '33

Repeated April 8th, '33

Repeated June 24th, '33

Repeated July 11th, '33

Repeated August 1st, '33

Repeated August 13th, '33

Repeated August 24th, '33

#514: Midnight, June 8th, '30

I walk, heart pumping in my chest
Hands dripping with sticky sweat,
A sickness rising in my stomach,
Towards her.
The headstone, dark gray, glimmers in the moonlight.
I extract a vial and kiss it gently.
I sip it.
It burns.
I cough.
I pour.
I whisper.
And a bright light explodes from the surface of the earth.
It pierces through my violet irises
And an intense burning rises within me.
I awoke and could not see, everything was black, momentarily clouded by the sheer intensity
of the light so bright in my nightmare, it blinded me in reality.

Repeated October 1st, '33
Repeated February 18th, '37
Repeated March 4th, '42
Repeated December 12th, '50

#556: 9 pm, April 23rd, '33

A tall, burley man stood with a lifeless figure at his feet. His fists were clenched, and his chest heaving. A shorter, thinner man stood beside him with his hand on the other's shoulder.

"We will find him, Brogan," the shorter man said.

"I want to kill him myself," Brogan said.

"You cannot, there is only one way."

"How?"

"Join us. Join the cause of your father and help to fulfill what he sought out to do, what he gave his life to protect."

Brogan nodded his head. "Tell me what I need to do."

In the shadows, I could hardly suppress my mocking smile.

#588: 4 am, April 19th, '35

The woman sits, clothed in black garments and huddled on the ground. She has her head buried in her knees. She swivels her body in a circular motion, slowly. A hand touches her shoulder gently and she looks up, revealing black sockets where her eyes belong. She begins to mumble unintelligibly, drool seeping delicately from the corners of her dry, chapped lips.

The sister, with her shimmering pink eyes, sits down beside the blind one and takes her hands. The pink-eyed sister rubs the hands, massaging away the nervousness and fret of the other. The pink-eyed sister turns her blind sister's hands over and places her younger palms on top.

Then, the blind sister's whole body wrenches forward and she screams and screams, rubbing her black palms on her face, leaving black soot behind on her aged cheeks.

#604: 7 pm, September 10th, '37

Darkness.

Cold.

Shimmering pink eyes in the distance.

She approaches, cloaked in darkness.

His luminous yellow eye shines as he reaches into his pocket.

He extracts a shimmering pink jewel that makes her eyes widen with greed.

She reaches inside her own cloak and reveals a radiant silver jewel.

Silver is traded for pink.

Each smile triumphantly.

I awaken and smile triumphantly.

#606: 10 am, November 11th, '37

A group of men sit at a bar.
They drink and laugh.
One has a luminous yellow eye.
Haram.
They swear, and smoke, and grab at a passing woman's breasts.
She turns to slap him, but he catches her hand.
He pulls he close to him and kisses her sloppily,
Then he slaps her across the face and pushes her away from him.
The men at the table laugh.
Amid the chaos
A little boy reaches his hand into Haram's pocket.
He grasps something, retracts his hand, and runs.
Haram jumps up from the table and chases after the boy.
They catch him quickly.
He is grabbed by the throat, and his little fist is forced open,
revealing a radiant silver jewel.
The boy is thrown to the ground,
and kicked,
and hit,
and the men laugh, and the boy cries.
Blood drips down his face,
and he cries.
and no one hears him,
but me, until I awaken.

242

#712: Two a.m., 31 July 4th, '44

My cabin, in the dead of night, an aerial view. Rain pouring down heavily amid clapping thundering and white hot lightening. Out of the darkness, a morphed shadow appeared atop the thatched roof. It was humanoid. Long, lanky arms and legs covered in black cloth. Skin, like white ash, pearly and smooth. Fingertips like nails that reach out as it slinks across the rooftop. It crawls, headfirst, down the side of the house, perfectly poised and not a slip of the body in the heavy rainfall. A spider in the night: long limbs curving upwards at impossible angles as it moves delicately, furtively, down towards the open window.

A pair of green eyes glimmers out of the darkness upon a man, in a dead sleep, in the room. Me.

It stares intently for a few minutes, then thin, blood-red lips curl into a smile revealing white, pointed teeth. A hand reaches down and lifts the window slightly. A second hand reaches in and slides through the small opening, followed by a head, then a torso, like a snake slithering through an opening in a fence . . . . then,

a crack

a hiss; Vesta

a screech, a whirl of faint wind

I awake with a start and stare at a slightly open window. I race to the window and look out into the night.

There is nothing but rain,

and thunder,

and lightening.

And those glowing green eyes, though now absent, burning an image in my brain.

#823: 10 pm, January 23rd, '50

The darkened street is quiet and modestly lit by a row of lanterns that line the sidewalk. A light breeze blows leave about, and they dance and swirl as they float down the street.

Locke appears, and he walks in the direction of the tavern. As he approaches the door, the loud cries of drunken men and the coquettish laughter of disreputable women can be heard from within. Locke pushes the large wooden door open, revealing a crowded barroom.

Locke makes his way to the bar and orders a drink. The tavern-keeper eyes him suspiciously but does not hesitate to serve him.

As Locke sips his drink hesitantly, he glances periodically at a group of men in the corner. They are sitting around a table, covered with coins and jewels, playing cards and pints of ale. The men at the table are all tanned and tattooed and scared.

One, in particular, has a shiny glass sphere replacing the left eye, which has a thick scar running over it. His other eye reflects a faint yellow in the dim bar-light. Haram.

A scantily clad woman, thick-set with huge breasts and heavy make-up, drapes her arms around his neck and whispers in his ear.

Haram looks up at Locke and smiles.

Locke turns away nervously, but it is too late. He is grabbed by the collar and pulled from his stool.

Haram, with Locke in his grasp, looks around the bar, surveying the other patrons who, having been startled by the commotion, are now staring at the two of them. He lets go of Locke's collar and pats him innocently on the shoulder.

Haram then yells aloud for all to hear, "Our ship leaves tomorrow, boy. We'd like you to come with us!"

"What?" Locke says, in utter confusion at Haram's pronouncement. He grabs Locke once more and pushes him towards the door. The men in the group get up from the table, leaving the disappointed harlot behind. They walked him down the road a bit, out of sight of passersby, and crowded around him.

Two men hold Locke against a brick wall of the building and pin his arms.

Haram takes a long drag off his cigar and blows the smoke in Locke's face. He coughs.

"I thought I told you not to come around here again, boy," Haram sneers. He leans in close; his glass eye, shiny and repulsive, reflects Locke's image back at him.

Locke tries to look unafraid, but his apprehension is evident in his speech.

"I'm not here to try and steal from you," he says.

"You think I'm stupid, don't you?" Haram says. "Every summer for ten years, whenever I come around here, I've caught your greasy hand trying to pick my pocket. I told you not to come around here again, boy, and apparently the last lesson I tried to teach you wasn't enough."

"What are you talking about?" Locke says.

But the answer did not come. For Haram pulled his fist back and released.

But before the weight of the blow could be felt by Locke, I awoke, and I curse that he has failed me yet again.

#828: Quarter to 5 am, August 3rd, '50

He enters his room and shuts the door behind him.

He is alone.

He removes his eye patch, revealing an empty socket vertically traversed by a thick scar.

He takes his index finger and rubs the inside of the hollow socket soothingly.

He reaches into his pocket, he extracts a radiant silver jewel.

He holds the jewel up to his glowing eye, and he laughs.

What he does with the jewel next is unknown, because the image quickly dissolved as I awoke in raging ire.

#844: Half past midnight, September 20th, '54

Darkness.

It lasts for several minutes, then disperses revealing two men standing outside a stone structure.

The men are brothers, nearly identical.

Identical brown eyes though one set are hard, one set are soft.

Identical faces.

Equally handsome.

But one is slightly larger in build as well as confidence.

The larger brother hugs the other, and pats him on the back. "Brother, the moon approaches."

"Worry not, brother, I shall not be long."

The younger steps inside as the larger rides off on his horse.

The view pans out revealing a large, medieval castle.

The towers extend high into the sky.

There are trees in all directions surrounding the structure.

At the highest peak, a silver flag flaps in the wind.

I awoke, heart racing, but with jubilation rather than fear.

They seek refuge at Morham Castle.

And the weaker has been left alone.

#846: Midnight, October 26th, '54

It is dark; a dense fog coats the ground.

Twelve sets of stiff boots clod upon the cobble-stone road as they head to the northern end of town, with torches ablaze, lighting a path as they march forward.

They come upon a door; a large hand pushes against it.

It is locked.

They bang.

They yell.

They pound.

Silence.

Suddenly, shattering glass. Hands reaching in through the broken window, a shard of glass slices neatly through thick flesh.

Soft red droplets drip slowly down the sill.

The door is unlocked. The men rush inside.

He is dragged, kicking and screaming in protest, from the dwelling.

He is kicked, punched, dragged for a distance, his legs and torso scraping across the road.

His pants tear, revealing scraped flesh.

The voices of the men are muffled, but threatening.

The voice of Janus is muffled, but frightened.

He speaks the words they want to here.

It is revealed by their triumphant smiles.

The tall one strikes Janus again, inflicting such terrible pain that he screams in agony.

A thick rope is knotted about his neck, the end of which is looped over a tall tree branch.

He kicks, he pleads.

The men grab the rope, tight in their hands, and pull, with brute force.

He flies up like a flag.

He struggles,

He chokes,

His eyes protrude slightly from their sockets, slightly pink

His fight becomes weaker, until . . .

The tall one wraps his arms tightly around Janus's swinging legs and pulls down, hard.

His neck snaps.

He is still.

I have awakened with a sickening feeling in the pit of my stomach.

I clutch at my abdomen and double over in pain. It churns and aches.

It is the sting of treachery: Janus, the traitor.

 I must do something about this . . . .

Locke,

    I am assuming that, by now, you have read through my manuscript. It is not the only gift I have left you with. You have the spark and, with time, you will learn how to use it. Also, if you travel back to Medea's house, you will find a handsome wardrobe. You may also find within it a small silver key. Go back and reread my diary entry dated February 13th, '31. The key unlocks a special box, the contents of which may be of great use to you.

Best of Luck,
Vincent